4|11

HEADS YOU LOSE

HEADS YOU LOSE

LISA LUTZ AND DAVID HAYWARD

G. P. PUTNAM'S SONS | *New York*

PUTNAM

G. P. PUTNAM'S SONS
Publishers Since 1838
Published by the Penguin Group
Penguin Group (USA) Inc., 375 Hudson Street, New York, New York 10014, USA · Pen-
guin Group (Canada), 90 Eglinton Avenue East, Suite 700, Toronto, Ontario M4P 2Y3,
Canada (a division of Pearson Penguin Canada Inc.) · Penguin Books Ltd, 80 Strand,
London WC2R 0RL, England · Penguin Ireland, 25 St Stephen's Green, Dublin 2,
Ireland (a division of Penguin Books Ltd) · Penguin Group (Australia), 250 Camber-
well Road, Camberwell, Victoria 3124, Australia (a division of Pearson Australia
Group Pty Ltd) · Penguin Books India Pvt Ltd, 11 Community Centre, Panchsheel Park,
New Delhi–110 017, India · Penguin Group (NZ), 67 Apollo Drive, Rosedale, North
Shore 0632, New Zealand (a division of Pearson New Zealand Ltd) · Penguin Books
(South Africa) (Pty) Ltd, 24 Sturdee Avenue, Rosebank, Johannesburg 2196, South Africa

Penguin Books Ltd, Registered Offices: 80 Strand, London WC2R 0RL, England

Library of Congress Cataloging-in-Publication Data

Lutz, Lisa.
    Heads you lose / Lisa Lutz and David Hayward.
        p.   cm.
    ISBN 978-0-399-15740-0
    1. Novelists—Fiction.   2. Brothers and sisters—Fiction.   3. Authorship—Fiction.
    I. Hayward, David, date. II. Title.
    PS3612.U897H43   2011   2010044999
    813'.6—dc22

Printed in the United States of America
10 9 8 7 6 5 4 3 2 1

BOOK DESIGN BY NICOLE LAROCHE

For Jerry and Linda

EDITOR'S NOTE

Dear Reader:

In the spring of 2009, the *New York Times*–bestselling crime novelist Lisa Lutz decided to collaborate on a murder mystery with a longtime friend (and ex-boyfriend), freelance editor and poet David Hayward.

The practical workings of the collaboration were as follows: Lutz would write the first chapter and all odd-numbered chapters thereafter. Hayward would write the even ones. They would not outline or discuss what they were working on. Each author would read the other's chapter "blind." Neither author was allowed to undo a plot development established by the other.

A few details about the presentation of the text warrant explanation: The footnotes within each chapter are comments made by the reading author. The authors also exchanged brief messages when a chapter was completed; these appear at the end of each chapter. The authors' initial messages to each other about the potential project are presented on the pages immediately following this Editor's Note.

Lutz told me she saw the project as an experiment, a challenge—a new way of writing that might spur creativity to higher levels. I leave it to you to judge the results.

For reasons that will become obvious, both authors refused to come together to revise their work. I present it to you in its original form. While unorthodox in structure, it is nevertheless a novel. It just happens to tell more stories than either author intended.

Signed,
The Editor

Dave,

I just finished the first chapter of a new novel—a real crime novel with a dead body and all—and I thought of you. And not in the way you might expect.

I'll cut to the chase: What would you say about making a go of another collaboration? And, no, I have not recently suffered a head injury. There's just something about this project that makes me feel like two heads might be better than one.

I know what you're thinking. Yes, our last attempt at collaboration, *The Fop*, was an epic disaster. A monthlong volcano of insults followed by a few years of complete silence qualifies, yes? Sometimes I don't know how we survived it (not to mention several other battles). But this is, what, thirteen years later? We're older, wiser, and probably too tired to fight with that level of vigor.

And maybe *The Fop* was doomed from the start. When it came down to writing it in the sober light of day, it might not have been the bulletproof idea it seemed over pitchers of beer at the Kilowatt. The story of a double-agent valet hiding behind the identity of his moronic yet flamboyant master is basically a B-movie version of *Jeeves and Wooster*. (Although, honestly, I still think there's something there. It just wasn't our fate to realize the vision.)

More importantly, we were writing that thing in the same room. Facial expressions can ratchet up an already stressful experience. I also think it's worth mentioning that this was back in your poetry days, and frankly, your touches of poignancy and high-art references were severely out of place in a broadly comic, mainstream undertaking.

Really, I accept equal blame for it. I had no patience and was often quite rude. Let me just offer up an overall mea culpa. But forget about *The Fop*. This is not *The Fop*. This is an as-yet-untitled crime novel that I think has some potential.

Okay, time to address the other elephant in the room. I know you're still bitter about you-know-what. It's true, in the very beginning, you helped brainstorm a few character details and offered some valuable footwear consultation. But it was always my screenplay, not a joint venture. And after the brutal struggles over *The Fop*, did you really expect me to ask you to collaborate again? Still, I know you felt betrayed, especially since *The Fop* went nowhere and my solo project got made (even if it did go straight to video). But that's all in the past. This is my olive branch to you. Maybe I'm a sucker for unfinished business, but I still believe we have some creative symbiosis.

If you're game, let me know and I'll send you the first chapter along with a few minor stipulations. If not, no offense taken. I'm sure I can find some other ex-poet interested in slumming it in the world of mainstream fiction.

> Best,
> Lisa

Lisa,

And hello to you, too. A word or two of personal greeting would have been nice—after all, it's been a few months since I saw you at Frank's. But I guess the businesslike approach is part of your strategy for this new project. I think I get it.

And we did almost have something with *The Fop*, didn't we? Clear away the romantic debris—and maybe the last half-hour of every writing session—and it really might have worked. I still laugh every time I think of the ski lodge scene (after he retrieves the monocle). Can you name a funnier movie sequence in the past decade? I can't.

But yeah, communication was never our strong suit. For example, the news that you considered *The Fop* a "broadly comic, mainstream undertaking" would have been useful in 1997. If I'd known we were aiming that low, I would have punched up the crotch gags, and maybe the last thirteen years would have gone differently for me. But let's leave all that in the past. I'm sorry, too.

I had a good laugh about my supposed bitterness over being shut out of your straight-to-video success. (Coincidentally, that's exactly as many laughs as I experienced watching the film.) A sliver of the money would have been nice, but you're right: That thing was all yours. I'm happy it led to better things for you. I'm over it. Let's not mention it again.

I don't know what your "minor" stipulations might be, but I have only one, and it's major: If we do this and it sells, we split the money down the middle. Given our history—not to mention your lifelong obsession with butlers and other menservants—I think this can work only if we approach it as equals. I realize you're the "name" here, but if I didn't have something you wanted, I figure you wouldn't be asking me.

If you agree to that, I'm game. And hopefully not in the hunting sense.

Dave

Dave,

I can handle the fifty-fifty split, but only with a couple of sensible amendments. First, I get top billing, since you agree that I'm the "name" author. Second, you may not discuss any aspect of our collaboration with our mutual acquaintances.

My final stipulation is that you simply correct my spelling and grammar, rather than mock me for it. You know what I've discovered in the world of publishing? Copy editors. They're totally awesome and they never insult me.

I just want to mention two more things: (1) Most people secretly wish they had a butler. I simply have the courage to openly voice my desire. (2) Read your description of *The Fop*. How was it not obvious we were talking about a broad comedy? I'm hoping the first chapter will make the tone of this story unmistakable, but if you're confused, please ask. Don't try to create a new genre.

So let's get started.

Lisa

Untitled

LISA LUTZ

with DAVID HAYWARD

CHAPTER 1

Paul flipped the coin and Lacey called tails. It was heads. Had the quarter made one more half-flip, who knows how differently things might have turned out? Paul could let things go; Lacey couldn't. But there's no point in thinking about what might have happened. Lacey lost the coin toss, so this is how the story goes.

Thursday was trash night. Lacey and Paul Hansen, grown siblings living under the same roof, had evolved tools for resolving simple disputes. In their childhood, they'd resort to wrestling matches or the slap game. But ever since their parents died, Paul had refused to engage in any physical altercation with his sister. Now that they were in their late twenties, the coin toss was the judge and jury in their household. Lacey grabbed her coat and slipped on her boots. She pulled the trash from the pantry and stepped out into the crisp California night. The sky was almost clotted with stars. She dumped the trash and dragged the bin down the long driveway and deposited it on the curb.

When she turned to look back at their house, a modest rambler lonely among acres of forest, all she could see was one dim light in the living room and the flicker of a television set. Paul was always watching TV. During the day, their home appeared ordinary and peaceful, if not a little weather-worn. A paint job wouldn't hurt. Though Mercer (pop. 1,280) was only a few miles away, it felt like they lived in the middle of nowhere. No other homes could be seen from their doorstep. As children they'd played in the forest that abutted their backyard, creating the footpaths that now guided them through the once-impenetrable terrain. Lacey had thought it was the most beautiful place in the world. Not anymore.

Now she mostly thought about how she would escape. Some days she pictured herself as far away as Italy. Other times she thought San Francisco would suffice. From there she could still keep a close watch on her brother. After their parents' death, she was the only real family he had. Even Aunt Gwen was gone, retired to Canada. And when Paul came back from college, his life didn't exactly fill up with friends. She stayed for him, she told herself. As far as Lacey could tell, Paul didn't want to go anywhere. He could see the entire world on the Travel Channel—what was the point of buying a plane ticket? Lacey no longer cared where she went as long as it wasn't Mercer. One day soon, this town would be a distant memory.

And one day, a coin toss wouldn't decide Lacey's destiny. It was a few hours to midnight (or prime time, as Paul called it) when Lacey heard the flies. She retraced her steps up the driveway and returned to the house to grab a flashlight. She tripped along the weeds and brush in their backyard, closing in on the stench. An animal must have died. Maybe a deer. But what would have killed a deer in the middle of their backyard? There was no hunting in these woods. Maybe the deer just died. Animals sometimes just die, like people, right? That's what she was thinking up until the moment she realized it was a body, a human body.

Her flashlight panned across the scene momentarily and she turned away. Just to make sure she saw what she thought she saw, she flashed the light on the body again, this time lingering on the head, or at least where the head should have been. She gagged. Then she decided she had seen enough. She ran full-speed back to the house.

"We have a problem," Lacey said to Paul, trying to sound calm and rational. She always liked people who were calm and rational, and adopted this persona whenever possible.

"Can it wait until morning?" Paul replied, staring blankly at the TV screen. "My program is on."

Had Lacey been in an argumentative mood, she would have reminded

Paul that "his program"—meaning any show he liked—was always on. This particular moment, his program involved men catching crabs in perilous conditions. Even Lacey liked this program.

"No, it can't wait," Lacey said, trying to keep her voice even.

"Can it wait fifteen minutes?" Paul asked, checking the clock.

"No," Lacey replied.

"Almost anything can wait fifteen minutes."

"Not a house fire," Lacey snapped.

"Is the house on fire?" Paul asked.

"No."

"Well then."

Lacey sat down on the couch next to Paul. She tapped her boot nervously on the hardwood floor—a habit of hers that could drive Paul to the brink of insanity. While the news could have waited fifteen minutes until Paul's program was over, Lacey didn't feel like waiting.

"There's a dead body in our backyard," she said. "I'm going to call 911."

Lacey slowly got to her feet and walked over to the phone. She picked up the cordless, but before she could dial, Paul snatched it out of her hand.

"Show me," he said.

"Well, he's definitely dead," Paul said.

"Thanks for confirming my diagnosis," Lacey replied. "Now what?"

"I'm thinking."

"That could take forever."

"Do you know him?" Paul asked.

"He's missing a head!" Lacey shouted. "How the fuck do I know if I know him or not?"

"Good point."

Despite the cold air, a bead of sweat dripped down Paul's forehead.

"He smells," Lacey said, fighting her gag reflex again.

"Agreed."

"Can we call the cops now?" Lacey asked. "I want him out of here."

"No, Lacey. We can't call the cops," Paul said, matter-of-factly.

"Why not?"

The reason was obvious, and on a normal day, a day when Lacey hadn't discovered her first headless body, she wouldn't have needed the reminder.

"Think about it," Paul said in his most condescending tone.

"Oh . . . right," Lacey sadly replied.

They couldn't call the cops because they couldn't have the law nosing around their property, an unfortunate side effect of their business. Like so many in their line of work, Paul and Lacey had fallen into it. Paul had grown his first marijuana plant in high school, but he didn't pursue it seriously until he came back from college short on savings and job opportunities. Five years later, the Hansens were a small but steady supplier. Lacey was interested in botany, but she never quite thought of herself as a pot grower. It was just something she was helping out with for now.

"Why here?" Lacey asked, her calm and rational persona fading fast.

"I don't know," Paul replied.

"Is someone sending us a message?"

"Still don't know."

Despite the smell, the siblings stood at the grisly crime scene and took in the sight of the uninvited guest on their property. The body, flat on its back, had on work boots, old blue jeans (the kind that got old from wearing them and working in them and then washing them), a plaid work shirt, and another layer underneath. It was once white. Now it was covered in dirt and blood and who knows what else.

"So what do we do?" Lacey asked, fighting back the urge to vomit.

"We have to move the body," Paul replied.

In silence, brother and sister returned to the house to prepare for the ugly task at hand. Lacey pulled her hair into a tight ponytail. She was twenty-eight years old, it occurred to her, and moving her first dead body. The calm and rational side of Lacey thought about DNA. She'd watched enough of those programs to know that she didn't want hers sprinkling all over the corpse. Paul donned a baseball cap. Lacey pulled two sets of dishwashing gloves from the pantry. Paul grabbed a tarp from the garage. Lacey poured peppermint oil on a pair of earplugs and stuffed them up her nose. She offered a pair of the same to her brother. The silence was briefly broken.

"These aren't used, are they?" Paul asked, holding the earplugs at a distance.

"What do you care? You've worn that same shirt for a week straight," Lacey replied. The shirt was a blue variation on Mercer's plaid flannel uniform. Last week it was red.

"I don't want your earwax up my nose."

"They're fresh," Lacey said. "I buy them in bulk. You have no idea how loud you snore."

"Well, you did play me that tape," Paul mumbled.

Another short patch of silence. Paul backed his blue Dodge pickup truck to the edge of the gravel driveway. He met Lacey beside the body. The tarp was laid next to the headless man.

"You can have the feet," Paul said, generously.

"Thanks," Lacey replied.

Paul grabbed the body by the shoulders; Lacey took his feet. Having never tried to move a body before, neither sibling realized how immovable dead weight was.

"Let's roll him," Lacey suggested.

Paul and Lacey each secured the tarp on the ground with one foot and, with all their force, they pushed the body over once, then twice, until it was resting in the center of the tarp. Then they wrapped the plastic around the body and secured it with duct tape so no fluids could escape.

They each grabbed a side of the tarp and lifted the body off the ground, carrying it to the truck. They dropped him on the ground to catch their breath. They had to somehow lift one hundred and eighty or so pounds onto the truck bed. Lacey was strong. Sometimes she had to carry giant sacks of soil amendments deep into the woods, but this would take all her strength. She rested for a bit on her haunches.

"On the count of three," Paul said. "One. Two. Three."

"Now what?" Lacey asked, after Paul secured the body in the truck bed.

"We dump him."

"Where?"

"Anywhere remote," Paul replied. "We're surrounded by acres of forest. If we pick the right spot, he might never be found."

"But don't we want him to be found?"

"Why?"

"Because clearly he was murdered, and we want the murderer caught so his family, if he has any, can have some peace."

"You don't even know the guy," Paul replied.

"Doesn't matter," Lacey said. "It's the right thing to do."

"I don't care where we dump him as long as it's miles from here."

"I know a place," Lacey replied.

Paul drove their truck down the dark road. He turned on the radio to a country station. He thought the music might help. Lacey hated this song—pop masquerading as country. She knew it would always remind her of this night, so she was glad it wasn't one she liked.

There was an eight-mile path off a rest stop about fifteen minutes from their house. It wasn't a popular hiking destination, but it got enough foot traffic that a decaying corpse would eventually be noticed.

Paul pulled the truck into the rest stop and breathed a sigh of relief when they saw the parking lot was empty. Lugging the body off the truck was easier. There was no point being gentle with a corpse. But still, the thud when it hit the ground sent a wave of nausea through Paul. He wished he'd brought a joint to calm his nerves. He wanted to stay calm for Lacey, but his calm was wearing off. They dragged the body about a quarter-mile down the trail, unwrapped the corpse, and dropped it down a short embankment. The body ended up facedown, or would have if it had had a face. Paul folded up the plastic tarp. He pulled off his gloves and told his sister to do the same.

"What will we do with all this plastic?" Lacey asked.

"Burn it," Paul replied.

"We can't burn plastic. Do you know how bad that is for the ozone layer?"

"Our DNA is all over the gloves, Lacey. The ozone layer can suck it."

"We should have worn cloth gloves inside the plastic gloves. Then we could have burnt the cloth gloves and left the plastic ones with the body or maybe in a dumpster somewhere," Lacey said.

"Let's remember that for next time," Paul replied, his patience waning.

Lacey took the flashlight from Paul's hand and said, "We better double-check and make sure we haven't left anything behind."

She beamed the light over the body, which was now tangled in brush. While Paul worked to dislodge a thick branch, Lacey gingerly hiked down the embankment to the side of the body. She scanned the area around the corpse with the flashlight. That's when she noticed it. The watch.

She'd seen it before, lots of times. An old Seiko with a new leather band. One of those watches that supposedly winds itself through regular movement, although most people end up shaking their arm to wind it up. It never kept exact time. Lacey studied the body again. It was the right size. The clothes were the same, although all the men in Mercer seemed to dress alike. Holding her breath, she unclasped the watch and viewed the inscription on the back under the glow of the flashlight:

4 D LOVE D

"Paul," Lacey said. Panic was edging into her voice, tears catching in her throat.

"Where are you?" Paul said, peering over the embankment.

He saw his sister standing over the corpse with the flashlight.

"We know him," Lacey said. "It's Darryl. It's Darryl Cleveland."

NOTES:

Dave,

Okay, back to you. I think it's time for a little backstory on the siblings. Maybe you can take care of some of that.

Also, I've decided Lacey should be studying botany. You might want to get started on the research since you're good at that sort of thing. Mind setting that up in your chapter?

Also, I didn't mention how the parents died. I'll leave that detail to you. I don't care how. Just don't go crazy. Leave the mafia out of it. Capiche?

Good luck,
Lisa

Lisa,

Nice job. I'm reminded how succinct and propulsive your writing can be. Don't worry about backstory—I've already got a novel's worth in my head.

Just a note for both of us to keep in mind as we continue: Let's make sure we don't start taking sides, with you favoring Lacey and me favoring Paul. That's the kind of predictable gender stuff that derailed us back in the *Fop* days (although I stand by my allegiance to Lucius Van Landingham). I think we're both above that now.

Dave

CHAPTER 2

"Dude grew fucking honeydews in Qua-*tar*."

That's what Paul's friend and mentor Terry Jakes used to say about Darryl Cleveland. Spoken in Terry's unplaceable twang, it was the first thing to pop into Paul's head when Lacey identified the body. Then he pictured Darryl in elementary school, a quiet blond kid always attached to his beat-up ten-speed. After high school, Darryl went straight into the Marines. "The few, the proud, the available," Lacey said at the time, though Darryl, a former mathlete and an instinctive gearhead, was in fact a pretty smart guy.

In the Marines, Darryl had worked on irrigation systems somewhere in the Middle East—maybe not really Qatar, but definitely not Iraq or anywhere too dangerous. He came back to take care of a family property up in Tulac. Now Darryl lived with his stepmom and worked for growers, including the Hansens, as a kind of overqualified freelance water consultant.

One of the more persistent conundrums surrounding Mercer was that the residents of so rainy a place could be so preoccupied with the acquisition, storage, and allocation of water. Another one was that the natural serenity of the place seemed to foment[1] anxiety and despair more efficiently than any urban housing project. A third was that no one seemed to ever visit or even talk about Mount Shasta, although there it always was.

Even before he enlisted, Darryl seemed to have a knack for getting water from one place to another. At one of Terry Jakes's most remote

---

[1] Take it easy, Dr. Thesaurus.

plots, the property owner kept chopping up the hoses they'd run from a nearby spring. Darryl had the idea of buying an old waterbed mattress, filling it up, and taking it to the plot on old fire roads in the back of his Chevy LUV truck. Darryl had paid Paul twenty dollars and all the PBR he could drink round-trip, to help him machete a couple of thick patches so the truck could maneuver to the plot. After that, the yield turned out to be a monster.

Paul remembered it so clearly because it was the first time he left the house after the cabin incident. He'd wondered at the time if Darryl had even heard about it. Bad news traveled fast in Mercer, but Darryl kept to himself. That made it easier to be with him than with any of Paul's real friends, who didn't have much experience hanging out with a seventeen-year-old whose parents had just died. And it beat hanging around the house with his comatose sister and the relentlessly nurturing aunt who'd come to live with them during "this challenging time." Aunt Gwen put a lot of stock in the healing powers of chamomile tea; Paul found Pabst more effective.

Paul and Lacey had both been relieved that they weren't expected to accompany their parents to the family's cabin down by Wallis, an hour south of Mercer. They needed some alone time, their parents said. Paul looked forward to a weeklong slow burn of a party. Lacey just welcomed the break in her mom's surveillance.

During the vacation, a generator under the cabin leaked carbon monoxide into their parents' bedroom. When a week passed and no one heard from them, Lacey and Paul called the sheriff, who drove up to the cabin and found the bodies. It was a couple of years before carbon monoxide poisoning became a big public health scare. And that was it. Their dad's sister came down from Bend, Oregon, to live with Paul and Lacey for the rest of the school year. Then Paul went off to college, and Lacey, with one more year of school remaining, moved in with her best friend's family in downtown Mercer.

Senior year Lacey met Hart, a sandy-haired rich kid from the Central

Valley with a rebellious streak. Lacey was the only girl in school who didn't seem impressed—a fact that drew him to her irreversibly. For Lacey, Paul thought, the appeal was just as simple. He was the one guy in Mercer who wasn't *of* Mercer. Hart had been all over, even to Europe, and loved to talk about the trips they'd take. Within a month, he and Lacey were inseparable. In two years, they were living together on the outskirts of town. Paul noted that Hart seemed more intent on traveling inside his head, via whatever substance was available, than ever taking Lacey any-where, but he kept his mouth shut. Once Lacey had made up her mind about something—in this case that Hart was what she needed—there was no point talking about it.

Five years later, Paul came back from college with some basic horti-cultural knowledge, but without decent job prospects. What he had was land and unlimited access to Terry Jakes, who seemed to know everything there was to know about growing pot, indoors and out. Darryl helped out with the water during a leave from the Marines. By the summer after graduation, Paul was in business. In the five years since then, he'd man-aged to build up a steady little client base. Lacey had been back with him almost a year. She didn't exactly embrace the business, but for now it was all they had. And at least she was back with family.

"I'm sorry it's Darryl," Paul said, standing over the body now. "But it doesn't really change anything. Put the watch back on him, leave him here, get rid of the tarp and gloves, wait for someone to find him."

"I guess. But I hate to think—"

"There's nothing to think about except getting away from this and stay-ing there."

Lacey returned the watch to Darryl's cold wrist and Paul gathered up the tarp. They got home with five minutes to spare before *Cud-gel,* the show where people tried to complete an obstacle course while being pummeled by giant mechanical clubs. A stocky receptionist from

Michigan took the early lead. The low-center-of-gravity types always beat the natural athletes, Paul noted to himself.

Lacey waited until the commercial break. "So, what now?"[2]

"Jesus. Is that your new catchphrase?" Paul replied.

"Nope. It's still 'Shut the fuck up.'"

"Standard," Paul said. "He's not going to get any less ripe, especially if it stays hot. I bet someone finds him and calls the cops before his step-mom even notices he's gone."

"What about the you-know-what?"

"The head? We're not being recorded, you know. I'll look around in the morning, but I doubt it's anywhere near here. Let's not go sneaking around with flashlights again."

After *Cudgel* they sat through a whole *Mythmatch* rerun, the one where Dracula beats Poseidon, a highly questionable upset in Paul's book. It was becoming clear that they were both just delaying going to bed. Not out of fear of a killer lurking in the woods—by now they were used to a sort of constant low-level fear ("alertness," Paul called it)—but because they knew what to expect in their sleep.

The only uncanny sibling weirdness they shared was that whenever something big happened, they had the same dream. Or not exactly the same dream, except for after the cabin incident, but always close enough to be creepy. "What are we, twins?" Lacey had said after the first time, echoing Paul's thoughts with irritating precision. They quickly discovered that the phenomenon was boring to reasonable people who had lives and endlessly fascinating to long-winded stoney types, of which Mercer had no shortage.

Paul started to drift off and Lacey hit the mute button, waking him immediately.

"So," she said. "Why did they cut off his head?"

Paul cleared his throat. "Either *a*. That's where the bullet was lodged

---

[2] *What Now?* could be a good title.

and they wanted to remove ballistics evidence, or *b*. Maybe they wanted a souvenir."

Among the many verbal habits of Paul's that irked Lacey, only a few inspired true loathing. Speaking in outline form was number one, followed by the use of horseracing odds to describe the relative likelihood of anything.

"They should have taken his fingers, too," Lacey said, without contemplating how ghoulish that sounded.

"Fingerprints only matter if he's in the system," Paul reminded his sister.

"Right. But why leave it on *our* property?" she asked.

"Either it was random or they knew what they were doing," Paul replied, trying not to think too hard about it.

"They, not he?" she asked.

"Darryl's not exactly svelte. Anyway, I'd make option *a* the 3 to 2 favorite, with *b* at 4 to 1. Anything else, *c* through *z*, 10 to 1 tops."

Lacey and Paul sat there in silence, but neither of them could settle into their usual state of benign mutual irritation. And for the first time, they missed it.

Paul gave in first, with his usual "Night, Lace," and then lay in bed thinking of the trident in Dracula's chest. The wrong tool for the job.

In his dream he was walking down rows of different kinds of melons. The oleaginous[3] redheaded detective from *NYPD Blue* and that forensics show was walking next to him in his sunglasses, whispering, "That's a cantaloupe, Paul. *That's* a casaba. Do you know the difference? Do you like casabas, Paul?" Lacey's dream was simpler. She was cutting up melons; inside was just sand.

It was still dark when she got up for her run. She felt the gravitational pull of the tarp and gloves in the garage but stuck to her standard route—they'd agreed to wait for burn day. Halfway through the run was a ridge

---

[3]Seriously.

where she always paused to look out over the house, the town, everything as the sun was coming up. She had an urge to get up there fast just to see if everything still looked basically the same. It did, which was no comfort.

For the rest of the run, she recounted the milestones of her days with Hart. She often did so when she started questioning her move back into her childhood home. First was "I failed Botany 1A at Las Piedras Community College," which had felt like the bottom at the time. Then it was "I lived in an actual trailer park." Finally, for the last few months of the relationship, it was "my perfect boyfriend Hart cooks meth." Yep, her current living situation was still better. But the past was narrowing the gap all the time.

When she came through the screen door, Paul perked up, just barely.

"Melons and Caruso?" he mumbled into his coffee.

"Just melons."

Then they both heard gravel spitting into mud flaps. Someone was coming up the hill.

NOTES:

Lisa,

You want backstory, you got it. I can already see how we're going to complement each other, what with your plotting expertise and my eye and ear for detail. I can't believe how easy this is. Although beginnings were never the problem, if I remember correctly.

Dave

Dave,

Thanks for all the backstory. Since it gives us a solid foundation, feel free to ease up on it a bit next chapter. Also, since I'm on the subject of cutting back, can we maybe keep the made-up TV show references to a minimum? A little goes a long way.

I also want to follow up on my request about Lacey's botany studies, given her sudden failure of Botany 1A. It's fine that you didn't go with my suggestion, as long as there was nothing passive-aggressive in your decision. We're in this together.

Terry Jakes is going to make an appearance, right? Let's not make him like Professor Solemni from *The Fop*—quoted but never seen.

Still, I'm feeling positive. We're off to a good start!

Lisa

P.S. I'm curious where you learned all this stuff about growing marijuana plants. It would explain some things in our history.

CHAPTER 3

Lacey ran to the window and peered through the blinds. Her heart was racing until she saw the mud-whipped truck. An old Ford, green beneath the dirt, but you'd never know that. From now on, every time an engine stirred in their driveway Lacey would assume it was the cops.

"It's just Rafael," Lacey said.

She returned to the kitchen, finished her toast, washed her plate, and topped off Paul's coffee. Paul had never been a fan of stimulants of any kind, but Lacey had discovered that caffeine had a slight impact on Paul's work ethic and so she pushed it like a regular old drug dealer. In fact, sometimes when she was feeling particularly hostile, she'd crush up NoDoz into his beer.

Approximately three and a half minutes after they heard Rafael's car in the driveway, the doorbell rang. The delay wasn't unusual for Rafael. Once Lacey timed him at four minutes and thirty-five seconds. Rafael could never leave his truck until the song on the radio was over—an isolated OCD tic. Lacey once wondered aloud whether Rafael maintained that policy even if he didn't like the song. Paul said he did.

Rafael Dupree handled half of the college circuit for Paul and Lacey, selling their product along the string of small schools to the south, as well as to other clients scattered around the area. He was a student at Sequoia State who didn't attend class much until he dropped out. Now that he was dealing, he audited lectures regularly. In fact, he'd even started supplementing his income by selling his notes.

The doorbell rang for a second time. Paul was sitting and Lacey was standing, so Paul assumed door-answering responsibilities fell to his sister, but he always assumed that. After their parents died, Paul fell into the habit of playing the adult in the family. Despite their mere thirteen-month age difference, Paul had always played the big brother. But now that Lacey had moved back in, protective had become bossy. Lacey had started to take a stand. Not answering the door was one way she asserted herself.

"I have to get ready for work," Lacey said. "Don't keep him waiting."

With that, Lacey walked right past the front door and into her bedroom. She put on her shoes and grabbed her purse. When she returned to the living room, Paul and Rafael were already on the couch, smoking a joint.

Lacey made a show of looking at her watch.

"It's nine-thirty in the morning," Lacey said.

Rafael launched into a coughing fit, then sputtered out, "It's medicinal."

Lacey eyed him quizzically and Paul explained.

"Look at his arm. Poison oak. This will help the itching."

It was true; Rafael's forearm was mottled with a familiar-looking rash. However, Lacey took issue with Paul's home remedy.

"You should foment that with vinegar and water and then take an antihistamine."

"Foment. *Fo-ment*," Rafael repeated like a chant. "Cool word. I'll have to remember that."

"Yes," Lacey replied. "However, in this case I'm using the less common sense of the word, which means to bathe in an ointment, not stir up trouble."[4]

"Okay," Rafael said, looking confused.

"We'll take care of it," Paul said. "You better run. Betty was hoping for her delivery this morning."

Lacey checked her watch.

"You could have mentioned that sooner."

---

[4]So you do still have that dictionary I bought you.

"I guess I could have. Sorry."

Paul then shifted his attention back to work, which bore no resemblance to work.

"How much do you need this time?" Paul asked.

"Just a half-o," Rafael replied.

"I'm leaving," Lacey said as she threw on her coat.

"Be cool," said Paul. "Know what I mean, Lace?"

"Yeah, I know," Lacey replied, lying.

After everything that had transpired the night before, Lacey marveled at how quickly Paul could return to business as usual. She knew there was no other way he should be, but still it got under her skin, like so many things he did.

Betty was a regular who didn't smoke. She was five-foot-ten and, at her peak, had weighed a solid one hundred and eighty pounds. She'd been one of the first woman loggers in the region. It took fifteen years to ruin her back for good. Even with regular visits to the chiropractor, there wasn't much she could do for the pain.

It was Betty who'd inspired Lacey to expand the business into baked goods. Betty worked part-time for the local physician, Doc Holland, billing and answering his phone. During an office visit, Lacey had noticed her popping pills and shifting uncomfortably. Betty had bought from the Hansens before, but didn't like smoking, having given up cigarettes five years ago. Lacey experimented with some recipes, and eventually found that cooking the pot in oil and using a box mix was just fine. In a pinch, even Paul could whip up a batch.

Lacey knocked on her front door. Betty opened the door holding a cup of coffee. She was wearing a light blue terry-cloth robe, her usual morning attire. The robe covered an ankle-length night dress with a ruffle around the collar. Betty had a few other versions patterned with flowers and one with bumble bees. Lacey was always surprised by the contrast between Betty's sleepwear and outerwear. Outside, Betty always reverted to her old logger's uniform: denim, flannel shirt, and hiking boots. Lacey preferred sleepwear Betty. She struck a far less intimidating figure.

"Darling, am I glad to see you," Betty said.

This was one part of the job Lacey didn't mind. Some people she was helping; she believed that. There were others, though . . . she didn't know what she was doing for them.

"Can you stay for a visit?" Betty asked.

"I'm already late for work," Lacey said.

"Have you heard?"

"I don't know," Lacey cautiously replied.

"I have news."

"What?"

Betty leaned in close, even though there was no one around for miles. "I heard Doc Holland sold his practice to some guy from the city."

"What city would that be?" Lacey asked.

"San Francisco," Betty replied as if that were an even bigger secret.

"Why would you move from San Francisco to Mercer? Isn't that suspicious?"

"He arrived yesterday," Betty replied. "You can make an appointment and start your investigation."

Lacey returned to her car. She'd already lost interest in the incoming doctor. Besides, she had always wanted the town to get a dentist. Sometimes it was just the sight of tooth decay that reminded her she was living in the sticks. The new doctor was one mystery she could put on hold. The other one, however, she couldn't let slide.

Darryl's house was just a quick loop outside of her route to work. She decided to drive by, just to see if anything was amiss. She slowed in front of his rambler. He had repainted recently. She noted other improvements as well. Maybe that's why he hadn't been seen around much. Maybe he was trying to make a break from the water business, keeping clear of his usual contacts. Lacey liked the idea—she could relate. Too bad he died. She couldn't relate to that. Darryl's truck was still parked out front, but there was no sign of anyone in the house. Why should there be? Darryl lived with his stepmom, but she worked full-time, and now most of him was lying alongside a hiking path twelve miles away.

Suddenly, Lacey felt tears streaming down her face. Last night she'd seen just a body, and not even a whole one. Today she realized Darryl was gone for good. It's not like they were close or anything; in fact, when he was around they hardly said a word to each other. But still, she had gotten used to him and now she'd have to get unused to him. Lacey wiped the tears away with her sleeve and kept driving until she reached the Tarpit. She'd never minded the name before, but today it reminded her that she was stuck and that it was time she got out of Mercer.

"I'd like a nonfat soy-mocha latte," Bernard, one of the regulars, said.

"What size?" Lacey asked.

"Medium, no, large."

Lacey poured a shot of espresso and mocha into the mug and steamed the soymilk, while starting another batch of espresso with her right hand. She looked at Bernard in his lumberjack shirt and work boots and wondered when it had happened—when he'd transformed from the guy who ordered black coffee and a bear claw to a man who buys city drinks that cost more than a full breakfast at the Jenkee's down the street.

Lacey kept this job because she thought she should have one on paper and she needed time away from Paul, but some part of her wished this town had stayed as it had once been—a town where people didn't need to use more than two words to order a cup of joe. The one benefit of the job was that the morning rush kept her mind so busy on the small tasks at hand that she didn't have too much time to think about her life and the mess she had made of it. Some days she still thought of Hart, but every day she got better at forgetting about him.

Lacey was loading mugs into the dishwasher and trying to solve the mystery of the headless body in her backyard when she was interrupted by an unnecessarily booming voice.

"Coffee. Black," said Sheriff Ed Wickfield, as if he were introducing himself.

Lacey turned around.

"Hi, Ed. How are you doing?"

"Surviving," Ed replied, with the tone of a cop whose work might involve undercover narcotics operations in Central America. In truth, Ed mostly dealt with traffic violations and run-of-the mill drunk and disorderly calls.

"Glad to hear it," Lacey said.

Then they did the dance of Ed trying to pay and Lacey waving him away. The owners of the café never let the sheriff or the fire marshal pay for coffee. Ed always put two bucks in the tip jar. Lacey wished that made her like him, but it didn't. She always had this unnerving feeling that Ed was waiting for the perfect moment to pounce and seize his glory with a massive bust.

She could never decide if his small talk amounted to innocent questions or thinly veiled interrogations.

"How's that brother of yours?" Ed asked.

"Okay, I guess," Lacey replied. "You'd have to ask him if you want the full report."

"Is he keeping busy?"

"It's all relative."

"How does he fill his days?" Ed asked.

While it did seem to be a pointed question, it was a question that a handful of locals asked. How Paul filled his days was a mystery to everyone except Paul. Since Paul didn't want to get a cover job, they decided to tell people that he was slowly draining his inheritance and killing time the way so many young men kill time—computers, television, and video games. Sometimes when Lacey was feeling hostile, she'd add that Paul had a minor addiction to porn. Mostly, she'd add this detail when speaking to any single, relatively attractive woman in the area. When she was feeling more generous, she told people that Paul was a nature enthusiast and spent hours studying the local flora. At least that was in the vicinity of the truth. Mostly she wanted to give him an alibi for when he didn't pick up the phone because he was in their basement tending to an entirely different type of vegetation.

Lost in the various thoughts clouding her head, Lacey forgot the question.

"I'm sorry. What was that, Ed?" she asked.

"How does Paul fill his days?" the sheriff repeated. The tone remained friendly.

"We have satellite TV," Lacey answered.

During her break, Lacey strolled the two-block stretch of Mercer that made up the town center. She picked up the local paper and opened the flimsy rag. Every day was a slow news day in Mercer. As far as she could remember there had never been a murder or a missing-persons report. She looked today and there was nothing to speak of. Not a single mention of Darryl Cleveland.

And why should there be when he was walking into the hardware store right in front of her.

Lacey followed him inside.

"Darryl?"

She knew it was him, but for some reason she had to say his name like it was a question. Darryl turned around and smiled. Lacey was so happy to see him alive and with a head and everything that she threw her arms around him and gave him a hug. Then she realized that she had never hugged Darryl before and stopped abruptly.

"It's been a while," she said, by way of explanation.

"I guess so," Darryl said, uncomfortably.

"How have you been?" Lacey asked, not sure what purpose the answer would serve.

"Surviving," he replied.

Lacey looked him in the eye. Something about him was off, but she couldn't put her finger on it. It could have been the unprecedented embrace, of course.

"So what's been happening?" Lacey asked.

"Same old, same old," Darryl replied.

"Are you sure?" said Lacey, knowing otherwise.

Darryl looked confused. "I ain't sure about anything, Lacey."

"Me neither," she replied.

It suddenly occurred to Lacey that Darryl's connection to the dead body might not be so innocent.

"Well, it's been really good running into you," she said abruptly. Then she made a quick exit.

"Yeah, nice seeing you too," Darryl replied.

But Lacey couldn't hear him. She was already out the door.

NOTES:

Dave,

In case you think I was trying to throw you a curveball with the Darryl thing. Nah, it just came to me suddenly. But I think I like it. Hope you agree.

A quick note for your next chapter: Sometimes your vocabulary feels a little high-end for this kind of book. It would be great if I didn't have to Google as I read.

Let's try to keep the momentum going with your chapter. For example, maybe a little more plot development and a little less background. Okay? I just want to keep this thing zipping along for the reader's sake. Another idea along those lines is to try to end each chapter with a bit of a bang (without overdoing it, of course).

Lisa

Lisa,

Looking good. That was a nicely handled moment with Darryl at the end.

I'll try to throw in a little more action to keep things rolling. Sorry about your Google problem. I can spell things out a bit more. I sometimes forget you were home-schooled. Ha ha.

Before we get too far along, how about a road trip up north? I think it'd be helpful to get a sense of the real-life places and people. What if we spent a couple days near Shasta soaking up the local culture? Separate rooms, of course.

Dave

CHAPTER 4

A little high, Paul went looking for the head, hoping not to find it. But he told himself he could handle it if he did. He was used to coming across various body parts of recently deceased creatures. Their cat, Irving, was an indiscriminate murderer of anything smaller than him: mice, squirrels, slow or overconfident birds. Lacey had once stepped out of bed onto the perfectly intact face of a vole. "Not the head, just the *face*," she kept saying. She had a point. It was almost like Irving was showing off. He was an outdoor cat after that. Maybe that suited him, anyway, given his rugged past. The girl at the animal shelter said Irving had been brought there after one too many run-ins with the area's most notorious feral cat, Bad Sue.[5]

The job fell to Paul, as usual, because Lacey was at her cover job, which in his book was a waste of time. If they needed a cover, Paul thought, there was nothing wrong with claiming to be caretakers—it was the stated occupation of plenty of Mercer-area residents, many of whom did, in fact, merely take care of a property. But that would have sounded too redneck for Lacey. As Terry Jakes, not exactly upper-crust himself, used to say, "Caretakers are just carnies who got off the ride."

Paul suspected that Lacey's barista (maker of coffee beverages)[6] gig was more about her self-image than actual cover. She couldn't even admit to herself that she was a pot grower, Paul thought. Facing facts had never been her strong suit. Even as a little girl, she seemed to have fun only when she was playing dress-up. But he was her big brother, and he'd help

---

[5]Hmm. Does the cat really need a backstory?

[6]Thank you for the explanation. I am aware of the term.

her out as long as she needed him. Maybe she'd go back to school after she saved a little money.

With Irving at his side, Paul started where they'd found the body, then proceeded in an outward spiral until he reached the property's perimeter. Irving trotted alongside him, more doglike than most dogs. Covering the property took almost four hours and yielded only an old badminton (a lawn sport resembling tennis)[7] set and some faded orange Hot Wheels tracks covered in pine muck.

He was back inside watching *Volcano Chasers* by the time Lacey stormed in.

"No head," Paul said.

"That's nice. I have a slightly larger piece of news," said Lacey. "I just saw Darryl Cleveland at Olmstead's Hardware. Head firmly attached."

"Are you sure?"

"Let me think about it. Yes."

"Did you ask him anything?"

"Like what? 'How do explain your incredible comeback?'" Lacey said, imitating a sportscaster interviewing an athlete.

"No. I mean like, 'Did you lose your watch?'"

"Of course not."

"Good. So we're done," Paul said.

"Jesus," Lacey said after a pause. "Could you be a little bit happy it's not Darryl?"

"I *am* a little bit happy about that. I'm a *lot* happy that the head isn't on our property. Now we can just sit back and watch what happens."

"How perfect for you," said Lacey. "'This week on *CSI: Mercer*, two pot-growing orphans stumble onto a body, changing their lives forever.'"

"Yeah, yeah," Paul said. "I gotta run. Senior Circuit today. You'll be okay around here, right?" It was a rhetorical question, and Lacey had stopped answering those.

---

[7]Okay. That's enough.

"Oh yeah," Paul added. "Feed Irving. It's been like a week since he's killed anything. Maybe he's depressed or something."

First stop on the Senior Circuit was Mapleshade, a nursing home/retirement tower that housed most of Mercer's hidden elderly population, the size of which helped to explain the success of Jenkee's Diner and two separate pharmacies. Sook Felton's room was on the top floor, overlooking the forest.

"Brought you some peaches from Lacey," Paul said in Sook's room, producing a little bag. Sook's biggest complaint about Mapleshade was the food.

"Great. They got a pint of vanilla stashed for me in the kitchen freezer."

"So how was the movie?" Paul asked. Paul always came on a Friday, and movie night was Thursday—most of the sentient residents would gather around the big widescreen in the community room.

"Lousy," said Sook. "Where is it written that old people in movies have to be cranky, adorable, or adorably cranky?"

Paul wasn't touching that one, though he had to admit Sook didn't fit into any of those categories. It was probably more weird than adorable that the thing Sook seemed to enjoy most in life, other than a bowl of high-quality pot, was chick lit. One of the nurses had hooked Sook on the genre soon after he'd arrived at Mapleshade a few years ago, bored out of his mind. Now it was an obsession. Hearing about Sook's literary preferences, Lacey had taken him to the movies to see, in her words, "*Divine Secrets of Your Sister's Pants* or whatever." (Not exactly her type of movie, but she adored Sook.) He'd hated it, and now avoided all film adaptations of books he liked.

For as long as Paul could remember, Lacey had been drawn to the elderly. "Because they don't give a shit," she explained. That was fortunate, since Mercer's demographics were heavily skewed toward high school kids, retirees, and a whole lot of not much in between. Her friends from high school were off in San Francisco or New York, working the jobs they got with their college degrees.

"So I'll take an ounce," Sook said, getting down to business. "We lost Bernice but gained a nurse."

"'Lost her she quit smoking' or 'lost her she died'?" Paul asked.

"The latter. She had a good run," Sook said, doing a little shrug. It was his usual response to a death at Mapleshade, and it was a safe bet that he felt that way about himself. Like most twice-widowed, Korea-vet, nature-loving, gun-enthusiast, bilingual, weed-connoisseur great-grandfathers of five, he'd lived a full life.

Sook sold Paul and Lacey's pot to a few residents, maybe half of the nurses, and at least one administrator. In return, the staff turned a blind eye when he ventured off the paved walking paths and into the woods, which provided plenty of shade despite a conspicuous lack of maples. They were also by far the best place around Mapleshade to be high.

"I gotta run," said Paul. "I'm due at the Gardens."

"All right. Thank Lace for the peaches. See you next month." Then Sook's face turned serious. "Hey, I hear Doc Holland split town," he said. "Know why?"

"Nope. Why do you ask?"

"No big reason," Sook said. "He owed me twenty bucks."

Sook was a bad liar, but Paul let it go. He'd always thought bad liars were kind of like honest people—you always knew where you stood. Paul wasn't big on judging people, as long as they didn't try to take what belonged to him. And if they did, he'd care about getting it back, not about bringing them to justice. All he really wanted, he told himself, was his patch of land and the freedom to do his job. And maybe a bigger TV.

"Just in time for fight night," said Lito, coming out to meet Paul's truck.

When Paul shut off the engine, he could hear the Babalato brothers arguing somewhere inside We Care Gardens, the assisted-living facility they owned. Jay and his younger brother Marvello (Big Marv) Babalato had run the place since their mom died a decade back. Things had gotten so bad between them that the complex was now more or less divided into halves—two houses run by Jay and two by Marv. Paul was reminded yet again why Lito did such a thriving business around here: Anyone within earshot of the brothers would have a steady supply of negative energy to deal with. Listening to them, Lito just shook his head and got in the truck. He was Jay's son, but he never took sides. No one did anymore.

We Care Gardens was just down the street from Mapleshade, and not by coincidence. It was perfectly positioned to receive people fresh off the Mapleshade tour and presentation, which concluded with a frank discussion of what Mapleshade would actually cost. In most cases, the sticker shock was still fresh as they pulled into the parking lot of the humbler, earthier alternative.

The Gardens' four little houses might have been shambolic (disorderly), but they were surrounded by a well-maintained collection of tropical and native plants. Throughout the compound you could always smell home cooking—the one facet in which We Care towered over Mapleshade. Sook said he could sometimes smell the cooking from his room.

Paul assumed that Lito sold to some of his sisters, who made up most of the nursing staff, and maybe some of the residents, but his main customers were probably through his other job out at the airport, where Lito was the entire maintenance crew.

After some small talk, Lito bought two ounces, his usual.

"Hey, you mind dropping me out at the airport?" he asked. "My sister took my truck."

"Sure, no problem," Paul said.

"I just need to grab something from inside. Be right back," Lito said.

Paul waited in the truck, listening to the rhythm of the brothers' argument. After a while it stopped, and then took a violent turn, like someone had bumped the volume knob. One of them was shouting at the other now. Somewhere in there, Paul thought he heard the word "Darryl."

Then he thought he must have imagined it. No more daytime smoking, he told himself, recalling his morning with Rafael. He had no intention of playing private investigator, but he couldn't stop thinking about how Darryl's watch and the headless body got introduced to each other.

Lito came jogging out, still shaking his head but not smiling anymore. "Man, get me out of here," he said as he climbed into the truck.

"So what was that all about?" Paul asked.

"Trust me, you don't want to know."

Paul couldn't argue with that.

He was glad to give Lito the ride because it gave him a legitimate excuse to drive by the rest stop to see if there were any signs that the body had been found. He'd made Lacey swear she wouldn't go anywhere near it, but hey, their top seller needed a ride—what could he do? As they passed the rest stop, Paul looked over casually, hoping for police tape and a couple of cruisers. Instead there was just an idling truck and a family at a park bench. Where was Sheriff Ed when you needed him? Probably intimidating some high school kids.

For a second as they drove past, Paul thought he caught a whiff of the body from all the way across the highway. Okay, he thought, *definitely* no more daytime smoking.

Mercer Airport looked more like a driving range, or an airstrip with a snack bar. A row of small, rusty hangars off to one side completed the picture. As the maintenance guy, Lito mostly had to keep weeds from overtaking the runway and replace burned-out runway lights. A large middle-aged woman named Wanda handled all the pilot communications and "air-traffic control" (a running joke, since there were at most only a few takeoffs and landings each day).

She was smoking a cigarette outside the radio booth.

"What's up, Wanda?" Paul asked.

"Nothing, unless you count Doc Holland selling me his Cessna for two grand." She sounded pleased but hardly excited. It wasn't the first time she'd taken a plane off the hands of someone who was leaving the area in a hurry. She'd either resell them or keep them around for parts. Diabetes had forced her to quit flying, but she still liked to tinker.

A small plane buzzed toward them in the distance.

"Who's that?" Paul asked.

"I don't know yet," said Wanda. "He wasn't in the log, but I cleared him. I guess we're about to find out."

Paul watched the plane's three blue lights teetering down against a blotchy sunset. The sky was clouding up. Tomorrow would be a burn day.

"Maybe it's the new doctor?" Lito offered.

Then the plane blew apart like a firework, and burning pieces of it started raining down all over Mercer Airport.

NOTES:

Lisa,

How's that for a bang?

Dave

Dave,

Wow. I wasn't expecting such a literal interpretation, but I appreciate the intent. I'm assuming that you have a plan for explaining the explosion, so I'll try not to step on that in my chapter.

At first I wasn't sure how I felt about all this assisted-living stuff, but I'm warming to it. It could broaden our potential demographic, and you've certainly increased our suspect pool.

No offense, but I say no to the road trip. Let's keep in mind, we're writing a crime novel here. I think we've already got plenty of local color.

I'm surprised you'd even suggest a road trip after what happened on our last one.

Lisa

CHAPTER 5

News of the plane crash tore through Mercer. Exactly twenty minutes after the fire was extinguished, Wanda was on the phone disseminating the news throughout the town. A plane crash will cause a stir almost anywhere, but in a place like Mercer it drew residents to the site like zombies to fresh brains. The Tarpit emptied in the time it takes to microwave popcorn. The only person not following the smoke plume was Lacey. The Tarpit's owners told her to close up shop as they hopped on their Harley and took off to join the town field trip.

As soon as it registered that virtually every inhabitant of Mercer would be otherwise occupied, Lacey formulated a plan. When she locked the front door, she took in the sight of Main Street, now a ghost town. She got into her ten-year-old Honda Civic and pulled out of the parking space without even checking her rearview mirror.

Ten minutes later, as she passed the dueling assisted-living facilities on her way out of town, a queasy sensation took hold. What if she never escaped Mercer? What if her final days were spent in Mapleshade, or worse, We Care Gardens? Lacey decided to shift her priorities. Solve a murder; get out of town. She wouldn't wait for that big crop and that big payoff that might never come. She'd do one last thing for her hometown, then she'd start a life somewhere else. How hard could that be?

An empty station wagon loitered in the parking lot of the otherwise deserted rest stop. She parked a few spots over, grabbed her backpack and water bottle from the trunk of her car, and entered the foul-smelling ladies' room to check for signs of tourist life. Nothing. She exited, scanned the area, and peeked inside the men's room, holding her breath the entire time. Also empty. She peered inside the station wagon and saw camping gear. They must be on the trail, she thought. Maybe they'll find the body, report it to the police. That's how it was supposed to happen, right?

Lacey returned to her car and had just started the engine when she caught a glimpse of hikers surfacing from the trail—a family of five, weary, but with the calm glow of nature and exertion. If they *had* seen a body, they must be in the mortuary business.

Shouldn't they have noticed something? The smell had been overpowering only two nights ago. It could have only gotten worse.

Lacey killed the engine and got out of her car. She smiled at the family and they exchanged friendly hellos. She watched them fill their water bottles from the fountain and return to their car. Lacey set out on the trail. In twilight, without a headless body in tow, it took no time to reach her destination. Lacey glanced at her surroundings. She felt an edginess take over, like she was being watched. Her eyes told her differently, but then she didn't trust her eyes.

She was sure this was where the body previously known as Darryl Cleveland was rolled. She knew this trail, day or night. You forget where you left your keys, that cup of coffee you were drinking earlier, but you remember things like where you dumped a headless body in the middle of the night. Lacey scaled down the incline and stared at dirt and weeds— a human-sized matted patch confirmed that she was in the right place. She kicked the dirt around, for no good reason. But then she noticed an unnatural little shape cresting to the surface. She brushed the top layer off with her hands and found a ring. She exhumed it, blowing dirt off the silver. She'd seen it before—a woman's wedding ring with a Celtic design, adorned with diamond chips.

It felt like every bit of air escaped her lungs. She inhaled as hard as she could, but it wasn't enough. A sense of terror swept over her. She stuffed the ring in her pocket, scouted the terrain for signs of life, then scaled up the embankment and ran back to her car.

On the drive home, the anxiety didn't abate. Lacey had watched enough true-crime TV shows[8] with Paul to know she was tampering with evidence. She was interfering with a criminal investigation that hadn't even started. And worst of all, Lacey might know the killer. He'd left his ring at the scene of the crime, after all. Well, his mother's ring, but he always carried it in his pocket. Lacey's next move couldn't be a hasty one. She had to think about her every step until this whole thing was over. Then she realized that if anyone connected the body to the second dump site, her footprints were all over it.

Lacey drove ten miles up the two-lane blacktop, five miles past Emery. A fleeting positive thought drifted through her as the woodsy landscape passed in her periphery. It could be worse. She could live in Emery and sling hash at Diner (they didn't even bother giving it a name). While driving, Lacey unlaced her shoes and slowed the car. When the coast was clear, she tossed them out the window one at a time.

"Where have you been and what happened to your shoes?" Paul asked when Lacey returned home.

"Driving," Lacey replied, sidestepping the second question.

Paul had always had a notoriously short attention span. In fact, no one would play basketball with him anymore—he kept forgetting which team he was on. Lacey figured a quick subject change and he'd forget all about her missing footwear. She wasn't sure she wanted to tell Paul about her excursion.

"Who crashed?" she asked.

"Don't know," Paul replied.

---

[8] Like *Nightcrimes*?

"Whose plane?"

"Couldn't say."

"You're just chock-full of useful information," Lacey said. Sometimes she had to pull teeth to get a complete answer from Paul. Other times he was as long-winded as a folksinger. When it came down to it, Paul had more to say on subjects he knew nothing about.

"A plane went up into a ball of flames. Just like in the movies. Where were you? The whole town was there."

"Not the whole town," Lacey replied.

"If you've got something on your mind, spill it," Paul said.

When Paul wasn't stoned, he could tune in to Lacey's moods like a transistor radio (which might explain why he smoked so much). But it had been a while since he was thinking clearly. It took her by surprise. Besides, she didn't like being in this alone. So she told him.

"Headless non-Darryl is missing from his second resting place."

Paul sighed. Lacey wasn't sure if he was sighing about the missing-body part or the Lacey-knowing-about-the-missing-body part.

"You returned to the dump site?" Paul asked, disappointed. "Good job staying under the radar."

"The whole town was occupied. I couldn't have manufactured a better scenario."

"Lacey, you have to let it go."

"A man is dead. I can't let it go."

"A man is always dead, Lacey. Is it your plan to start investigating them all?"

"If they're dumped on our property, yes," Lacey replied.

Paul took a hit from the pipe he kept in his pocket. He reached for his beer, clumsily knocking it over. Paul righted the bottle and saved the few ounces that remained. Lacey jumped up to grab a rag from the kitchen. Then she stopped herself halfway to her destination and said, "You spilled it, you clean it up."

Lacey's brief assertion was followed by the sound of an engine barreling up the driveway. If both siblings had been hooked up to an EKG, the thing would have exploded.

"Shit," Lacey said, not even knowing who they'd find on the other side of the door.

The engine died suddenly, so they knew it wasn't Rafael paying another visit. Paul approached the curtains.

"Don't peek," Lacey said. "It looks suspicious. Just act normal."

"Normally, I'd peek through the curtains," Paul replied.

Lacey watched the beer drip onto the shag carpet. She shook her head, returned to the kitchen, and grabbed a sponge and dishrag. She cleaned up the mess, waiting for the doorbell. Despite expecting the unnerving buzzing sound, both siblings jumped as if they'd been stung by a bee.

Paul looked through the peephole.

Who is it? Lacey mouthed. Paul's complexion whitened even beyond his usual indoor tan. *Sheriff Ed*, he mouthed back. Paul hid the pipe and pulled the can of air freshener from the pantry, loading the room up with the scent of a mountain breeze, whatever the hell that was. Lacey answered the door, despite her recent stand against it.

"Sheriff, to what do we owe the pleasure," Lacey said.

Paul rolled his eyes out of sight. Lacey had never used that phrase before, especially not to law enforcement.

The sheriff nodded at Paul and remained in the foyer. Lacey wondered whether the sheriff was smelling mountain breeze or mountain breeze masking the scent of marijuana. When Sheriff Ed's nostrils flared and he shot Lacey a glance, her question was answered. She always had a feeling he knew what was going on in the basements and backwoods of Mercer, but he usually seemed to turn a blind eye. His reticence unnerved her, but she channeled her energy into making a show of tidying up after Paul's beer spill.

"It's like living in a frat house," she mumbled.

"I wish," Paul replied.

"You seen Terry Jakes?" the sheriff asked.

Lacey was hearing about Terry Jakes all the time, but she had to pause to remember the last time she'd actually seen him.

"He came into the café a week ago maybe."

"How about you, Paul?"

"I talked to him on the phone Monday night."

"How'd he sound?" the sheriff asked.

"You've talked to Terry before," Paul replied. "You know what he sounds like."

Paul's habit of occasionally taking questions too literally was yet another trait that Lacey loathed. She shot her brother a glance loaded with both embarrassment and hostility and clarified the question in the most condescending manner.

"He means, did he sound normal? Was anything strange about your conversation?"

"You could be a detective, Lacey," the sheriff replied.

"Don't encourage her," Paul replied.

"Do you recall what you and Terry talked about?"

"He was working on his *Survivor* application. He wanted to know if I'd shoot the video for him again."

Ed and Lacey sighed in unison.

"I wish he'd give up on that," Ed commented, looking to the ceiling as if that wish were just as hopeless as Terry's dreams of fame.

"They always have one redneck per season. Terry doesn't see why it can't be him," Paul said.

"Why are you asking about Terry?" Lacey inquired.

"He's been missing forty-eight hours. His ex-wife called and asked if I'd locked him up for the usual and then we had a talk. I made a few phone calls. He might have taken a vacation. You know Terry. He's unreliable on a good day. But still, let me know if you hear from him."

With that, Sheriff Wickfield departed. Lacey double-bolted the doors and joined her brother on the couch. The silence between them was as unnerving as a jackhammer right outside your bedroom window. Paul turned on the television and ramped up the volume. He didn't want Lacey to ask the question she was going to ask.

"Do you think—"

"No," Paul replied with the speed of a man drawing his gun.

"They're about the same size," Lacey mumbled.

Paul turned up the volume even higher. Lacey shot up from the couch and manually turned off the television, although it took her a minute to find the button, not having done that in years.

"Have you heard anything about Hart lately?" she asked, sitting back down on the couch. They looked like two spies meeting on a park bench, avoiding eye contact and speaking under their breath.

"Why are you asking about Hart?"

"No reason," Lacey replied.

"There has to be a reason," Paul said, and you could tell he was curious about that reason since he didn't turn the television back on.

"I haven't heard from him in a few months. Wondered if anybody else had."

If Lacey told Paul the truth, that she had Hart's ring in her back pocket, they might have reverted to their childhood selves and gotten into a wrestling match right then and there. It was unfair, Lacey thought, that a man whose primary forms of exercise were fetching beer from the fridge and hopping into his truck could outfight her. But it was one of those hard facts women live with.

Paul looked at his sister askance; his brain played with just a few pieces of a puzzle.

"Did Hart steal your shoes?"

"Why would you ask that?"

"Out of the blue you start asking questions about Hart. And your shoes have mysteriously disappeared and you won't talk about it. I'm just trying to make the facts add up."

"Listen, Sherlock, that's probably the worst example of deductive reasoning I've ever heard."

"Then enlighten me."

"There's trouble brewing, so it's only natural that Hart comes to mind," Lacey said. While it was true that trouble seemed to follow Hart around, when they were a couple, she couldn't see it until the very end. Hart let you see only what he wanted you to see. Eventually Lacey accepted that he was a skilled con artist, but she never remembered feeling like she was being conned. He'd made her feel like she was always the only person in the world.

"What happened to your shoes?" Paul asked.

"My footprints were all over the second dump site. I got paranoid and decided to get rid of them."

"Where?"

"I tossed them in the Diner dumpster in Emery."

"Really?"

"Yes."

"You wouldn't lie to me, would you, Lace?"

"No."

NOTES:

Dave,

While this is the first time I've indulged in a traditional who-dunit, I do know that we should be sprinkling the story with clues, to move things forward. You have to admit you have a tendency to become infatuated with characters at the expense of story.

Still, I think we're generally heading in the right direction. Good luck dealing with that plane crash. If you're having trouble sorting it out, let me know and I'll help.

Lisa

P.S. Can we meet Terry Jakes, please?

Lisa,

Thank you for your generous offer of help. But keep in mind that it's still early. Try to be patient. I'm reminded of all the weak lukewarm tea you've served me because you couldn't wait for the water to boil.

Don't worry about Terry. Once you meet him you're going to want to feature him in all your chapters.

As for the road trip, I would think after all this time you'd have a few fond memories of it. I know I do.

Dave

CHAPTER 6

Late Saturday morning Paul stood at the base of a thirty-foot wooden ladder in the forest, looking up.

"So this is your idea of irony," he shouted up at the platform above him. "Lying low above it all."

No response.

"Terry!" he shouted.

"Terry no here! You come back later!" came the answer from above, in a ridiculous accent alternating between Beijing and Edinburgh.

"I'm coming up," Paul shouted. At the top of the ladder, he nudged his head up through the wooden hatch. It landed with a whack as his head popped up through Terry's floor.

"Hey, little brother," Terry said to the head.

"Sheriff Ed's looking for you," said Paul. He smelled chili, Terry, and gin, in that order.

"And I'm all the way out here. What a coincidence. What did he say?" He was slurring his words.

"Nothing, just if I'd seen you."

"What'd you tell him?" Terry asked.

"The truth."

"Hmm. An interesting gambit. I'll look into that," Terry said, offering his hand to Paul and helping him up into the shed.

The forest service fire observation tower was Terry's retreat whenever the pressure of work, ex-wives, or the "powers that be" tripped his hair-trigger instinct for self-preservation. Not that he was selfish—when Terry had taught Paul the business, he did so with no expectation of reward.

"You don't owe me shit," he once told Paul. "I take that back. When I'm old and pissing myself, you got to pull the plug." Even early on, he never asked Paul about his parents. Terry knew he was no one's idea of a father figure, and he never tried to fill that role. As a result, in a weird way, he partly did.

Paul took a seat at the tiny wooden table. The shed was just big enough for the table, a stool, a cot, and the hatch. Surrounding the shed was a rickety observation deck. The whole thing felt like a crow's nest on a pirate ship.

"So what brought you out here? Hard time from the ex-wives club?" Paul asked.

"Just protecting the citizenry, as usual," Terry said. His voice was shaky, and not from the gin—Terry usually got louder and more articulate when he drank. "Me and Smokey taking care of business."

"Glad you're okay. I—"

"You're just in time for happy hour," Terry interrupted. "I forget—how do you take your martinis?"

Paul thought for a second, taking a seat on the stool. "Warm, bone-dry, not shaken or stirred, served in a plastic Thermos cap. Preferably Winner's Cup. Failing that, Bombay Sapphire."

"That's a can-do," said Terry, and poured them a round. "Here's to the survival instinct," he said, tapping his camping cup against Paul's Thermos cap and spilling a little gin.

They knocked their drinks back. Paul grimaced and Terry refilled them.

"So. Catch the fireworks yesterday?" Terry asked, trying to sound casual.

"Yeah. In fact, I had front-row seats," said Paul.

"What the hell happened?"

"They don't know," Paul said. "A little plane just blew up. You know anything about it?"

"No idea," said Terry. He let out a theatrical sigh. "I'm too young to be sayin' I'm too old for this shit."

"Actually, you've been saying that since I was twelve," said Paul. "What shit, exactly?"

"Just the usual times a hundred, alimony and whatnot. You know me—shit reaches shin-level, I can wade. When it gets to be a shit Katrina, I head for higher ground."

Terry was fading, leaning to one side and closing one eye, a sure sign that he was only a couple of units shy of matriculating[9] to the next level of drunkenness. When that happened, he'd be beyond human comprehension. If Terry had any beans to spill, Paul would have to get them spilled soon.

"So, have you talked to Darryl lately?" Paul asked.

"Look, man, I don't know. He's in the wind as far as I know," Terry said, leaning a little farther toward his sleeping bag.

"What?"

"Just a figure of speech, man. Like 'Heads are gonna roll.'"

Paul felt that one at the base of his neck. He grabbed Terry's hand. "Terry, what the fuck's going on?"

With his other hand, Terry gulped down the rest of his gin. "Remember that favor I did for you?"

"Which one?" Paul asked.

"All of them, man. I'm calling 'em in. I need you to take something over to Tate at the Timberline."

The Timberline was a bar downtown; Tate was its owner and daytime bartender. Paul didn't relish the idea of interacting with him, but the errand sounded simple enough.

"No problem," Paul said. "What is it?"

"Two grand."

"Uh, okay," Paul said, glancing around the shed. Stacks of money were not in evidence.

"The other part is I need to borrow two grand," Terry said. "No joke. If he doesn't get it today—" He interrupted himself to look Paul in the eye, asserting his lucidity. Paul had spent enough time with drunk Terry to know when he was bullshitting. He wasn't.

---

[9]How about you matriculate into a plain English course?

"What's going on? Why do you owe Tate so much?"

"Like fresh milk, a bad deed does not turn at once," said Terry.

Paul was silent. He'd learned that responding to one of Terry's maxims only led to more of them.

"Just can you do it or not?" Terry asked, flopping back onto his sleeping bag.

"I can do it," Paul said. "But I need to know what's happening. What's going on with you and Tate? Why's Sheriff Ed asking about you?"

Terry was done talking. When Terry went down, he stayed there. It was only midday, but Paul guessed he'd be out until the next morning. Terry was prone to passing out suddenly, but when he woke up, he'd remember every detail of their conversation.

Then Terry mumbled something that sounded like "Hotels going up on Atlantic and Ventnor."

"What the hell? Terry?" Then the snoring kicked in, overwhelming the cheery clamor of the insects and birds below. Paul sat with him for a while, then found an old wool blanket in a corner and covered him up.

Paul lifted up the hatch in the floor and climbed down the ladder. His truck was parked a mile away on an old fire road. The hike gave him time to think about the errand. Two grand was a major hit these days, but it was way less than he'd borrowed from Terry when he was getting started. And an unhappy Tate, he knew, was a dangerous thing. By the time he reached his truck, he felt like he'd sweated out all the gin and most of the anxiety. He thought about stopping by the Tarpit to talk to Lacey, but decided it would be simpler to keep her out of it. She had a way of complicating things. Paul pointed his truck downtown, where his bank and his bar were next-door neighbors.

The teller didn't raise an eyebrow; in Mercer, cash transactions were still the norm. With a fat front pocket, Paul went next door. The Timberline was the default bar for most locals, having outlasted numerous fringe bars that were trendier, more upscale, more violent, more granola, more whatever. Back when Paul and Darryl were regulars, the tree in its green neon sign used to grow, fall, and regrow in blinking cycles. Now it stayed fallen, but at least it was still lit.

Tate wasn't behind the bar, which meant he was probably in the office in back. Paul had never seen him hurt anyone firsthand, but there was almost a hum of violence about him. Like a lot people around Mercer, he had a side job that was more lucrative than his main one, as a kind of supervisor—more like pimp, Terry liked to say—for the couriers who took product back and forth between L.A. and the north. He had a stable of drivers of all ages and backgrounds, and was quick to let them go if they didn't execute perfectly.

Paul sat down at the bar, feeling the envelope in his front pocket bend. He smelled menthols and perfume. The woman on the next stool spun to get a look at him. It was Deena, Terry's first ex-wife.

"Well, if it isn't Mr. Paul Hansen, Jr.," she said, in her sultriest voice.

"Mrs. Robinson, are you trying to seduce me?" It was their running joke.

Paul was glad to see her. If anyone knew about what was going on under the surface in Mercer, she did. She had a fat man's capacity for booze and a marine's discipline when it was time to stop.

"Seen Terry lately?" he asked her.

"Nope."

"Is he behind on his checks again?"

"Nope. Maybe he took a run up to Spirit Rock, for old times' sake." Spirit Rock was the Indian casino outside Tulac. "If you see him, give him a kiss."

Before Paul could get the bartender's attention, Deena said, "Two more John Dalys"—Arnold Palmers with vodka. They made small talk for a while. When it became clear she wasn't going to dish up the gossip, he asked her what the latest was.

"Hmm, I guess nothing. Unless you count 'Mysterious Plane Explodes.'"

"Come on, there's always something."

"Okay," Deena said in a stage whisper, leaning toward him. "But this one is *not* for general consumption."

"Agreed," said Paul.

"You know Sheriff Ed's hot little wife? Turns out she might have dipped a toe into some very, shall we say, *deep* waters. From what I hear, things could get really complicated really soon for her. I really shouldn't be talking about this." Then she drained her drink. "You know, I think I just reached my quota. See ya, sweetie."

Paul turned to the bartender on shift. "Tate around today?"

"Your name?"

"Paul Hansen."

Without another word, the bartender went to the back of the bar and into the office. He came out and gave Paul the okay with a thumb over the shoulder.

Paul went back and through the open office door. Tate was sitting behind a big metal desk.

"Have a seat," Tate said, and Paul did.

"I have some money for you from Terry." He handed over the envelope.

Tate didn't even look inside. "Where is he?" he asked.

"No idea," Paul lied. "He dropped this off at my place."

"How much is here?"

"Two thousand."

Tate shook his head a little. "One more time. Where is he?"

"If I knew, I'd tell you," Paul said, looking him in the eye but not overdoing it. He could lie okay.

Tate lowered his head, put his elbows up on the desk, and stroked his ponytail hand-over-hand.

"Can I go?" Paul asked.

Still no reply. After a few moments Paul tentatively stood up and started back toward the bar. Before Paul reached the door, Tate said, "Tell Terry I won't take any more payments."

"Okay," Paul said. When he got Tate's meaning, he added, "How much is the whole thing?"

Tate gave him a look like it was an interesting philosophical question. "All of it," he said.

Paul sat in his truck, trying to pull himself together. His first impulse was to get out of there, to just flee from whatever insanity had overtaken Mercer. If he had been alone, he might have done it, too—headed to the coast for a few weeks. But Lacey depended on him to keep the business running, and money was tight even before the day's unexpected expense. Paul decided to go straight to the only person who was tied to the body. Whatever was going on, Darryl was involved in it, and probably deeper than Paul was.

Paul hadn't been out to Darryl's house for almost a year—not since he and Darryl had argued about the best way to water an associate's big hillside plot. Darryl was the best irrigation guy around, but he was also well aware of that fact, and very touchy about his methods. It shouldn't have been a big deal, but they'd been distant ever since.

Paul pulled over a few houses down the street, not wanting to give Darryl a chance to slip out the back door if he didn't want company. As he sat there thinking about what he'd say, he noticed a little guy in a baseball cap creeping along the side of Darryl's house, ducking low to avoid the windows. Except it wasn't a guy. It was Lacey. He watched her unlatch the side gate and disappear into the backyard. Paul sat there for a moment. Then he put his truck in reverse, backed away down the block and around the corner, and drove away.

NOTES:

Lisa,

I think I'm getting the hang of this clue business. Let me know if you need me to spell out the Monopoly reference.

To respond to your last note, you've always had this notion that plot and character are two separate entities. In the *Fop* days you bulldozed characters in the name of moving the plot forward. The croupier, for example, was a casualty we couldn't afford. When the casino burned down in the third act, he would have been the natural choice. Instead we had to conjure a suspect out of the blue.

If our book doesn't have the requisite number of kills and thrills, who cares? The reader will remember the characters long after they've forgotten who done it.

Dave

Dave,

Thank you for your thoughts on character and plot. But I kind of want my readers to remember "who done it" rather than who drinks warm gin in a Thermos cap and calls it a martini. It's a nice detail, but even the finest martini could use an olive. Meaning something to chew on.

By the way, did we ever find out whose plane crashed? We might want to clear that up one of these days. As for your "clue," a Google search informed me that Ventnor and Atlantic Avenues are real estate on a Monopoly board. I have no idea where you're going with that. Do you?

On a positive note, I don't believe you mentioned Irving the cat even once.

Lisa

P.S. I didn't mean to imply that the road trip was all bad. Reno was awesome. Especially when we won the football bet. I just don't know why you refused to get gas. We could have died out there.

CHAPTER 7

When Lacey heard a truck idling down the desolate street, she slipped between a set of bushes, scratching the exposed skin on her neck. A breathless and eternal minute passed until the truck rolled away. She circled the perimeter of Darryl's house, searching for a better view inside. She didn't know what she was looking for, but an investigation has to start somewhere, right? And the only two people linked to the body were Darryl Cleveland and now Hart Drexel. She started with the easy one. Darryl. At least she knew where he lived. Besides, she had spent all day batting away dark thoughts like flies. But whenever you try not to think about something, that's when you can't escape it. So she let herself think, just for a minute.

Hart's ring had been left behind at the second crime scene. From the moment she'd found it, the ugly thought had stuck with her. *Hart was the killer.* But then she cooled down and figured there had to be another explanation. Hart was trouble, sure, but mostly she remembered all the little things he used to do for her—checking the oil in her car so she wouldn't burn out her transmission, bringing her coffee in the morning. Once he even tried making chicken soup when she had a cold. Lacey had to pour it out the window when he wasn't looking, but still.

Could she have really spent three and a half years with a murderer?

A light shone from the living room, offering a fish-tank view. Darryl was sitting on his couch, a beer in one hand and the other hand tucked into his jeans. Lacey had seen men sit like this many times before, even when they weren't alone. Still, she felt more like a peeping tom than a private detective. The show on TV was *Cudgel*.[10] Lacey recognized the contestant and even noted that it was a rerun—how tragic was that? She was definitely getting out of this town.

Fifteen minutes passed without any action except on the TV screen. Then the telephone rang, which made Lacey jump. But not Darryl. He just sat there as if he couldn't hear it. When *Cudgel* broke for a commercial, Darryl got up from the couch and pressed a button on his answering machine. Lacey assumed someone had left a message and Darryl was listening to it. She couldn't make out the voice, only that there was a voice.

Then Darryl looked at her, or right out the window to where she was lurking. Only it was dark outside and light in the house, so she knew he couldn't see anything. Still, from the way he was looking, he knew someone was out there.

Darryl killed the lights and Lacey made a run for it. This time, she exited through the backyard, scaling the chain-link fence. On her way down, she sliced open her left arm. She felt the pain, but refused to utter a sound.

Darryl peered through the living room window, then raced into the kitchen in the back of the house and saw a shadow escape through his backyard. He'd never be able to identify her. In fact, if pressed for details, he'd say a male, approximately fourteen years of age, wearing a baseball cap, a black shirt, and blue jeans, was casing his home for a burglary. But only because that's exactly how Paul described the suspicious individual when he left a message on Darryl's answering machine, explaining that he just happened to be driving by. Had a delivery and couldn't stop, but he thought he'd be neighborly, even though they weren't exactly neighbors.

Lacey sprinted to her car, just a few blocks away. Once safely inside, she flipped the light on and got a good look at her wound. There was

---

[10]What, you can't come up with one of your own?

nothing clean around to stanch the bleeding, so she removed her sweat-shirt and wrapped it around her arm. The blood kept flowing, and Lacey was starting to feel queasy and a little faint. She thought about calling Paul but knew that he would ask questions that she wasn't about to answer. The closest emergency room was over twenty miles away. She didn't think she could make it.

"Are you the new Doc Holland?" Lacey asked, standing in front of the old Doc Holland's residence/office, trying not to drip blood on the front porch.

"I guess so," the sleepy-eyed male replied.

"I'm sorry to bother you so late, but I didn't think this could wait until morning."

The new Doc Holland, who was wearing scrubs that most likely per-formed double duty as pajamas, unwrapped the sweatshirt from Lacey's arm and studied the deep cut.

"I'll meet you at the office in one minute," he said.

Lacey walked ten paces to the adjacent building and sat down on the stoop. In that brief passage of time, the new Doc Holland threw on a lab coat, brushed his teeth, and walked through the interior door that con-nected his new home to his new office. He invited Lacey inside, turned on the blinding lights of the examination room, and began pulling sup-plies from the metal chest.

"We haven't been formally introduced," the new Doc Holland said. "I'm Matthew Egan."

"Nice to meet you, Dr. Egan."

"You can call me Matthew."

"Nah."

"And you are?"

"Sorry. Got distracted by all the blood. I'm Lacey Hansen."

"Nice meeting you, Ms. Hansen."

"Don't call me that."

"How did this happen?"

"Climbing a fence."

"Why were you doing that, this time of night?"

"I don't know. Just felt like it, I guess."

"When was your last tetanus shot?"

"A while ago, I think. I'll probably need one."

"This is going to hurt."

"It usually does."

While Dr. Egan injected lidocaine around the jagged edges of the cut, Lacey gritted her teeth and took inventory of the room and the new doctor. The room had been repainted a soothing blue, a great improvement over the sour, paint-chipped yellow that was Doc Holland's brand. Also, the supply closet appeared to have been either scrubbed or replaced, and the entire examination room had the sterile scent that one comes to expect from a doctor's office if, say, your doctor isn't Doc Holland. The improvements didn't end there. Other than the dark circles under his eyes and a nose that had clearly been broken once, maybe twice, the new Doc Holland, Dr. Egan, could easily be described as handsome. Also, unlike Doc Holland, there was no discernible odor emanating from the new doctor, except maybe the smell of fresh toothpaste. She guessed his age to be about thirty-five.

Right about then was when Lacey got suspicious.

While Dr. Egan waited for the lidocaine to take, he tried to make casual conversation, a skill Lacey never quite got the knack for.

"So, Lacey, how long have you lived in Mercer?"

"Too long."

"You have family?"

"I live with my brother."

"That's nice of you."

"Why? Oh, I see. You got it all wrong. Paul doesn't have special needs or anything. Well, sometimes it seems like he does."

"I see."

"It's just a convenience."

"Sometimes that's a good thing."

"Sometimes it isn't. What happened to Doc Holland?"

"He wanted to retire."

"He never mentioned it before, and he sure skipped town quickly."

"Sometimes people make snap decisions."

"Did you make one?" Lacey asked.

"I'm going to start stitching now. You should just feel a tug. No pain."

"This isn't my first time."

"I didn't think so," Doc Egan replied. "First-timers expect the stitches to hurt, not the painkiller. You gripped the side of the table when you saw the lidocaine needle."

Lacey looked directly at the wound while Egan started stitching.

"Do you regret your decision yet?" Lacey asked.

"Excuse me," Doc Egan replied.

"You know, moving here."

"No. Why do you ask?"

"Because everybody wants to get out of here. But you, you move from a perfectly nice city like San Francisco to a town like Mercer."

"Maybe I needed some clean air and some country living."

"There's better country than this. In fact, you could probably throw a dart at a map and find it."

"Doesn't seem so bad to me."

"You must be running away from something," Lacey said.

Doc Egan looked her in the eye and sighed.

"You sure get to the point, don't you?"

"Not always. But I like a good story when I'm getting stitched up."

"No story. I got divorced," Doc Egan explained. "It was unpleasant. The city reminded me of . . . everything, so I decided to get out. Now does it make more sense?"

"Yes. I'm sorry about that."

An uncomfortable silence set in. Lacey felt bad for digging until she hit a nerve, so she decided to dig where the new doc probably didn't have any nerves.

"You're better at this than Doc Holland," Lacey said, commenting on the repair job.

"Thank you."

"You should see the scars he's left behind in this town. Sometimes you had to wonder if he was really a doctor. Where is he now?"

"He asked me not to tell," Doc Egan replied.

Lacey got the feeling she was playing with a puzzle where half the pieces were missing. She was pretty sure Doc Holland fit into it somewhere, but she couldn't construct a scenario that fit with the few pieces she already had.

"Did you ever meet Doc Holland in person?"

"Of course," Egan replied.

"What did he look like?"

"You know what he looked like. Are you feeling okay, Lacey?"

In truth, she wasn't. She hadn't had dinner, and the blood and the pain and the vague sense of doom were making her nauseous, but she pressed on.

"I'm fine. What did he look like?"

"About sixty-five, average height, slight paunch, almost completely bald except for a patch of gray hair on the top of his head, bulbous nose, crooked smile."

"That's Doc Holland, all right."

Doc Egan finished stitching and then dressed the wound. He looked at Lacey with concern. She was staring blankly at the ceiling, trying to make sense of this mixed bag of facts that didn't add up.

"Now how are you going to get home?" Doc Egan asked.

"Same way I got here," Lacey replied, sitting up on the table. She didn't mention that the room was spinning.

"I don't think you should drive. Can you call your brother?"

"I'd rather not. Besides, he's probably drunk by now," Lacey said.

"Then I'll drive you."

"Totally unnecessary, Doc. I have a car and I'm perfectly fine."

Doc Egan reached into his pocket and held out Lacey's keys.

"I have your keys," he replied. "You can pick up your car tomorrow."

Lacey slipped off the table, took the bloody sweatshirt from the edge of the table, and tossed it in the trash. Contemplating the bandage on her arm, Lacey tried to figure out how she could hide the accident from Paul. She was not in the mood for his questions.

"Doc, I'm cold. Do you have a shirt I can borrow? One with sleeves?"

Lacey waited on the front porch while Doc Egan locked up. He handed her a baseball jersey, which she pulled on over her T-shirt. It just covered the last strip of tape on her forearm.

The drive to the Hansen home was silent, minus Lacey's terse directions.

"Here," she said, as they approached the home. One light as usual was on in the living room, punctuated by the flicker of a television set.

"Looks cozy," the new doc said.

"Hmm," Lacey replied.

"You should take the painkillers I gave you before bed. It's going to smart in a few hours."

Lacey opened the car door. "Thanks for the ride, Doc."

As Lacey strolled up the steps to the house, Doc Egan shouted, "See you tomorrow."

"Tomorrow?"

"Don't forget to pick up your car."

"Right."

Inside, Paul stared with rapt attention at the TV screen. It was an act. They both knew it. Under normal circumstances, Paul would have asked

Lacey where she had been. But neither said anything, because one was tired of delivering lies and the other was tired of hearing them.

"Night, Paul," was all she said.

As predicted, Lacey woke up in the middle of the night with her arm burning. She grabbed two Vicodin from her dresser drawer and walked into the kitchen for a glass of water. As she gulped the water, she heard a car pull up in front of their house and stop. She looked at the clock: 3:12 a.m. Adrenaline pumping, she tiptoed over to the window. Just before she parted the curtains, the car screeched away.

Lacey opened the front door and turned on the porch light. She walked a few paces toward the curb. That's when she saw it. Lacey raced inside the house and shook her brother awake.

"He's back," she said.

Paul stood over the even riper corpse.

"Who is doing this to us?" she asked.

"I think we can rule out Darryl, since he'd probably think to remove his family heirloom. Is it still there?"

"Yes."

"Let's keep him out of it."

Both siblings held their breath as Lacey aimed the flashlight and Paul bent down to remove the wristwatch. Something familiar caught Lacey's eye. While Paul gazed into the distance, devising another plan, Lacey knelt down and lifted up the sleeve on the corpse. Just a few inches above the wrist, she found an amateur tattoo of a four-leaf clover.

Lacey got to her feet, took a deep breath, then choked on the stench and turned away. She silently handed Paul the flashlight and strode back into the house. Five minutes later, she returned carrying two of Paul's marijuana plants from the basement. She put them in the back of his truck.

"Lacey, what are you doing?"

Lacey ignored her brother and reentered the house, exiting once again with two more plants. Paul followed her as she put them in his truck bed.

"Lacey. Talk to me," Paul said, as if his sister had turned into a zombie. She didn't look right.

"I just called the cops," Lacey said in a monotone. "Leave now while you can. I'll tell the sheriff you're staying with Terry at the lookout tonight. Go," she said, tossing him the keys to the truck.

"Lacey, what's gotten into you?"

"The dead body is Hart Drexel. I'm not moving him again."

NOTES:

Dave,

    Back to you. Seven chapters in and we finally know who our dead body is. I'm sure I'm stating the obvious, but now would be a great time to start figuring out who killed him and why.

    I really wanted to bring the Babalato brothers into the mix, but all I could think about was family counseling and meds and that didn't fit in with moving the plot forward.

        Lisa

Lisa,

    I wasn't expecting the leisurely detour into romantic comedy territory, but I enjoyed it. I can't wait to see what's in store for Lacey and the hunky doctor. Maybe a quirky gay neighbor?

    With regard to suspects and plot advancement, I'm not saying I have it all perfectly mapped out, but I assure you there's plenty up my sleeve. Remember how I came up with the haberdasher gambit to get the fop out of Zurich? You never saw it coming, and it saved the whole first half of the script.

        Dave

P.S. We didn't die, did we?

CHAPTER 8

"Have you lost your mind?" Paul said in a furious whisper. "Call the cops *first*, then decide what to do? Did you ever think to maybe talk it over with me? I know it's three a.m. and you're scared. But did it occur to you that maybe we should get our stories straight?"

Lacey looked woozy and focused at the same time. "Here's the *story*," she said. "My ex-fiancé is dead in our driveway. The end. This has to stop."

"*You* have to stop. It's like you've been trying to get us deeper into this mess ever since it started."

"I'd love to chat. Fact is, the cops are on their way," Lacey said wearily. "Do you want to help me load up the rest of the plants or not?"

She had a point. Paul shook his head and returned to the basement. He put the cops' ETA at twenty minutes. This time of night, first on the scene would likely be Deputy Doug Lund.

Thirteen minutes later they'd hauled out all the plants, as well as a few Tupperware containers full of finished product, but there was no way they could dismantle the lights and water lines. Neither of which was illegal, but still. Terry had taught Paul to never relax about attention from the law. Even if the sheriff's department seemed to turn a blind eye, you never knew when higher authorities would decide to assert their power. Just ask anyone who was allowed to open and operate a dispensary in L.A. just so they could be brutally raided by the Feds after building a thriving business.

Paul had designed the room so it could be taken down completely on a day's notice. The best they could do was sweep up, take all the tools and soil amendments, and pile everything into the truck with the plants. He ran to the barn for a tarp, realizing on the way that the only one he'd find was the one they'd wrapped the body in three days ago. That wasn't so bad. The tarp was one more thing they didn't want to be here when the cops started poking around. Not something Lacey would have thought of.

He called her over to the truck and they unfolded the tarp. They both gagged as the smell jumped out from it. They stood on opposite sides of the truck bed and passed the rope back and forth until it was firmly in place. Paul looked at his watch.

"Okay, it's three thirty-eight," he said. "Don't take this the wrong way, Lace. But I think it'd be awesome if the person talking to the cops didn't have dilated pupils or a mysterious arm wound. How about you take the truck, I stay here and answer questions?"

She threw the rope back over to Paul's side. "But *I called*," she said, plainly. "They know I'm here."

"Uh, good point." Paul didn't do his best thinking in the middle of the night. "Okay . . . but don't tell them I'm with Terry. Tell them . . . I have a new girlfriend up in Tulac."

Lacey just gave him a raised eyebrow. It was the middle of the night, they were tying down an illegal load before the cops arrived, and her headless ex lay a few yards away, but some reflexes were automatic under any circumstances. "Hmm," she said.

"What!? I could actually have one up there now, for all you know."

"You're right. My bad."

"What about your arm?" Paul said, pointing at the bloody bandage peeking out from the sleeve of her new baseball jersey.

"I'll think of something."

"That's what I'm afraid of," Paul said. "Just stay calm."

"I am calm. You have to go now."

Paul took her by the shoulders and looked into her eyes. "We'll get through this."

He got in the truck, took off down the hill, and turned away from town.

He didn't know where he was going, but he didn't want to pass a sheriff's cruiser on the way.

Lacey sat on the porch swing for a while, not rocking, just thinking about how this could have happened. Back in high school, all Hart seemed to need was to make her laugh. He used to do impressions of anyone in town on command. Terry Jakes was her favorite, followed by Sheriff Ed and Paul. For the past few months, every time she went to town, she expected to run into Hart. Half hoping, sometimes. Now that would never happen. After a while, she got up, went inside, and put a sweatshirt on to hide her wound.

"Not so lucky after all, I guess," said Doug the deputy, leaning as close as he could to the body's crude clover tattoo.

"Jesus, Doug, Hart's dead," Lacey said. "You knew him."

It had been well after four by the time he'd arrived, giving Lacey a solid half-hour alone with Hart. After Doug had taped off the crime scene, she'd told him the basics—how she knew it was Hart (the tattoo), but didn't know what he was up to lately. She hadn't seen him since spring.

She figured she'd probably have to repeat the story later to Ed or some other higher-up. Hopefully that would be the end of it. She went with the truth.

"Sorry. I'm not exactly used to this kind of thing," said Doug, who had already demonstrated that fact with some vigorous barfing around the side of the house as soon as he'd come within smelling distance of the body.

"So, who gets called in for a thing like this?" Lacey asked.

"Everybody, I guess," said Doug. "Ed should be here any minute. The crime-scene guy is coming down from Orendale."

Lacey guessed that Sheriff Ed had instructed Doug to not fuck anything up, and above all not to touch the body. He'd succeeded on the second count, at least.

"Where's your brother?" Doug asked.

"Up in Tulac. At his new girlfriend's place."

"How about that!" Doug said. "Good for him."

Later, Lacey watched from the porch swing as Sheriff Ed finally showed up, just beating the sun. He gave her a sad little wave from across the yard, then went about checking out the body and its surroundings. Deputy Doug handed Ed his notepad and the sheriff proceeded to ask Lacey all the questions over again and a few more. Doug didn't seem to notice that his work was being redone. He pulled out another notebook and copied down the sheriff's interview verbatim. Lacey wondered why the sheriff had even allowed Doug to be first on the scene.

She knew Hart had some history with Sheriff Ed, and what Hart had told her about it was probably the tip of an ugly iceberg. With Hart, that was usually the case.

"Lacey," he said, with an empathetic look as he approached the porch.

"Nice of you to join us, Sheriff," Lacey said as he walked up the steps. She'd had enough of recent events.

Ed ignored the barb. "Where's Paul?" he asked.

"New girlfriend."

The sheriff raised his eyebrows a bit. "Well, I'll be damned," he said. "Lacey, I have to ask you to come down to the office this afternoon. Just a formality. Until then, you look like you could use some sleep. Will you be okay till Paul gets back?"

"Sure," she said. She planned to stay on the swing until they left.

The crime-scene guy had arrived, and was now taking photos and samples. He seemed just as interested in the tire tracks as the bodies. Maybe Doug had blundered after all—it looked like he was getting chewed out for driving right up to the scene. Paul, for all his supposed level-headedness, had peeled away with their plants, leaving another, even fresher set of tracks that would be easy to match, even for Mercer's finest. Maybe this would escape their attention—they hadn't exactly been meticulous so far. No one had asked where *her* car was, for example.

Finally, the crime-scene guy wrapped up the body and he and Doug carried it to the cruiser. Maybe now it would stop following her around, Lacey thought. She had to remind herself that it was Hart.

Doug came up to the porch to say good-bye. "Lace, it was good seeing you. I'm so sorry for all this. I hope you know we'll find whoever did this."

He looked like he wanted to give her a hug but glanced back at Ed over by the cruiser and reconsidered. Instead, he reached for her hand and gave it a tender shake.

Then Doug looked at his palm. There was a little smear of blood on it. Lacey gave him a pleading look.

"Irving had a fight with a feral. I tried to separate them and I got clawed," said Lacey, pulling up her sleeve to show him the bandage, from which a rivulet of blood had meandered down her forearm. She must have agitated the wound loading the truck with Paul. "I swear, Doug."

Doug gave her a long, queasy look as if he was about to throw up again. Then he composed himself. "Next time, use a hose," he said. "Old-fashioned, but it works." He wiped his palm on the inside of his jacket and walked out to the cruiser. After Doug left, Lacey rolled a joint and sucked it down. Then she went back to bed.

Paul turned off the road onto the dirt driveway of Terry's place. He hated doing this without asking permission first, but what could he do? Terry was probably still at the fire tower, out of cell phone range, and even if he wasn't, Paul wasn't about to make a call. He'd seen way too many guys get triangulated on *ThugTracers*.[11]

And besides, Terry had just called in all the favors Paul owed. So he

---

[11] I suppose I should be grateful that you didn't waste a paragraph summarizing an episode.

didn't owe Terry anything. He knew there was space in one of Terry's grow rooms, and the security here, for anyone who didn't know all the combinations like Paul did, was impeccable. As long as no one came poking around while Paul unloaded, he'd be fine.

It took Paul a half-hour to carry in his plants, set them all up under the lights, and water them by hand. They'd be fine for a while.

As mad as Paul was about his sister's decision to call the cops without consulting him, he wasn't surprised—it was typical impulsive behavior for Lacey. And it hadn't really made things worse. The return of the body made things about as bad as they could get, short of actually implicating them in the murder. What were they going to do, move the body again and wait for the killers to move it back? As to why the killers would want to involve the Hansens, Paul was at a loss. Did someone hate Hart so much that they wanted to hurt the woman he loved—even after he was dead? Or was someone getting back at both Hart and Lacey?

The truck bed was empty now except for the tarp and a tire jack. Paul hesitated for a second, then decided not to leave it with his plants. He folded it up and put the tire jack on top of it. When he got into the truck, he felt Darryl's watch in his back pocket as he sat down in the driver's seat. The truth was, he'd made his own rash decision to remove the watch—it was instinctive, and maybe dumb. There was only one way to find out.

On the way to Darryl's, he thought about his alibi for the night. What Lacey didn't realize was that if the cops questioned him, there *was* a woman in Tulac who'd vouch for him. But hopefully it wouldn't come to that. There were some things he wanted to keep to himself.

This time he parked right out front of Darryl's and went straight up to the door. Darryl answered the knock in a few seconds.

"We need to talk," Darryl said immediately as he opened the door, and gestured him into the house.

"Couldn't agree more," Paul said.

They walked through the carpeted living room and into the bright kitchen. It was a distinctly parental home out of a nineties sitcom. Despite Darryl's relative success, he still lived like a teenager. His stepmom cooked all the meals and kept up the house. There was an actual list of chores on the fridge. She was apparently out with her new boyfriend.

They sat at the table. Darryl went first.

"So. You don't seem too curious to follow up about the so-called prowler you saw," he said. His voice was shaking a little. "What was up with that? You just happened to be driving by out here? I know we haven't been on great terms for a while, but if someone was breaking into my house and you noticed it, why not at least scare them off?"

"I think the real question," Paul said, "is if you were home, why didn't you pick up the phone?"

"Look, man, I'm in full turtle." It was a phrase of Terry's that meant maximum retreat.

"That's funny. Terry's been turtling pretty hard himself," Paul said. Darryl gave him a blank look.

"Listen," Paul continued, "I have something of yours. I'll give it to you in exchange for some information."

"Keep it, man. I got no information that wants to be shared."

Paul put the watch on the table in front of him.

"Holy shit. Where'd you find that?" Darryl reached for it and Paul snatched it back.

"Come on," said Darryl. "Someone stole it out of my truck a few weeks ago."

"Tell me the truth, man. Why was Hart Drexel wearing your watch?"

"Drexel? Fuck. No idea. I haven't talked to that dude in years. That's the God's honest," Darryl said.

Paul believed him. He'd seen Darryl lie more than once—it was an occupational hazard they shared—and this was different. Darryl was scared, but he wasn't lying.

"There's a little more to it," Paul said. "Hart's dead. Somebody cut off his head and dumped his body on our property. He was wearing your watch. I took it off before the cops came. I'm trying to help you."

He held out the watch. Darryl suddenly wasn't so keen on taking it—or even touching it. Paul put it down on the thick vinyl tablecloth.

"Jesus," said Darryl, shaking his head. "What else can possibly . . . I'm sorry man, uh . . . thanks."

"Okay. Now it's your turn. Why are you and Terry so freaked out?"

"Let's just say I found out some stuff I didn't mean to find out. As long as I keep it to myself—and certain people *know* I'm keeping it to myself—I'll be fine. You gotta believe this: I can't tell you more without sharing my problem with you. And it sounds like you have your own unrelated shit to deal with. As for Terry, who knows? If he's in the same boat I am, that's news to me."

"What about Tate?"

"At the Timberline? Not involved, as far as I know. That dude's okay with me."

It wasn't much, but Paul was relieved to hear it. He convinced himself he'd gotten all he could get out of Darryl. If he had secrets, Paul didn't care to hear them. The ball was in the cops' court now anyway. "Okay," he said.

On the way out, Darryl stopped him. "Hey, bro, thanks for what you did for me. Not sure it was the smartest move in the world, but it took balls." He sounded a little surprised, Paul noticed. "We solid?"

"Yeah," said Paul, and gave him a quick dude-hug. "Let's stay in touch, though. Keep that watch somewhere safe."

"I will. If anywhere's safe," Darryl said, and closed the door.

At least now he and Lacey weren't alone in this, Paul thought as he climbed back into his truck. He was glad to be rid of the watch and he felt good about what he'd done for Darryl, but he still had a distinctly fragrant tarp to get rid of, as well as no idea whether the Tate–Terry business was related to the killing. It was mid-morning now, and Paul wanted to get back home before his absence seemed more suspicious than it already did—not to mention to be there for his sister, who'd just been through the worst night of her life. Then again, she might have been through plenty of worse ones with Hart. Paul was glad he didn't know.

On the drive home, Paul's thoughts turned back to Terry's drunken babbling up in the fire tower. Maybe the thing about "some heads are gonna roll" was just an unfortunate coincidence? After all, Terry was known to karaoke the Judas Priest song of the same name. But what about the weird Monopoly stuff?[12] He'd mentioned "Atlantic" and "Ventnor." Paul hadn't played in years but he could visualize the board. What was the other one—the most expensive of the three?

With a couple of miles to go, it hit him: Marvin Gardens. There was only one Marv in Mercer. And only one Gardens.

[12]Indeed.

NOTES:

Lisa,

Okay, I feel like I just wrote *The Brothers Karamazov*. In quantity, if not quite in quality. Don't worry about matching the length of this chapter. I'm fine with splitting everything fifty-fifty even if I'm putting up most of the words.

Anyway, I think I've found a balance between developing the characters and the story. I hope you can step up your game.

Dave

Dave,

For the record, if we were in a word count competition you'd find that we were neck and neck. But who's counting? Oh wait, I am.

Lisa: 8702

Dave: 8394

If you're Dostoyevsky, I'm Tolstoy.

I think we're making progress and I'll see what I can do about my "game."

Lisa

P.S. And please, no more with the Monopoly. You keep that up, I might have to give Terry a disease that compromises his mental state. Don't worry, I'll pick something that has a cure. Syphilis?

CHAPTER 9

Lacey smoked pot only as a sleep aid, but it worked. She crashed for four hours. During that time Paul tried to untangle the fuzzy town conspiracy that he felt certain would eventually surface. He returned home and waited for Lacey to wake up. Lacey woke in a haze, so Paul started with an easy question.

"Lacey, where's your car?"

Lacey looked at her watch. She was supposed to meet the sheriff in twenty minutes.

"You need to give me a ride," she said.

As Paul drove Lacey to the new doc's office, he didn't even bother asking why her car was left behind. Instead, he focused on more important matters, like Lacey's upcoming police interrogation.

"Just be cool," Paul cautioned.

"What does that mean?" Lacey replied.

"That means don't tell the sheriff that we found the body three days ago and moved it and then went poking around at the second crime scene and then, when it showed up at the third crime scene, removed evidence."

"Oh that," said Lacey. "Anything else?"

"You might not want to mention that we're marijuana growers."

"I won't," Lacey replied. "But for future reference you're the grower. Not me. I'm retiring."

Paul had come to see marijuana cultivation as a career. Lacey always saw it as temp work, something you did after all other options were exhausted. Besides, there was no temp agency in Mercer.

"Whatever you need to tell yourself, Lace. We'll talk more later."

"Sure. Right after my police interrogation."

"Who do you think did this?" Lacey asked.

"That's what I'm trying to sort out," Sheriff Ed replied.

"Could it be drug-related?"

"Could be any number of things," Ed said, not showing his cards.

"Or personal. Do you know anyone who had a beef with Hart?" Lacey asked.

"Well, that was one of the questions I was going to ask you."

"I didn't know him as well as I thought," Lacey replied.

"Did you know he was making methamphetamine in his basement?" Sheriff Ed asked.

"No," Lacey lied. She wasn't sure whether knowing someone was making meth and not reporting it was a criminal offense.

"Now how did that slip by a smart girl like you?"

"I've been asking myself that ever since. How did you know?"

"It's my job to know what's going on in this town."

"Then how come you never arrested him?" Lacey asked.

"He cleared out the basement before I had a chance," Ed replied. Clearly the question had gotten under his skin. Ed had tried to run Hart out of town for years.

"So somebody snitched on him. Who was it?"

"Sweetheart, that's classified information."

"Aha, so there was a snitch. I was just guessing," Lacey said.

Sheriff Ed looked over the single sheet of legal paper that contained all the information he had on the Hart Drexel murder. He let out a frustrated sigh and tried to take the reins on his runaway interrogation.

"Did Hart owe anybody money?" the sheriff asked.

"He owed me a hundred and fifty bucks," Lacey replied. "But I wouldn't kill him over that. Do you think he was sleeping with somebody's wife?"

The sheriff cleared his throat a few times and turned the question around, "A good investigator doesn't speculate too soon. Now have you heard rumors about an affair?"

"I think Hart was seeing someone on the side back when we were together."

"Did you ever confront him?"

"I didn't make anything of it at the time," said Lacey.

"Who was it?"

"Don't know. But he used to come home smelling like some kind of flower. If you can find her, she might know something, but I guess that's not much to go on."

"What brought her to mind?"

"I'm just thinking about reasons why one person might kill another. Crimes of passion are the most common, right?"

"People kill each other for all kinds of reasons."

"Don't you think it's suspicious that Doc Holland went missing and then Hart's body turned up?"

"Doc Holland retired. I'm not sure that I see the connection."

"I'm just brainstorming here," Lacey said.

If she were in full disclosure mode, she might have mentioned that Hart always had a thorn in his side when it came to Doc Holland. In fact, whenever Hart needed minor medical attention, he'd visit the osteopath in Emery rather than drive a mile to Holland's place. If Lacey asked about it, Hart would always change the subject in the special way that only he could.

"Thank you for your time," said Sheriff Ed.

"You should look for the woman who smells like some kind of flower," Lacey said.

"I think that's all for now, Lacey," Sheriff Ed quickly replied, getting to his feet.

Lacey remained seated.

"Why do you think they took his head?" she asked.

"Too soon to tell," the sheriff replied. "Let me walk you out."

Lacey noticed the sheriff's weary tone and slumped posture as he walked her out of the building. He looked as tired as she felt. She figured he'd been up all night. She wondered what theories he had been hiding from her.

"Will you call me if you hear anything?" Lacey said as she got in her car.

"Take care of yourself, sweetheart," Ed replied as he returned to the station.

Paul, deciding he'd better secure his alibi for the night in question, drove twenty miles to Tulac and knocked on Brandy Chester's front door.

"*Paauul,*" Brandy squealed when she saw her beau. "Why didn't you tell me you were visiting? I would have made you a tuna casserole."

Paul had once made the mistake of complimenting Brandy's signature dish. Truth was, he found it almost inedible, but he didn't want to hurt her feelings. Since then, she made the meal whenever she knew he was stopping by. That's when Paul's surprise visits commenced. Brandy and Paul embraced in the doorway; then he followed the woman in pink into her pink abode.

Aside from the white carpet, which was stained from years of abuse, Brandy's home looked like it had been decorated by a deranged ballerina. For the first few weeks they were dating, Paul wore sunglasses inside, but slowly he got used to it. Truth was, he liked Brandy. She had a good heart. A heart of gold, you might say. They'd met at Olmstead's Hardware when Brandy asked for his help finding the right screw.

Brandy was big-boned, full-lipped, and blond all over. She was the kind of woman who was always bleaching something. Brandy began most of her sentences with "Back when I was dancing . . ." although you could tell from her frame that she was never a Rockette. Three years ago, Brandy's career was sidelined by a pole-dancing injury, which is far more common than you might expect. The accident left her with a permanent limp. Paul never minded the limp. In fact, he found it rather fetching.[13]

Brandy prepared a grilled cheese sandwich while Paul explained his need for an alibi. It didn't require too much explaining. Brandy agreed as if people asked her for an alibi every day.

"Sure thing, sweetheart. I'll tell the cops I made you a tuna casserole and we had a cozy night in watching *Mythmatch*."

"Let's first make sure we know which episode was on that night," Paul replied.

"You think of *everything*," Brandy said, smothering her man with a kiss.

Lacey swung by the Timberline after her interview with Sheriff Ed. Hart used to kill hours at this place. He and Tate were tight. Lacey had never liked the man, but she figured she should give him the news.

She went straight back to the office and knocked twice on the closed door.

"Enter," said the gravelly voice on the other side.

Lacey caught Tate in his undershorts and T-shirt.

"I would have waited until you put some clothes on," Lacey said, averting her gaze.

"My clothes are at the laundry-mat."

"All of 'em?"

"If you must know, Lacey," Tate impatiently replied, "my woman kicked me out with the shirt on my back. Those clothes got to be washed sometime."

Lacey noted that Tate's couch was made up as a bed.

---

[13] I hope you enjoyed yourself here.

"What about your underwear?" Lacey asked. "Doesn't that have to be washed?"

"I bought another pair of shorts. Now what can I do for you, Lacey?"

"Hart's dead."

"Your Hart?"

"He's not mine anymore. Or anybody's."

"What happened?"

"Murdered."

"How?"

"Don't know."

"I'm sorry for your loss," Tate said. The news shook him, but he was the kind of man who tried not to let on what he was thinking, even in his underwear.

"When was the last time you saw Hart?"

"You investigating me?"

"Just asking an innocent question."

"About three weeks ago, maybe," Tate replied.

"What did he want?"

"A drink," said Tate. "What else?"

Lacey's thoughts turned to the other mystery that had surfaced recently.

"Do you know why Doc Holland skipped town so fast?"

"Nope."

"Do you know where he went?"

"Wish I did."

"Why?"

"Because he left town with an unpaid debt."

"He was gambling? What was his game?"

"He had no game. It was just a friendly loan."

"Really? What's your friendly interest rate?"

"Why? You need a loan?"

"No. Just curious."

"You might want to keep that in check," Tate replied. "See you around, Lacey."

Lacey took the cue and left.

Instead of grieving for Hart, Lacey figured she could do the next best thing: Find his killer. While Tate had an angle on everyone in Mercer, he wasn't the talkative sort. But she knew who was.

Lacey drove to Betty's place to see whether a gossip exchange could uncover any new leads. Besides, on TV it's always two disconnected clues that intersect in the end. Maybe there was some connection between Doc Holland and Hart Drexel.

"I am so sorry, honey. Are you okay?" Betty asked, when Lacey told her the news about Hart.

"I think so," Lacey said.

She had wondered why she felt nothing. She'd even repeated those three words in her head again and again to induce a reaction: *Hart is dead.* No matter how many times she said it, she still couldn't feel that it was true.

Betty served Lacey a mug of hot chocolate with a layer of miniature marshmallows.

"This'll make you feel better," she said.

Lacey was doubtful, but drowned the marshmallows in the brew and then let them dissolve in her throat.

"Have you heard from Doc Holland since he left?" Lacey asked.

Betty was surprised that the conversation leapfrogged over Hart so quickly. It took her a moment to comprehend the question.

"No. I haven't seen him since he left. Why do you ask?"

"There's just something suspicious about the way he skipped town without a forwarding address. Only the new Doc Holland knows where the old Doc Holland is living."

"Have you met him?"

"Who?"

"Doc Egan."

"Oh yeah. He stitched me up."

Lacey pulled up her sleeve to reveal her bandaged arm.

"What happened to you?"

"Gardening accident."

"You should be more careful. How—"

"Let me ask you a question. You handled Doc Holland's bills. Was he having financial problems?"

"He wasn't flush."

"What does that mean?" Lacey asked.

"Well, he had a lot of bills. Whatever came in every month, left. And then some."

"Did anything strike you as unusual?"

"I don't know."

"Think."

"Why are you so interested in Doc Holland?"

"I'm trying to take my mind off Hart," Lacey replied.

"Let me see," Betty said, consulting the back of her brain. "He had a thousand-dollar payment every month to Mallard Corp."

"What was it for?"

"When I asked him, he said it was supplementary malpractice insurance."

"For Mercer!?" Lacey exclaimed.

"Yeah, I thought it was on the pricey side," Betty replied.

"What does Doc Egan pay?"

"Don't know. He only asked me to handle his patient billing. He's got his own computer program and stuff."

"Thanks for the cocoa," Lacey said, standing abruptly.

"Leaving already?" Betty asked.

"Sorry to run. I forgot that I told Sook I'd pay him a visit this afternoon."

Lacey was out the door before Betty could offer her a slice of the lemon meringue pie she had just baked.

———

"Lacey," Sook said, slowly getting to his feet. He was wearing his usual tan cardigan that always smelled like mothballs. "Where have you been turtling yourself?"

Lacey knitted her brow and froze it there for full effect.

"Sook, I don't care how many times Terry or my brother say 'turtling.' It's not a word in the dictionary, so stop using it."

"Terry says if you use it enough, it becomes a word. And since it's a word based on a word, how bad can it be?"

"What if we all started making up words all the time, Sook? Then nobody would understand what anybody else was saying."

"Did you come here to tell me to stop using the non-word 'turtling'?" Sook asked.

"No. I'm taking you on an excursion."

"Count me in," Sook said. "Closest we have to drama around here is the latest escapee from We Care down the street. Poor old gal in her nightgown woke up the whole damn place banging on our front door at two a.m. last night. Half the We Care staff were out looking for her. You ask me, something must be messed up over there if people are trying to break *into* this place."

"Well, beats prison, right?" Lacey asked.

"Let me get back to you on that," said Sook. "Anyway, I do believe I'm up for an outing. Are we going to the movies?"

"Nope."

"Diner? I could use some of those fries. Wouldn't mind a chocolate shake, either."

"No, we're not going to Diner."

"Then where are we going?"

"I'm taking you to the doctor," Lacey explained.

Sook sat back down in his chair. "That sounds about as fun as a bee sting."

"Would you rather stay here?"

———

On the drive to Doc Egan's office, Lacey informed Sook of his symptoms.

"What seems to be the problem?" Doc Egan asked when Lacey and Sook arrived in his waiting room.

"I have no appetite and my ears are ringing," Sook said.

"What's your last name, Sook?" Doc Egan asked on the threshold to the examination room.

"Felton," Lacey answered.

"Hang on a second," Doc Egan said, "I'll get your file."

Egan disappeared behind the door only to return empty-handed.

"Were you a patient of Doctor Holland's?"

"Nope," Sook replied.

"You weren't?" Lacey asked.

"No. I used to go to that osteopath in Emery."

While Lacey tangled with the idea that both Sook and her ex (or *the* ex-Hart) were patients of an inconveniently located osteopath, Doctor Egan attached a pen to a clipboard and passed it to Sook.

"Once you fill out the questionnaire, we can start the exam." Doc Egan turned to Lacey. "Have you cleaned and re-dressed your wound yet?" he asked.

"What wound?" Sook asked.

"I got into a knife fight with Big Marv Babalato," Lacey said, pulling up her sleeve.

"Come into my office," Doc Egan said.

While Sook reminisced about his medical history, Doc Egan redressed Lacey's wound and she interrogated him about his financial responsibilities.

"Just out of curiosity," Lacey asked. "How much is malpractice insurance?"

"Depends on where and what kind of practice."

"Well, for example, how much would malpractice insurance be in a town like Mercer, with your current patient load?"

"Can I ask why you're asking?"

"Will you answer if I don't?"

Matthew Egan sighed, washed his hands in that special way that only doctors do, and removed Lacey's old wound dressing, tossing it in the bin.

"I think it runs around three thousand," he replied.

"A month?"

"No. A year."

The patients then swapped places. During the half-hour that Sook was getting poked and prodded, Lacey excused herself to make a phone call and slipped into Egan's private office. Technically, it was a closet converted to an office. Her first day on the job, Betty lasted a full two hours in the four-by-six-foot space before her claustrophobia took charge. After that she worked from home, accessing Holland's voicemail and scheduling appointments.

Eventually Lacey located Egan's check register and saw a payment to Kimbell and Company for $750.00, which was listed as a quarterly insurance payment. Just when Lacey was about to start hunting for the bill in the file cabinet, she heard voices in the waiting room.

Lacey checked the office for signs of disruption, adjusted the calendar, and closed the desk drawer. She exited the office just in time to take a seat on the threadbare couch.

"So, how is he?" she asked.

"Starving," Sook replied.

Lacey shot him a hostile glance.

"Your friend is fine," Doc Egan said. "Maybe he could get a little more exercise."

"We'll work on that. Oh, before I forget," Lacey said, reaching into her bag, "Here's your shirt. It's clean and everything."

"I'll see you in eight days, Lacey."

"Why?"

"To get your stitches out."

"Right. See you later, Doc," Lacey said, ushering Sook out of the office.

Sook and Lacey sat in the corner booth of Diner, feasting on chocolate shakes and french fries.

"How come you never went to see Doc Holland?" Lacey asked.

"Don't know," Sook replied. "Habit, I guess."

"No, that's not it," Lacey said, sliding Sook's fries out of arm's reach. "You should tell me the truth. Otherwise, these Diner visits might become very infrequent."

Sook drained the last bit of shake from his tall glass, making that annoying sound. He put the glass down, consulted the ceiling, and finally spoke the truth.

"Sometimes people aren't who you think they are."

"Get to the point, Sook."

"Doc Holland wasn't a real doctor."

NOTES:

Dostoyevsky,

Back to you. Just a quick refresher: We have a murder to solve—a dead body and a killer on the loose. I've been looking back at some of your previous chapters. Your storyline with Terry Jakes is bordering on incoherent. How about we keep him out of the picture for a while and work on creating more viable suspects?

Also, let's work on making this more cinematic, but not like *The Fop*. There was way too much drinking and talking in that script. In fact, that sounds like a fitting description of our whole relationship.

Lisa

Lisa,

You know what would help me create suspects? If you stopped turning all my potentially threatening characters into stuffed animals for Lacey to play with. Tate, for example, is supposed to be a menacing badass. Now he can't even manage to wear pants or pronounce "laundromat"? Also, I seem to remember introducing Sook as a multifaceted war veteran, not a cuddly grandpa. I'd retaliate, but I wouldn't even know where to start. Actually, I do, but I'd hate to see Dr. Dreamy end up in a ditch somewhere.

It's funny that you remember our relationship as consisting entirely of drinking and talking. I remember it as drinking and listening.

You want cinematic, keep reading.

Dave

CHAPTER 10

Leaving Brandy's Sunday night, Paul decided to confront her the next time they met. He'd been hoping she respected him enough to divulge her secret, but it was getting to the point where it was either stop with the charade or good-bye. The first sign was the biography of Wittgenstein he'd found under her bed. Then it was the game theory podcasts on her iPod. Her computer even had a bookmark for the Quorum Group, apparently a club for brainiacs who didn't deign to mingle with the dim bulbs of Mensa.

On his way out of Tulac he stopped in an underlit park and slid the folded-up tarp into a trash bin. Lacey would be pleased to know he'd spared the ozone by not burning plastic. On the highway back toward Mercer, his mind wandered to Brandy again. Did she even like *Mythmatch,* or was she just patronizing him? She probably liked it, he decided. It was pretty sophisticated if you thought about it.

Paul's cell phone interrupted his thoughts with the opening riff of "American Woman." That could mean only one thing.

"Terry."

"Don't use names," Terry said.

"You're calling my personal cell phone from your personal cell phone."

"We'll have to do something about that," Terry said. "You'll never believe this, but while I was gone twenty beautiful Kush plants and a dozen Trainwrecks spontaneously germinated in my grow room. I shit you not. Somebody up there likes me."

"Ha ha," said Paul. "I'm coming by."

"I'll be here," said Terry.

———

When Paul arrived, Terry was at work in the basement, trimming Paul's plants. Wearing a Tulac Titans cap and a chipper expression, he bore no resemblance to the babbling mess he'd been the previous morning out at the tower. But that was typical. Terry could do a complete emotional 180 faster than anyone Paul knew. In another twenty-four hours he could be fetal again.

"To what do I owe the pleasure of these ladies' visit?" Terry asked.

"I'll explain later. I do appreciate the babysitting, but I need some explaining from you first. First, what's going on with you and Tate?" Paul said.

"You give him the money?"

"Yep, but he wasn't happy. He says no more partial payments. How much are you into him for?"

"Don't worry about Tate. I wouldn't say he's all bark, but he's not going to bite the hand that feeds him. I only owe him a little more. The two K will buy me enough time."

"Time for?" Paul asked.

"A nice business deal I've been working on for a while. It's in the closing stages. When it wraps up, I'll have more than enough to pay Tate. And you, of course. Thank you, my brother. You know I'd do the same for you."

"Wait a minute—this isn't another koi breeding venture, is it?" Paul asked. He flashed on a memory of Terry screaming obscenities at a pond.

"Absolutely not," Terry said. "Fish can go fuck themselves."

"What about that Monopoly stuff—Marvin Gardens? I know you were talking about Marv at We Care Gardens. Don't tell me you owe him, too?"

"I don't," said Terry.

"Come on, Terry. Don't shut me out. Maybe I can help."

"It's best if I keep it need-to-know. You're going to have to trust me for now. You know I'm good for the two grand. Within a month, scout's honor."

"I'm not worried about the money right now."

"Good. So what's with the plants?" Terry asked.

"Long story short, we found a dead body on our property Thursday night."

Terry's eyes went wide. Apparently it was news to him.

"We moved it to keep the cops away," Paul continued. "Then it paid us a return visit Saturday night. Lacey figured out that it was Hart Drexel, flipped out, and called the sheriff. I cleared out my plants before they came. You were still at the tower, I guess, and this is the only place I could think to bring them."

Terry made the *ert-ert-ert* backing-up sound. "You found a dead body three days ago and didn't tell me? Man, who's shutting out who?"

"You weren't exactly primed to process that kind of news yesterday. What were you so freaked out about anyway, if everything's going so great?"

"I thought the aforementioned business deal had been compromised," Terry said. "At the same time, Tate was starting to make angry sounds about his money. You know me, I'm sensitive. Thankfully, you came through for me. Even when you were facing a much hairier situation of your own. I'll never forget it."

"Me neither," said Paul.

Terry waited as long as he could, then added, "We just need to do this last bit of due diligence on the deal."

"'We?' I thought you used up all your favors yesterday."

"Come on, P-Funk. I'm not complaining about taking care of your plants. Indefinitely, I might add. We'll be back here in an hour."

"We're doing due diligence at night?"

"Night time is the right time," said Terry with a grin.

Terry hopped into Paul's truck and said, "Head north."

Paul took a right when he reached the highway. After twenty minutes Terry said to pull over, pointing to a little inlet off the shoulder.

"We're about a half-mile from We Care Gardens," Paul said. "That's where we're going, right?"

"Yep," Terry admitted as they pulled to a stop. He unzipped his backpack and pulled out what looked like two small welder's masks.

"Put these on," Terry said.

"What are they?"

"Night-vision goggles," Terry replied.

"Why do we need them?"

"Because the human eye lacks a *tapetum lucidum*," Terry deadpanned.

"Of course," Paul said. "Look, Terry, remember when I mentioned the corpse that keeps coming back to my property? This is not a great time for me to get arrested."

"Not gonna happen," said Terry. "I just need a lookout. You've done most of your job already—I couldn't risk driving my own car here. This deal is going to be worth it for everyone, man. You and Lacey included. I guarantee you."

Paul just looked down at the goggles he was still holding.

"I need this, brother," Terry pleaded.

Paul and Terry crept through the woods toward We Care.

"What are we doing on the Babalato property?" Paul asked.

"Need-to-know," Terry repeated.

When they were within sight of the rear office, Terry ripped off his goggles.

"Damn it, there's a light on," he said.

Paul moved his goggles down around his neck.

"What's the problem?" Paul asked.

"I got to get in there," Terry said.

"Why?" Paul asked.

"I just need some information."

"Can you ask for it?"

"Nope."

A figure passed by the window.

"What's the plan?" Paul asked.

"Follow me," Terry replied.

They snuck over to the building, then duckwalked around the side. Standing on their toes they could see through the window. An old man in a wheelchair was facing Jay Babalato, who sat behind his desk. The conversation was barely audible above the chirping crickets.

"We Care takes care of its own, Mr. Portis," Jay said. "There's no need to worry about the IRS."

"I don't want to go to jail," Mr. Portis said, and shook his head sadly.

"No, of course not. And we don't want that either. I just need a little more information from you about your financial affairs. Then we can provide the IRS with all they need to sort out this little mess. Of course, that will require some work by a professional, which isn't free."

"What do you want from me?" said Mr. Portis.

"A check made out to Franklin Fisher for twenty-five hundred dollars. He's our community accountant. He'll sort out this matter for you. He'll simply need your bank statements for the last few years."

"My son usually handles that stuff. This doesn't feel right."

"Why don't you give me his number and I'll explain everything to him."

The sound of heavy footsteps on dry leaves interrupted the eavesdropping. Paul turned his head to the left, toward the approaching sound, and then froze with fear. When he managed to turn his head back toward Terry, Terry was gone. Paul started scurrying toward the trees.

He'd gone a couple of steps when Big Marv turned the corner and caught sight of him in the light of the window. Marv just stared at him silently, then walked over slowly.

Paul waved casually, but he couldn't hide his nerves. Or the night-vision goggles around his neck.

"Hey, Marv."

"What are you doing here, Paul?"

"I was just hiking around, trying out these goggles. I thought I'd stop by and show them to Lito. Is he around?"

"Nope," said Big Marv, cocking his head to the side. "You alone?"

"Yeah."

A cat howled and Paul jumped. Marv didn't take his eyes off him.

"That's Mr. Skittles," Big Marv said.

"Ah. Who?"

"We Care's longest-residing resident," said Big Marv with a smile.[14]

"All right. It's been nice running into you," Paul said.

"My pleasure," Marv replied.

Big Marv seemed more bemused than angry. He took Paul by the shoulders and looked him in the eye.

"Listen, Paul. I know you sell pot at my place, and I let you do it. I have no problem with it. I suggest you take a similar attitude toward my affairs."

"Okay," said Paul. The clear thing to do was to leave it at that and hope to slink away unscathed. But something about the man in the wheelchair wouldn't let him. He heard himself adding: "It's just that . . . these people have put their lives into your hands. I just hope—"

The last thing Paul saw was Marv's eyes closing as they launched into Paul's forehead.

Paul woke up standing with his cheek against a hard wall, wearing an uncomfortable scarf, and then realized he wasn't standing, the wall was a parking lot, and the scarf was his night-vision goggles. He rolled over and recognized that he was in the parking lot at Diner, a good twenty miles from We Care. His cell phone and wallet were in one front pocket.

Paul dusted himself off and went into Diner. He sat down and ordered a coffee and fries. In the reflection of the napkin dispenser, Paul saw the welt on his forehead, shining like a supermarket Braeburn.

---

[14]Maybe you should just get a cat so you can stop writing about fictional ones.

Paul had never been headbutted before, or even knocked out. His introduction to both experiences was serving as a convincing argument to heed Marv's suggestion to mind his own business. Paul could take issue with Marv's chosen manner of punctuating it, but the suggestion itself had some indisputable merit. Maybe it was time to start acting like a minor-league pot grower again. No more trying to help anyone out but himself and Lacey.

After he finished his fries and coffee, Paul went outside and called Terry on his cell. No response. As he hung up, he noticed Diner's dumpster—the one where Lacey had allegedly tossed her shoes two nights before. It was padlocked tight.

NOTES:

Lisa,

Sorry to interrupt the Nancy Drew escapades, but I thought we could use a little more serious action. I wasn't deliberately ignoring your request—Terry Jakes was simply the right man for that job. In fact, he's the right man for many jobs.

And nice try with Brandy Chester, but you can't keep a smart woman down. My hope is that your Brandy defeat will convince you to build up some compelling characters of your own rather than trying to tear mine down.

Dave

Dave,

Bravo with Brandy. You know what, in the interest of a peaceful collaboration, you can keep her IQ points. But remember, I can take them away anytime I want.

Sure, I'll give the story a bit more edge if you think that's what we need. Although I'll probably steer away from headbutting. I've never understood that as a mode of assault. It has the element of surprise, but it's like punching yourself and someone else at the same time.

I'm hopeful that you're going somewhere with this Babalato business.

Any news on the plane crash?

Lisa

CHAPTER 11

Paul scrolled through his internal Rolodex, deliberating over the right person to call when you're stuck at Diner and you've just been head-butted unconscious by Big Marv Babalato. The obvious choice was Lacey, but he needed to keep her as far from this entanglement as possible, or he'd just have another knot to undo. He also didn't want to bring Brandy into the whole mess.

"Darryl, I need a ride," Paul said, after surveying the parking lot for cell reception.

Paul provided his coordinates and Darryl promised to leave right after his show, *Pulverize That*,[15] was over. The series involved men (generally unemployed engineers) building giant, state-of-the-art blenders and trying to decimate items that you wouldn't think could be decimated. Since the show had no narrative hook and a website where you could learn whether the indestructible item was destroyed or not, it troubled Paul that his friend wouldn't skip thirty minutes of watching an easy chair transform into a smoothie to help him out. Paul reentered Diner and ordered fries and a bag of ice.

Paul sat at the counter, resembling a man with a red welt on his forehead minding his own business. But he couldn't escape the quiet echoes of conversations that traveled through the bright lights of the dingy eatery.

"Did you hear there was a murder in Mercer?"

"Serial killer, they say. He cuts off their heads."

---

[15]I'm flattered by the homage, but who would watch this? It sounds like a rip-off of *The Uncrushables*.

"Mercer has always been a magnet for the unwashed and unwanted."

"I heard it was drug-related. Somebody stepping on somebody else's turf."

"I wouldn't live in that shithole if you paid me to."

Paul felt the usual Mercer loyalty and it took all his will to control his urge to set the Diner patrons straight. Hell, they came from a town that consisted of a gas station; a motel; Diner; and a mailbox, photocopy, and pet supply store all under the same roof. Who were they to judge? In Emery, there were only fifty people total to kill. Paul had had his fill of Diner, but when Darryl arrived, he was hungry, so Paul sat and waited while Darryl ate his fries.

"What happened?" Darryl asked.

"Don't ask," Paul replied.

"Okay," Darryl said, dunking his fry into a soup bowl of ketchup.

Paul thought a real friend would ask again, but then he realized he didn't have too many real friends, except Terry, who was feeling more like an albatross every day. He tried Terry one last time and left a message explaining that Darryl would drive him back to his truck.

While her brother was trying to escape from Emery, Lacey was at the Timberline, drowning her confusion in whiskey and beer.

A patron or two asked her where she'd been turtling herself, to which she replied, "Look it up in the dictionary. It's not a word!"

Tate served Lacey another drink. Her manners surfaced long enough for her to say, "Thank you."

"I see you've reached the anger stage of grief," Tate said.

"I'm not angry," Lacey replied, sounding angry.

"Well, you're something," Tate replied.

"I'm determined, that's all."

"Determined to do what? Drink yourself blind?"

"I'll be fine once I figure out who killed him."

"Maybe you should leave that to the cops."

"Murder is not their specialty, Tate."

"Is it yours?" Tate asked.

"Now it is."

For the next hour, Lacey roamed the bar like a drunk Columbo and made casual conversation. Then, as she moved on to the next patron, she would say, "One more thing . . . when's the last time you saw Doc Holland?"

Lacey's interviews offered no new information and so she sat back down at the bar, pulled out her notebook, and started compiling a list of people who required interviewing in Mercer. Too bad she couldn't locate Doc Holland, because he was number one on her list. Next was Marybeth Monroe, Hart's mom, who lived on the side of the mountain with her second husband. While Hart and his mom had never been close, Lacey wasn't sure who he was close to. She then listed Darryl as a person of interest and, finally, Terry, although she doubted she could extract any relevant information from him. Sometimes you couldn't even have a lucid conversation about the weather with Terry.

Lacey could feel the air in the room shift. Part of it was the breeze from his sheer bulk, but also his presence made everyone catch their breath for a second. Lacey knew of no specific crimes that could be attributed to Big Marv, but he always made her uneasy. Judging from the slight hush that took over the tavern, she was not alone.

Big Marv sat down on the adjacent barstool. Lacey shifted a few inches over to give him a wide berth. Besides, he smelled like his usual cheap cologne. Despite the layers of body odor that floated through the bar, Big Marv's scent was the most oppressive.

"Lacey," Big Marv said.

Lacey was never sure whether Big Marv approved of his nickname. Certainly he knew he was enormous, but sometimes enormous people don't like having attention drawn to that fact. Or maybe that was a woman's take on the matter.

"Mr. Babalato," Lacey said, just to be safe.

Tate served Big Marv a shot of the best whiskey in the house on the house and said, "Do me a favor, just don't ask her where she's been turtling herself."

Big Marv downed the whiskey in a single gulp and slid the glass forward for another pour. Tate obliged, grudgingly.[16]

"You want something for that?" Tate asked, referring to the red mark on Marv's forehead.

"Nope. I'm good. You should see the other guy," he said, grinning at Lacey.

She was trying to mind her own business with her note-taking.

"What you got there, Lacey?"

"Nothing. Just a to-do list," Lacey replied, snapping her notebook shut. "Can I have another?" she said, pointing to the glass.

"Are you sure that's wise?" Tate asked. The tension on the adjacent barstools was impossible to ignore.

"Give her a drink, Tate. It's on me," Marv said, showing no sign of reaching for his wallet.

Tate served the drink; Lacey tossed a bill on the bar; Marv slid the bill back in Lacey's direction.

"I said, I'm buying."

"Everybody knows you don't pay your tab," Lacey replied.

Marv swiveled his wrestler-gone-to-seed physique around on his barstool and looked Lacey dead in the eye.

"What has gotten into you people?"

"You people?" Lacey asked. "What do you mean? Humans? Women? People who pay for their drinks?"

"I just had a chat with your brother, and now you seem to be hunting for trouble. In your case I'm going to let it slide, what with your recent loss and all."

---

[16]I almost forgot that Tate was such a pushover. I just hope Lacey doesn't find out in an even-numbered chapter that he's a little tougher than this.

"What kind of chat?" Lacey asked.

"Nothing major, but you might want to make sure he stays awake for the next twelve to twenty-four hours."

Only then did Lacey realize that her brother probably had a matching welt on his forehead.

"Where is he?"

"Last I saw him he was at Diner."

"What did you do to him?"

"I gave him a piece of friendly advice."

"What?" Lacey asked. "Wear a helmet?"

"The problem with you people is that you're always nosing in other people's business. And when I say you people, I mean all you Hansens. Your mama and daddy were the same way. It's a shame what happened to them. So unnecessary."

Lacey felt a shiver run up her spine. She wanted to smash a beer bottle over Marv's head, like you see in the movies. Instead, she bought him a beer, laying her money on the bar.

"How about a peace offering," Lacey said. "A pint on me."

Tate poured the pint and slid it in front of Big Marv. Lacey got up from her barstool, and as she tossed on her coat, she made sure her arm swung in the perfect angle to knock over the glass and let the beer fall on Marv's substantial lap.

"I'm so sorry," Lacey deadpanned. She tossed another bill on the bar. "Let me buy you another."

Big Marv's face turned bright red. If Lacey had been a man, you could bet another headbutt would have been in the cards. Despite what women will tell you, there are more than a few perks.

Lacey took in a deep breath when she stepped outside. She held her hands up and watched them shake. She walked to her car, counting her drinks, wondering if she should call Paul and what state she'd find him in.

"There ain't no way in hell I'm letting you drive home."

Lacey spun around in the Timberline parking lot, which was really just an amoeba-shaped patch of gravel. Deputy Doug, in his off-duty denim and plaid, nodded in the direction of his pickup truck.

"Whether you spilled that drink on purpose or not, you've had a few too many."

Lacey hopped into his truck without any argument. At the moment, she didn't have any words left in her. But Doug had a different agenda. He started up the truck and turned onto the dark Mercer road.

"You okay, Lacey?"

"Uh-huh."

"You want to talk about it?"

"Nope."

"If you ever want to talk, I'm here."

"Unlikely."

"If you change your mind."

"Okay."

"I mean it. Anytime."

Lacey grunted some acknowledgment that's hard to spell. Doug remained silent until they reached the Hansen home. He had almost run out of material. But he hung in there as long as he could.

"I'm sorry about Hart. That must be hard."

"Thanks."

"But maybe it's for the best," Doug said. "I always thought you could do better."

"Not every thought in your head should be spoken, Doug."

Lacey reached for the car door before Doug had pulled to a complete stop. The door was locked from the driver's-side panel.

"Can you unlock the door, please," Lacey said.

"Maybe we can do this again sometime?" Doug said, not unlocking the door.

"Do what?"

"Have a drink sometime."

"We weren't having drinks together."

"Well, we could."

"Anything's possible."

"You know me, Lacey. I'm a nice guy."

"I'm sure you are."

"We could go to a movie, maybe."

"Are you going to unlock the door?"

"Maybe just something simple. Like dinner."

Lacey reached across the cab, pressed the lock release, and jumped out of the truck.

"Thanks for the ride," she said, deciding to end on a polite note since she'd already made one enemy that night. Something was up with Doug; she just didn't have the energy to contemplate it. She pushed the door shut with both hands.

Blaring music from the radio and a blinding light flashing on his eyes woke Paul. Lacey studied the solid welt that had formed and concluded that her brother was in danger of a concussion and needed to be awake. Plus, she had some things on her mind and needed to talk.

"Big Marv said something strange to me," Lacey said.

"My advice to you would be don't talk to Big Marv," Paul replied.

"What happened, Paul?"

"I tripped outside of Diner and fell on my head."

"What were you doing at Diner?"

"Eating fries."

"Alone?"

"Uh . . . yes."

"If I went into Diner and asked if you were alone, would the employees corroborate your story?"

"You're going to start investigating *me* now?"

"If you keep lying, I will."

"Lacey, we have got to let the cops do their job and just mind our own business, all right? I'm sorry Hart is dead. But he spent a lifetime making enemies. It's not so hard to believe that one of 'em finally killed him."

"A long time ago, I thought I'd spend the rest of my life with him, and now he's dead. I just need to know who did it."

Paul got two beers from the fridge and passed one to his sister. He turned on the television and found a rerun of *Nightcrimes*. They sat in silence for as long as Lacey could stand it.

"Did anyone ever investigate our parents' death?"

Paul muted the television and turned to his sister.

"What's got you asking about that?"

"Big Marv. He made it sound like maybe it was no accident."

NOTES:

Dave,

Look, I watered Big Marv and Doc Holland, and planted more seeds of suspicion. I even included my own fake TV show to try to maintain some sense of consistency for the reader.

In return for these olive branches, I have two minor requests for chapter 12: How about a Terry Jakes–free chapter and no wayward clues? Let's build on the core mystery here, rather than inventing new diversions.

      Lisa

Lisa,

Big Marv and I both appreciate your acknowledgment of his existence. I'll see what I can do about your requests, but doesn't telling each other what to do violate the spirit of the project?

Remember what happened when you refused to let go of the whole Baccarat showdown in *The Fop*? Sometimes you have to trust someone else to get the job done. You wouldn't remove your own appendix, would you?

      Dave

CHAPTER 12

"No shit," Tate said, putting his crossbow down in the dewy grass. "The boars would come right into the village?"

"They'd come right through your front door if they felt like it," said the old man on the other end of the log. "It got so bad that we had to call a truce and team up with the Commies just to clear them out. We spent a whole day with 'em driving the pigs back into the forest, picking off as many as we could. At the end of the day we roasted them up together and drank a few barrels of beer. The Koreans were better shots. Our GIs would shoot 'em up so bad there was hardly anything left to eat."

Tate just nodded.

"Two days later was the battle of Longsing. My battalion was wiped out. I lived in the forest for six days after that," Sook said. "That's when I really learned about them. Some say you have to learn to think like they think, well that's bullshit. Best you can do is just be quiet and patient. Korean wild pigs are some smart, persistent assholes, but they don't hear so good. They might smell you, but they won't pinpoint you unless they can hear where you are. First time I caught one I dropped my knife. That's a wrestling match I don't care to repeat."

A man learns a lot about himself when his only weapons are silence and a knife, Tate thought to himself. He'd slept only a couple hours after his shift at the Timberline, but he felt alive out here, ready to do battle. Wild pig season was only a few weeks long, but it was his favorite time of year.

"The thing about the Korean ones, though," Sook continued, in an elegiac tone, "they were almost blond. Beautiful. Soft hair like golden sheep. *Sus scrofa coreanus*."[17] He said it like the name of a high school sweetheart.

Sook was the only guy in town Tate could stand hunting with. For everybody else, it was a chance to get drunk and bitch about their wives. Fucking tea party. Even at his age, Sook could still easily handle a bow with a hundred-and-fifty-pound draw.

"So does Mapleshade know you're out here freezing your wrinkled ass off?" Tate asked.

"Don't ask, don't tell," said Sook, shrugging as he stood up from the log. "I help to smooth things out around there, they stay out of my affairs. As far as they know, we're getting the early-bird special at Diner with the rest of the bluehairs."

Tate picked up his crossbow and the two headed farther into the forest. "So that little Hansen girl's had a rough time lately," he said.

"Seems to think she's Nancy Drew," said Sook.

"Who?" said Tate.

"Never mind. Anyway, Lacey took me to that yuppie doctor, figured she could use me as a rent-a-grandpa. She's poking around in there, looking through Doc Holland's old records. Egan doesn't have a clue. I guess he's sweet on her."

"Little bitch came sniffing around the bar last night," said Tate. "You'd think after everything that's happened, she'd start minding her own business."

"Maybe that's the problem—she doesn't have any business to mind."

"I'd just hate to see a nice girl like that lose her head," said Tate.

"Take it easy," said Sook. "I pointed her in a certain direction. You shoulda seen her eyes light up. It should keep her busy, but she won't get anywhere with it. Good girl, but not quite as smart as she thinks."

"What about the brother?"

---

[17]Are you insane? Latin?

"Grows great Indica," said Sook. "Seems like the type to know when to walk away. But I'm keeping an eye on him."

Sook's ears perked up and he gestured silently to Tate. A doe nosed out into a small clearing in the distance. Tate raised his bow, then lowered it—deer season had just ended.

The doe turned its face to the two hunters as Sook's arrow split its forehead.[18]

Paul woke from a deep sleep. Across the room, his cell phone was playing "American Woman" from inside his pants.

On his way to the phone, Paul caught a glimpse of his forehead in the mirror. The welt had gone a weird subfusc[19] purple.

"Terry," Paul said flatly.

"Hey, my man. You okay?" Terry said.

"I'm alive. Marv knocked me out."

"I . . . yeah, I know."

"You *know*? I thought you took off."

"I found a vantage spot maybe fifty yards out. Jesus H., that sound was sickening. Like a baseball bat on a soft coconut. Look, brother, I hope you understand I couldn't be seen up there. I'm sorry I had to leave you there."

"Whatever. No more favors, Terry."

"Not a problem, amigo. Hey, you're not going to believe this," Terry said. He couldn't disguise his glee.

"Try me," said Paul wearily.

"I got all the info I needed. I waited in the woods till all the lights were out and Marv drove you to wherever. In and out in five minutes. So we're golden. Mission goddamn accomplished. All thanks to you."

"So where the hell were you all night?"

---

[18]What the hell is going on here? Is this the same novel?

[19]We'll talk about this later.

"Took me most of the night to hoof it to the road and catch a ride. My feet are swoll up like brined hams. When I got your message, I knew you were okay, so I let you sleep it off."

"How thoughtful," said Paul. "I think you owe me this much: What's going on with you and the Babalatos? Why are you fucking with them?"

"Like I said, we're closing in on a business deal. I just needed a little more information from their office."

"There's more, obviously."

"Okay, here's what I can tell you. Couple weeks ago Marv wanted to discuss the possibility of establishing some plants out at their place—they got a couple acres behind We Care, north of where we were last night. I went up there with him to check it out. A couple days later I went back to check out an old spring to see if it was still usable, which would make things a whole lot easier for Darryl when it came time to get the place irrigated."

"Cut to the chase," Paul said.

"I found a bag of teeth," said Terry.

"What?"

"I found a Ziploc sandwich bag full of human teeth."

When Lacey woke, it was late morning and Paul was gone. She'd slept off most of her night at the Timberline, but what remained in her brain was asperous.[20] When a long shower failed to smooth things out, she found herself rooting around in the closet for her old bong, an eighteen-inch purple monster from the Hart days. The Purple People Eater, he'd called it. She filled it and took a massive hit. Maybe she was feeling nostalgic. Or maybe she just wanted to get back outside of herself. For all of Lacey's derision of pot smokers and unease about the family business, she didn't hesitate to partake when she felt the need.

---

[20]And this.

But as soon as she felt the hit, her thoughts turned back to her list. She knew what she'd be doing today. She called first to see if it was okay. Marybeth Monroe answered on the first ring, with a somnolent statement of fact: "This is Marybeth." She was surprised to hear from Lacey but said it'd be lovely to see her.

The Monroes' house was a half-hour out of town, up the side of the mountain. Lacey drove the winding road through big, beautiful lots that had sat empty for years. No one seemed to be sure why, or even who owned them. That was one mystery she could let slide.

Eventually she emerged from the mist and could now look down onto it, a tattered blanket covering Mercer. She found the house, a caliginous[21] shingled thing half perched on stilts. Back when Lacey was in high school, Hart's mom had just starting dating Dick Monroe, a big-time lawyer.

Marybeth came out to the porch as Lacey exited her car. "Oh, Lacey," she said, and gave Lacey a long embrace. "So good to see you."

After an awkward silence, they walked through the front door and into a *Sunset* photo shoot. They sat down on a big white couch in front of an impressive stone fireplace embedded in blond wood.

Marybeth filled her in. She had a boy and a girl in private school up in Orendale, which had just resumed the previous week. She worked from home some days, real estate something or other. Dick was busy but made it home most nights. Lacey thought she seemed to be holding up well, given the recent news. Maybe she was a little medicated, or a little religious, or both. Whatever works, Lacey thought.

"I always liked you, Lacey," she said, sadly. "I thought you were Hart's best chance at happiness. I guess maybe I was right."

She didn't mean for the words to sting, but they did. Lacey never signed up to be a lifesaver.

"Well, I don't know what to say," said Lacey. "I'm sorry it didn't work out. I can't imagine how horrible this has been for you."

---

[21]I'm not even going to bother looking this one up.

"I know you cared for him deeply. You know, Hart had a lot of love in him once you got past the outlaw act. He just couldn't quite seem to use it on himself, you know?"

Her voice was unaffected, but tears were streaming down her face.

"I want to show you something." She got up and took a photo binder from the bookshelf. She started showing Lacey pictures of Hart as a young boy. When she saw little Hart on his dad's shoulders on the family farm, Lacey gave in. It was the first cry she'd had since the whole mess had started four nights ago. In fact, it was the first cry for a long time before that, too.

When the sobbing subsided, Lacey asked, "So, does Hart's dad know?"

"I doubt it. I haven't heard from him since the day he left. He thought of himself as the last cattle baron. Went to Texas to become a bigger one. Last I heard he was in Argentina, running a big beef operation. If he never finds out, that's fine with me."

She turned the page to a picture of Hart as Darth Vader on Halloween, and another in a straw cowboy hat on the back of a big brown steer. Even the steer looked happy.

"After his dad left he started getting quiet," Marybeth said. "One day a farmhand came to talk to me. Apparently he'd seen Hart running into the cattle fence. He'd get knocked off his feet, then get up and do it again. I looked in his drawer and the back of his shirt was singed. When I asked him about it, he admitted to it. 'I don't know, I just like it, I guess,' he said. Like it was normal. He was twelve.

"He called me now and then over the last couple of years," Marybeth continued. "He sometimes sounded sober, sometimes not. He worked construction for a while and then a few other odd jobs. I know he spent some time working for the Babalatos out on their old property, hauling old junk to the dump. A few months ago a lady called and said she had some mail for him under the name of some company. I forget what it was called."

"Can you do me a favor and let me know if you think of the name?"

Marybeth gave Lacey a concerned, motherly look. "Lacey, promise me you'll be careful. You don't owe Hart anything. He was blessed to have you in his life, and now he's gone."

"Have you talked to Sheriff Ed yet?"

"I went down to the station yesterday. Sheriff Ed always seemed to have it out for Hart. I guess he figures he finally got what was coming to him." Then she broke down again. "I'm sorry, I think I need to lie down."

"Anything I can do?" said Lacey as they both got to their feet.

"Just pray for his soul. It was wonderful seeing you, Lacey. God bless," she said as she hugged Lacey good-bye.

"Yeah, um, you too," Lacey said.

On the drive back down the mountain, the driver's side was the cliff side, where you were farther from the ledge yet more aware of it. The sun had burned off the mist, and all of Mercer was spread out beneath her: downtown, their place, the rest stop, Mapleshade, everything. But all Lacey could see was Hart running toward that fence, turning at the last second as he threw himself into it. Then picking himself up, walking back to where he'd started, and doing it again.

When she was halfway down, her cell phone rang. She put her headset on with one hand and answered it.

"Lacey, it's Marybeth. I thought of that name. It was Merganser, Inc."

"Mer-what? I missed that," said Lacey.

"Mer*gan*ser. Like the duck."

NOTES:

Lisa,

I thought it was time to bring a couple of my characters back to reality, and to introduce a little more danger and intrigue. I figure you didn't collaborate with me just to hear echoes of your own voice.

Dave

Dave,

I'm speechless. Wait, no I'm not. I just don't know where to begin. Your whole chapter was like a headbutt. Did you just watch *Deliverance*? Might I remind you that we're *collaborating* on a novel together, not playing a high-stakes poker game. What has gotten into you? What has gotten into Sook? Why in God's name would you use the words "subfusc," "asperous," and "caliginous" in a freaking crime novel? Here's a rule worth following: If the spell-check doesn't recognize the word, don't use it!

I brought you into this endeavor to improve it, not sabotage it. I just know James Patterson doesn't have to put up with this shit. In the next chapter, I'm getting this book back on the rails. I hope we can keep it there.

Lisa

P.S. No, I wouldn't remove my own appendix. But I wouldn't let you do it either.

CHAPTER 13

Another idiotic duck reference was all Lacey had to show for her visit with Marybeth Monroe. Lacey thought for sure Hart's mom would have a little more information. In fact, on the drive home she had to wonder why she'd even bothered with the visit, which was an utter waste of time. It was as if some outside element were at work, temporarily putting the brakes on her investigation.

There were questions that needed asking. For instance: Who were Hart's known associates? Where had he been living these past six months? Were there any conflicts she knew of? Was he dealing meth again, or even using his product? Was he having money troubles? Marybeth, from what Lacey recalled, was always good for a few grand. These questions would have to linger for a while. Lacey couldn't bring herself to return to the Monroe household just yet. Instead, she dropped by Mapleshade for a debriefing.

Once again, Lacey had enlisted the cuddly badass Sook in her investigation. Against her better judgment, she'd asked the old man to invite himself on an early-morning hunting trip with Tate—a reconnaissance mission, of sorts (though not the wisest activity for a man who had his driver's license revoked due to poor eyesight). After Lacey's dead-end visit with Marybeth Monroe, she hoped that Sook might offer some new revelation.

"My, it was cold out there. I'm afraid I don't have much to report," Sook said, looking a bit haggard. "You might want to steer clear of the Timberline for a while. You've really gotten under Tate's skin."

"Could he be the killer?"

"Lacey, he's not your killer. He was talking too much. Your murderer would keep his trap shut. Besides, Tate's basically harmless. Everybody knows that. Hell, he can't even get his wife to give him his clothes back. He's been wearing the same pair of pants for a week now. When he wears pants."

"He should just buy another pair," Lacey said.

"Agreed."

"I still think he's hiding something."

"We're all hiding something, Lace. But sometimes when you're foraging for mushrooms, you find wild nettle instead."

"I used to do that with my mom," Lacey said, recalling afternoons spent on their property while her mother showed her the difference between the King bolete, an edible fungus, and its close relative, Satan's bolete, poisonous until cooked. But still, who wants to tempt fate?

"Do what?" Sook asked, as Lacey's mind wandered.

"Do you remember when my parents died?"

"No. I was turtling hard back then."

"I thought we talked about that."

"Sorry. I was keeping to myself, mostly. It was around the time Loretta got diagnosed with cancer. I wasn't paying attention to much else."

"Sorry, Sook. I forgot it was around then."

An awkward silence started to take shape, but Lacey put it out of its misery.

"So, if Tate's a dead end, where should I look next?"

"Maybe nowhere. You ever think about giving this thing a rest? Why don't we play a game of gin rummy," Sook suggested.

"I regret spilling my drink on Big Marv," Lacey said, ignoring Sook's suggestion. "It would be nice to have a friendly conversation with him. I guess there's no turning back. Maybe I can break into his office in the middle of the night."

"Lacey, you're talking crazy. It's one thing messing with no-pants Tate. But Big Marv is *all* bite. That man don't even bother barking."

While Lacey was lost in thoughts of breaking and entering, Sook walked over to his bureau, withdrew a shoebox, reached under a mass of old photos, and pulled out a handgun. He passed it to Lacey, holding it by the barrel.

"You know how to use this, right?"

Lacey's uncle Duke had taught her to shoot during a visit right after their parents died. But when Paul started growing pot, he established a no-guns policy. It was the one part of Terry's advice he'd ignored as he set up the business. There'd been enough death in his life already. Lacey hadn't held a revolver in her hand since she was seventeen. But she most definitely knew how to use it.

"I remember," Lacey replied.

"For emergencies only," Sook said, returning the shoebox to the drawer.

While Lacey cradled the gun and imagined herself in a movie-style shootout, Sook rummaged through the other drawers of the bureau, tossing socks and faded T-shirts onto the floor.

"What are you looking for?" Lacey asked.

"My teeth," Sook replied.

"Excuse me?"

"This might surprise you, but these alabaster marvels are dentures. My real teeth I keep in a bag in my dresser. Only they're missing."[22]

"Why would you keep your old teeth?" Lacey asked.

"I don't know," Sook replied. "Maybe I was hoping for a windfall from the tooth fairy."

On the road back from Mapleshade, Lacey's mind cycled through the grab bag of useless information she'd acquired. Tate had only one pair of pants. Sook saved his old teeth and lost them. And, of course, there

---

[22]At some point you're going to run out of leads to destroy.

was that one juggernaut of a clue—Merganser, Inc.—courtesy of Hart's mom.

It occurred to Lacey that this crime was keeping her tethered to Mercer. She'd have to step up her investigation if she was ever going to get out. Without any other ideas up her bandaged sleeve, Lacey decided to pay another visit to the new doc, angling for more information.

"Lacey," Doc Egan said. "How nice to see you."

"Can I come in?"

"Of course."

Lacey strode directly into the office and parked herself on the examination table.

"Are you feeling all right?" Doc Egan asked.

"I'm fine. I'd like my stitches out now."

"It's too soon."

"It looks like my skin is sticking together just fine."

Lacey ripped off the bandage to show the doc his handiwork.

Doc Egan swabbed the stitches with alcohol and said, "Eight days. That's the rule. You have six more to go."

"Okay. Whatever," Lacey replied, quickly giving up.

There was another reason for her visit. Unfortunately, she was too worn out to orchestrate a subtle transition to the point of it.

"I accidentally got a piece of Doc Holland's mail."

"How did that happen?" Doc Egan asked.

It was a fair question, since they lived miles apart. Lacey had to think hard and fast for an answer.

"Hansen. Holland. I think we're the only H's in town," she said, surprised by her skillful prevarication.

"I see," Egan replied.

"So, maybe you could give me his forwarding address and I'll pass it along."

"Or you could leave the letter with me and I'll forward it to him."

"I'd feel more comfortable taking care of this matter myself," Lacey said.

Egan found Lacey's persistence equal parts bizarre and amusing.

"Maybe we can come to some kind of understanding," Egan said.

"I don't see why not. What did you have in mind?"

"I have some patients who could use a certain kind of medication."

"Why don't you write them a prescription?"

"The closest compassion center is a three-hour drive. Most of my patients can't drive. I need another option."

"Are you a cop?" Lacey replied.

"No, I'm a doctor."

"Sorry. I had to ask."

"Do we have a deal?"

"I'll comp the first batch. After that, you need to pay."

Doc Egan re-dressed Lacey's wound while she provided a complete price list. When he was done, he returned to his desk and on a prescription pad wrote out an address and passed it to Lacey. She looked it over.

"Wait a minute," Lacey said, "I thought he'd at least left the state. This is just a P.O. box in Tulac."

"I doubt he's living in Tulac. He probably has his mail forwarded to wherever he went."

Lacey hopped off the table. "Nice doing business with you, Doc."

Egan walked Lacey to the door.

"Want to catch a movie sometime?" he asked.

"Did you know that the closest movie theater is a forty-minute drive?" Lacey replied.

"I didn't."

"You should have looked into that before you moved here."

"That doesn't answer my question."

"Sure. Why not?" Lacey replied.

"This week sometime?"

"I'm busy this week."

"Doing what?" Egan asked. As far as he knew, she had all the time in the world.

"Solving a murder. I thought my brother would help me, but he's totally useless. It's kind of taking up most of my time."

"Why don't you leave that business to the cops?"

"It's personal," Lacey replied.

On her way home, Lacey dropped by Betty's place. She wanted to check on the address of Mallard Corp., the apparent provider of Doc Holland's supplemental malpractice insurance. If that's what it was. Lacey couldn't articulate a connection, but two operations named after ducks couldn't be a coincidence, could they? Betty still had Holland's accounting data in her computer and had no problem accessing the address, a mailbox in Emery, just north of Mercer. Betty served Lacey a mug of hot tea. She was itching for the latest town gossip, but Lacey was more interested in old news. She hoped Betty's memory was better than Sook's.

"Do you remember when my parents died?" Lacey asked.

Betty and Lacey's mom had been close. Their friendship arose out of proximity rather than common interests, but what eventually tied them together was trust. Betty was a woman you could rely on. On occasion she used to babysit the Hansen children. After Sheriff Ed broke the horrible news to Lacey and Paul, Betty was the first person to bring a casserole to the house.

"Of course I do, darling. It was a terrible day for the whole town."

"Was there an investigation?"

"I'm sure the police looked into the matter, but I don't think anyone thought it was anything more than an awful accident. Nobody had those carbon monoxide detectors back then. Come to think of it, I don't have one now. Do you?"

"Yes," Lacey replied. "Paul changes the batteries twice a year."

"I'm glad to hear it."

"Did my parents have trouble with anybody?"

"Everybody loved the Hansens."

"Everybody?"

"I think Big Marv had some sort of scuffle with your dad."

"What kind of scuffle?"

"Remember that fifteen-acre lot your family owned just on the city line between Mercer and Emery?"

"Vaguely."

"Well, Big Marv wanted to buy it. For years, he kept making offers and your dad always said no. Figured it would be worth something one day. 'Once the suburbs ooze their way out here,' he used to say. They still haven't spread this far. Still, it's a nice piece of property."

"So what happened to it? We don't own that land."

"After your folks passed, your uncle wanted you and Paul to have some savings, so he sold it."

"To Big Marv? That's awfully convenient."

"No. Marv tried to buy it, but Terry Jakes outbid him."

Lacey's head was swimming with inchoate clues. No matter how she twisted the facts, she couldn't figure out how she and Paul were connected to Hart's murder. She only knew that there was a connection.

Sheriff Ed's cruiser was parked in the Hansens' driveway when Lacey returned home. She sat in her car composing herself for a minute. While there were a number of questions Lacey wanted to pose to the sheriff, she would have preferred doing it on his turf. Lacey started to get out of the car, but remembered the gun in her purse. She stuck it in the glove compartment and then braced herself for whatever was happening inside the Hansen home.

The last thing Lacey expected to find was Sheriff Ed and Paul planted on the couch watching a repeat of *Brainfreeze*, a short-lived game show in which contestants ate a pint of ice cream and then had to answer reading and arithmetic questions.

"Hello?" Lacey said.

"Welcome home," Sheriff Ed replied.

"What's going on?" Lacey asked over the whimpering of a contestant trying to divide forty-nine by seven.

The sheriff picked up the remote control and turned off the TV.

"Have a seat," he said.

"This sounds serious," Lacey replied, following his instructions.

A glazed expression had taken over Paul's face—the same one as when Paul first discovered that you could slice earthworms in half and they'd live. That was one long summer.

Sheriff Ed cleared his throat and said, "Lacey, we found some of Hart's personal effects in our investigation."

"Like what? Do you know who the killer is? Where was he living? I forgot to ask Hart's mom, like a complete moron."[23]

"I'm not here about that, Lacey," the sheriff abruptly replied. "Did you know that Hart had a life insurance policy?"

"He was only twenty-eight. Why would he have that?" Lacey asked.

"I don't know," said the sheriff. "You didn't know about this?"

"Well, we hadn't spoken in six months."

"He took the policy out two years ago, right after you got engaged. A hundred thousand dollars," Sheriff Ed said, looking at Lacey for a hint of surprise. Whether he saw any was hard to gauge. Lacey had been working on her poker face since this whole business began.

"Oh," Lacey replied.

"You're his sole beneficiary."

---

[23] It was a highly emotional situation, and Lacey's not a professional detective.

"I don't understand."

"Just fill out the paperwork," the sheriff said, handing Lacey a manila envelope.

With that, Sheriff Ed got to his feet, tipped his hat, and departed without another word. Once the sheriff's car was long gone, Paul brought out the Purple People Eater and took the biggest bong hit of his life.

"Congratulations," Paul said flatly. "You know what this means, right?"

"Yes," Lacey replied. "I am now suspect number one."

NOTES:

Dave,

Back to you. I tossed in a few fancy words to illustrate how unnecessary they are. I am sanguine that you will agree. For the record, I took three years of Latin in high school. Still, I managed to keep it out of my chapter.

I don't want to harp on the insanity of your last chapter, but we're supposed to be building on each other's work. When I make a suggestion, please take it seriously. I know what I'm doing here.

Lisa

Lisa,

Three years of Latin, wow! Do you mean Latin Dance?

I can't help but admire your skill in turning all my ominous revelations into jokes so the reader wouldn't be distracted from another chance to watch Lacey flirt with Doc Egan.

As for the vocabulary, I'll try to turn it down a notch.

Dave

CHAPTER 14

Terry was cutting the pretty plants. *Cut, cut, cut,* went the scissors.

Paul was visiting his friend Terry.

"Terry, why did you not tell me this before?" asked Paul.

"Do you mean about the teeth?" asked Terry.

"Yes," said Paul. Paul was watering the pretty plants.

"I did not want to scare you," said Terry.

Paul was scared. He rubbed the bump on his forehead.

"Do not be scared of Marv," said Terry. "Your sister's new friend is more scary."

"Who is my sister's new friend?" asked Paul.

"I will give you two clues," said Terry. "Clue number one: He lived in a large city, but now he lives in the country."

Paul thought and thought.

"I will give you another clue," said Terry after a while. "He is a doctor."

Paul thought some more. "Is it Doctor Egan?" Paul asked.

"Yes," said Terry.

Paul had solved the riddle!

"Doctor Egan seems nice," said Paul.

"He may seem nice, but he has not been telling the truth," said Terry. "The new doctor has many secrets."

"What should we do?" asked Paul.

"I am going to visit the doctor," said Terry.

"Good," said Paul. "Let us visit the doctor."

"I must go alone," said Terry.

"Okay," said Paul. "I will talk to you after your visit. Good-bye, Terry."

"Good-bye, Paul," said Terry.

The two friends shook hands.

Paul felt tired. He drove his truck to his house.

Irving the cat was on the porch. He was eating a dead bat. *Chomp, chomp, chomp,* went Irving.

Paul petted Irving. "Hello, Irving," said Paul.

"Meow," said Irving.

NOTES:

Lisa,

Here you go. Hope you were able to follow along without pictures.

Dave

Dave,

My thoughts, in chronological order: 1. Fuck you. 2. Seriously, fuck you. 3. I wonder what John Vorhaus is up to these days. I never did call him. 4. What was I thinking collaborating with an unpublished, narcissistic poet? 5. We've sunk three months into this and there's still a mystery to solve.

I am reminded of that standoff during *The Fop* over whether Claude Hindenberg would smuggle the bomb in his tuxedo jacket or a loaf of pumpernickel. You conceded to my logic—who brings bread to a catered ball? But every scene you wrote after that featured a loaf of fresh pumpernickel. You're wasting our time mocking me instead of getting the job done.

I had always hoped this project would provide some kind of reparation for the slight you felt over that thing I did without you, but I have to question at what cost. I think we've sunk enough time into this project that it might be worth it to keep going, but you need to be on board with that.

If chapter 16 is replete with more Dick and Jane nonsense, then we'll call it a day. Until then, I've decided to overlook this snag in the creative process and get back to work. We will repair it during revisions. Along with the repeated cat references and "subfusc."

I do hope we can get past this.

Lisa

CHAPTER 15

When Terry was seventeen, he fell out of a tree, hit his head hard, and was never the same again. No thought that issued from his lips could be trusted as sound. That said, occasionally one of Terry's paranoid theories would land in the general vicinity of the truth. But it was always a gamble with Terry, and Paul was happy to stay out of the whole business.

Because Terry had never visited a doctor without an appointment, he made one for four p.m. the same day—the only available opening. Perfect, he thought. An afternoon nap, a stiff Bloody Mary, and he'd be at the top of his game.

"Terry Jakes?" Doc Egan asked on the threshold of his waiting room.

"The one and only," Terry Jakes replied. "At least the one and only in all of Mercer . . . and probably Emery."

"Nice to meet you, Mr. Jakes," Doc Egan said, extending his hand.

"Wish I could say the same," Jakes replied, sizing up the doctor as a crafty adversary.

Terry never trusted educated men. He read constantly to overcompensate for his own lack of formal education, but his reading comprehension was, to be polite, quirky. For instance, Terry had once read that the bathroom was the most dangerous room in one's home, so he had his own bathroom knocked out and built an outhouse instead. The project was one of many grounds cited for his second divorce.

When Terry entered Egan's office, instead of planting himself on the exam table, he sat down on the doctor's rolling stool. Egan had heard rumors about Terry and so he took the move as an innocent mistake rather than passive aggression.

"You might find the exam table more comfortable," Doc Egan suggested.

"I might," Terry replied. "But I've never gone in much for comfort."

"I see," Egan replied.

"I see you see," Terry replied.

"What can I do for you?" Doc Egan asked.

"It's what I can do for you," said Terry.

"Oh. You're not here for a medical concern?"

"No, sir. Terry Jakes is fit as a fiddle."

"I'm glad to hear it."

"Are you now?"

"Yes, I am."

"We cannot enter into alliances until we are acquainted with the designs of our neighbors. Sun Tzu," Terry said, sliding the chair right up to Doc Egan. But Doc Egan was standing, so Terry was in a supplicant pose. He quickly straightened up to compensate.

"I'm not sure what you're getting at," Doc Egan said.

"I know about your side business," Terry whispered.

"I don't have a side business."

"We're not being recorded, but I understand your concern. I'll do the talking."

"Oh good."

"Secrets are a man's only hope for survival."

"Is that a saying?" Doc Egan asked.

"I just said it, so it is."

"Fair enough," Doc Egan replied, searching the room for an escape route.

"I can keep secrets," Terry said, knocking his index finger on his head.

"Good."

"Think of me as a double agent."

"That sort of contradicts what you just said," Egan replied.

"You know what I'm here to talk about?"

"I don't."

"I understand you had to say that for the recording."

"You said there is no recording."

"No. There isn't. But you think there is."

"What are we talking about?" Egan asked.

"We're talking about one hand greasing the other hand."

"Whose hand is greasing whose hand?"

"Let's call one hand the Falcon and the other hand the Snowman."

"Okay."

"I know all about it. You're the new Falcon."

"Are you sure?"

"I'm sure."

"What does that mean?" Doc Egan asked.

"You know what I'm going to do about it?"

"What are you going to do about it?"

"Nothing. Absolutely nothing."

"Okay."

"Make sure you tell the Snowman."

Lacey drove to the Mallard Corp. address in Emery, where Doc Holland had been sending all those inflated malpractice checks. As she expected, it was just a mailbox depot combined with a pet supply store. Lacey knew that the proprietor would refuse to divulge the name of the owner of box 483, so she went in with a plan.

"Is box 483 available?" Lacey asked.

The clerk opened a file and reviewed the spreadsheet. Lacey tried to read it upside down, but the clerk snapped the file shut before any information registered.

"It just freed up," the clerk replied.

"It did?" Lacey asked, briefly stumped.

She'd planned to ask the clerk to contact the owner to see if they could work out a swap because Lacey just had to have that box—483 was her lucky number, or something. But now her next move was much simpler.

"I'll take it," she said.

She paid the seventy-five dollars, took her key, and left. On the way home she devised a new plan.

Sitting at the kitchen table, Lacey drew a simple diagram. All the random clues and duck references were starting to jumble in her head. Paul looked over her shoulder and asked her what she was up to.

"I'm organizing my thoughts," Lacey replied.

"I wish you wouldn't do that," Paul said.

Lacey ignored Paul and brainstormed out loud: "It appears that someone using the name Mallard Corp. was blackmailing Doc Holland. It also appears that a corporation called Merganser was somehow employing Hart. Do you think Mallard and Merganser are connected?" Lacey asked.

"Why would they be?" Paul replied.

"Merganser. Mallard. Ducks? Hello, Paul? Two corporations named after ducks—one is blackmailing a fake doctor—a quack. Get it? Paul, why don't you care about this stuff? Don't you want to know who killed Hart?"

"Sure, but only so I can steer clear of him."

"But what about justice?" Lacey asked.

"Bartenders serve booze. Baristas make coffee. Doctors treat patients. Cops solve murders. Lawyers prosecute and defend. Judges and juries mete out justice. You and me, we grow weed to chill all those folks out. Let's let everybody do their own job."

"Don't you want a better job?"

"I work with something I love and I get to make my own hours. I'm not sure how much better it can get."

"And it's illegal."

"Sometime in the future we might go legit and grow for those compassion centers."

"There's no *we* in this future. I don't know how you can settle for so little. I'm out as soon as I solve this murder."

"You should just let this thing go, Lacey, and learn to live your life."

"We can't, Paul. Whoever killed Hart was sending us a message. I, for one, want to know what that message was. Why don't you?"

"Because, Lacey, I've already translated that message. It reads, 'Keep out of it and you'll keep your head.'"

"You really are absolutely no help at all to this investigation. In fact, if you took a long vacation right now, I don't think anyone would notice."

"A long vacation sounds nice, Lace. Unfortunately, I can't go anywhere because if I leave you alone, you're likely to get yourself killed."

Paul then pulled out the Purple People Eater, got massively stoned, and watched four episodes in a row of *Flowers of Evil*,[24] in which a borderline-sociopath horticulturist critiques the works of amateur suburban gardeners. The following morning, Lacey tossed the PPE in the neighbor's trash and drove to work.

Lacey arrived an hour early at the Tarpit. She started the coffee brewing, took down the chairs, and used the office computer to type up and print a brief note to Doc Holland.

> *Dear "Doc,"*
> *We have some unfinished business. Please contact me for a meeting at your earliest convenience.*
>
> *Best Regards,*
> *The Mallard*

During the brief morning rush, Lacey got a much-needed respite from the investigation, which had been bouncing around in her head like a violent game of handball. Familiar faces smiled with either concern or satisfaction, asking about her well-being—some with genuine concern,

---

[24]Give it up.

others without. While coffee was poured and milk was steamed, Lacey gazed around the café, realizing how little Hart's death mattered to anyone. Come to think of it, Hart had only started meaning something to her again after he died. She'd been close to forgetting all about him. What surprised her was that when the memories surfaced, they were usually the good ones. Maybe that was the best way to think of the dead.

When the morning patrons began to disperse, Lacey cleaned up her station and sat down at one of the tables for a short break. She stared into the distance until she spotted a familiar face entering the establishment.

"Doc Egan," she said, getting to her feet and marching around the counter. "What can I get you?"

"Coffee, I guess."

"You came to the right place. What kind?"

"Regular. Black."

"Seriously?" Lacey asked.

"Yes."

"Wow. That almost never happens anymore."

Lacey poured the coffee and handed it to Egan, marveling at how simple an exchange it was. She served maybe one cup of straight coffee a day. It always lifted her spirits for some reason.

"Do you have a minute?" Egan asked.

Lacey's eyes darted around the empty café. "I might have ten," she said. "What's up?"

"I had a very strange conversation with Terry Jakes yesterday."

Lacey and the new doc sat at one of the back tables while Egan shared the details he could recall from his peculiar meeting with Terry.

"It didn't make much sense," Doc Egan said.

"Not much makes sense with Terry. But there's usually a kernel of truth in there somewhere. Give me the bullet points."

"He said something about one hand greasing the other. He knew about my side business, only I don't have one. He promised to keep my secret.

He called me the 'New Falcon' and he told me to say hello to the 'Snow-man.' Does that mean something to you?"

"No," Lacey replied. "I think it's just more Terry nonsense. He hit his head when he was young."

That was, of course, a lie. Not the head injury part, but the part about Lacey thinking it meant nothing. She wondered whether Terry was clued in to Doc Holland's Mallard problem. Although she was grateful that there were no more duck references.

Egan finished his coffee and there was an awkward pause before he left.

"So next week, Lacey—do you think you might be able to take a break from crime-fighting?"

"Maybe," Lacey replied. "I mean, if other people decide to chip in, who knows—we might have solved the mystery by then."

After work, Lacey dropped by the Timberline, nodded a polite hello to Tate, and found Deena, Terry's first ex, sitting at the last barstool.

"You doing all right?" Deena asked. She was sincere.

"I'm fine," Lacey replied.

"Men," Deena said. "Can't live with 'em."

She left it at that.

"I'm looking for Terry. You know where he is?"

"He came down from his perch for a couple days, but then he got spooked again and holed himself back up in his lookout tower."

"Thanks," Lacey said. "You got a message for him?"

"Yeah," Deena replied. "Dry up," she said, taking another sip of whiskey.

Lacey dropped her letter in the mailbox and headed out of Mercer to Terry's hideaway. She parked her car on the fire road and hiked the last mile to the tower.

"Hey, Terry," Lacey shouted.

She shouted his name again.

She approached the wooden ladder and shouted again.

"Wake up!" she said, banging on the bottom rungs.

From inside the lookout, Lacey heard some stirring and a groggy voice reply, "There ain't nothing wrong with a grown man taking a nap."

"Can I come up?" Lacey said.

"I'm indecent," Terry replied.

"I'll wait, then," Lacey said, quickly striding away from the tower.

A moment passed and Terry poked his head out of the primitive window.

Terry smiled warmly. His nap must have quieted his demons for a spell.

"Miss Hansen," Terry said. "To what do I owe the pleasure?"

Just then an unnerving squeak pierced the forest. The entire tower seemed to buckle to the right. Lacey screamed Terry's name and instinctively started toward the tower, then backed away. She could still see Terry's surprised face in the window as the whole thing collapsed.

Lacey watched until all the debris had settled. She approached slowly, easily finding the bright red of Terry's long johns among the planks. His neck was bent at an unnatural angle.

"Terry?" She said. His eyes were open, but there was no response. He stared directly into the sun.

Lacey checked her cell phone, but she knew there was no reception in these parts. She raced back to her car and started the engine. Leaving a plume of dust in her wake, Lacey drove a mile down the main highway until the cell towers kicked in. She called Sheriff Ed directly.

"Terry Jakes is dead."

NOTES:

Dave,

Please accept my condolences for your beloved Terry. I assure you, it was a purely professional decision. It was time to raise the stakes in the story. And it was Terry's time. He's in a better place now.

With Terry gone, maybe "Paul" can refocus—or rather focus—his efforts on the investigation. I'll admit that Terry grew on me in the end, but he was a terrible distraction.

All right, let's let bygones be bygones and finish this damn book. What do you say?

Lisa

P.S. While I long ago developed an immunity to your conveyor belt of insults, I do think it would be wise to use that creative energy toward the book and not in belittling me.

Lisa,

This is how you kick off our detente—by killing my (and no doubt the reader's) favorite character? If that's the way it has to be, I can take this one for the team. Just let me know ahead of time if you're planning to kill Paul next.

I admit I went a little overboard with the Dick and Jane stuff. Though I have to say it felt good to blow off some steam. You keep assuming I'm harboring resentments from the past. I can assure you that they're all freshly minted. But I feel like I owe it to my surviving characters to see this project through. I'll try to be less touchy if you try to moderate your hostility toward them.

Re: Paul, I've just been waiting for an organic point in the story for him to take an active role. Now that we've reached that point, I think you'll be pleasantly surprised.

Dave

P.S. I take exception to the "unpublished" jab in your previous note. Hello? *Harper's*, May 1996, page 32.

CHAPTER 16

The first Tuesday of every month was School Supplies Day—the day Paul drove down to the string of colleges a couple hours south of Mercer and distributed to his dealers there. He hadn't heard whether Terry had talked to Doc Egan yet, but he doubted doing so would make things worse. Somehow, he always landed on his feet. "Like a cat," Paul had once told him. "Or a puma," Terry had replied.

On the highway down, Paul felt more relaxed than he had since they'd found Hart. The familiar anxiety of driving around with a pound of pungent marijuana under his seat was almost reassuring compared to the way things had been going around Mercer lately.

The college market made up the most reliable chunk of the Hansens' customer base. There was plenty of competition, but also a giant, unwavering demand. Paul enjoyed that all these Tylers and Hunters and Masons were paying for his own kids' college education—if he ever had kids, that is. And if those kids had Brandy's genes, Paul thought, they'd probably need Ivy League money.

Over the next few hours Paul made a couple of transactions at smaller schools. The largest and last on his schedule was Sequoia State, Rafael Dupree's domain—he lived just off campus. As always, they met at the Sickly Thistle, a pub near campus.

Finding Rafael in a back booth, Paul was about to shake his hand but pulled up dramatically at the last second. "Hey, how's that rash?"

"Aw, man, don't be like that. All cleared up. Question is, how are you? I heard about Hart," Rafael said.

"I'm okay. Just trying to keep the doors open, you know?"

"How's Lacey holding up?"

"Let me get back to you on that one," said Paul. "Not sure she's really processed it."

"So, who do you think did it?" Rafael said.

"I have no idea. Not in a hurry to get one, either."

"Right," Rafael said, sounding not quite convinced. Then he offered his take on the suspect pool. "With somebody like Hart, it could be almost anyone. A recent business associate, someone from his Bakersfield days, back when he was doing business with gangs, a jealous husband, a jealous *sheriff* husband—"

"Yeah, yeah," Paul said. "For now I'm just letting it unfold how it does."

"That's very stoic of you, Epictetus." Rafael liked to show off what he'd picked up in the classes he was auditing.

"I got your epic teats right here," said Paul. "Come on, man, just let me have my beer."

"Yeah. Best to let bygones be bygones."

"What does that mean?" Paul asked.

Raf shrugged. "Nothing, man, just that you can't fix the past."

"Uh, yeah. Well, shall we?" Paul said, motioning to the door.

They went out to his truck and made their standard transaction. Rafael left for a medieval philosophy lecture.

As much as he liked Rafael, Paul was glad to be free of him. An idea had occurred to him during their conversation. He took out his cell phone and noticed that the battery had died. He used the pay phone at the back of the pub to call Lacey's cell. Her outgoing message came on immediately.

"Lace, it's me," Paul said, his voice quavering a little. "Hey, I just talked to Rafael. Listen: He says Hart was mixed up with a gang called Los Chungos from way back in the Bakersfield days. Apparently he was working off some money he owed them. I'm trusting that you'll . . . register the seriousness of this and act accordingly. To summarize: Hart, Los Chungos. Spanish for 'We kill nosy white girls.' Okay? Be careful."

Paul felt a little uneasy about using an honest guy like Rafael as part of the lie, but it was for a good cause.

It was shaping up to be a successful day for Paul's top two imperatives: keeping Lacey and the business out of trouble. He decided to check out a little liberal arts school nearby where he didn't have customers yet. He hung around the campus health food store, just getting a feel for the place—the same way he'd met Rafael a few years ago. Judging from the concentration of white dreads, it was a promising target. He'd ask Raf to check it out.

As Paul got on the highway to head back to Mercer, his focus on business as usual started to drift. He knew he'd pass the exit to the old family cabin halfway home. While he remained committed to steering clear of the Hart/Babalato mess as much as possible, he couldn't forget what Big Marv had insinuated to Lacey about their parents' death. He had to do something about it.

Paul could already see himself pulling off at the exit and, for the first time since before the accident, going to the cabin. If there *was* something to find, he wanted to find it before Lacey did. Given her recent behavior, she'd no doubt be snooping around soon enough.

His mind drifted back ten years to the days in the wake of the accident. He remembered it was like waking up on a different planet. The whole town seemed to go mute—even Terry was speechless for once. Paul remembered lying awake hearing Aunt Gwen through the wall, quietly repeating, "Thy will not mine be done," until she fell asleep again. All he could let himself hope for back then was that Lacey would be okay. Then Hart came along and Paul went off to college. In the weeks before he left, he'd felt a brotherly instinct to try to protect her from Hart, but he didn't push it, figuring she could make her own decisions. It occurred to him now that it was the worst mistake of his life.

When he came to the Wallis exit, Paul took it without thinking. He was surprised to remember all the turns it took to reach the cabin. Taking a deep breath, he pulled into the gravel driveway. No cars were out front, and it looked like no one had been there for a while. He had expected everything to look tiny, like nostalgic settings usually do, but it all looked normal. The cabin was nothing special, but it was nestled in a beautiful little valley crowded with redwoods. Not bad for a park ranger and a fish hatchery receptionist, Paul thought.

He went around the back and climbed in one of the windows on the back porch. There was never anything inside worth stealing, unless you had a thing for mismatched furniture from the seventies, so no one had ever bothered getting locks on all the windows.

Before his feet hit the floor, Paul was transported to his childhood. On the wall in front of him was the big, dopey felt sign his mom had made: two pine trees, with WINO spelled out in stylized letters between them, purportedly representing a hammock. The Wallis International Nature Organization, his parents' casual co-op of friends who shared the cabin. The club seemed to exist mostly to facilitate jokes about the club (which was "International," for example, because one of the men was Canadian). The sign used to hang in the entryway but had been moved here to the laundry room, apparently by someone who didn't have the heart to throw it away after the accident. Paul wondered if some of the same folks still had a stake in the place.

But Paul wasn't there to reminisce. He decided to get the worst part out of the way first, taking a quick look through the bedroom where his parents had been found. The furniture seemed to have been updated by a decade or so, but nothing else struck him. He went through the rest of the cabin.

In the hallway between the bedrooms Paul came across the big maple desk. Paul's dad was the type of man who recorded everything, even noting his mileage in a little notebook he kept in the glove compartment. If there were records for the place, this is where they'd be. In the back of the drawer, in a manila folder marked WINO, he found a sheet of names, addresses, and phone numbers. Three couples were listed: Jasmine and Walter Blakey, Grace and Victor Collaspo, Mal and Mel Sundstrom. Two of the couples rang a distant bell. He copied down the names and addresses, all of which were within a hundred miles of the place.

Suddenly feeling like an intruder, he went out the way he'd come in and got back on the highway. Instead of obsessing on the names and what he was going to do with them, he decided to go to Brandy's for some comfort.

Up in Tulac, she greeted him warmly, and he didn't mind when he noticed her furtively shutting down her computer—probably to hide some controversial chess gambit from the nineteenth century or something.[25] Confronting her about the intellectual stuff could wait, though.

Later that night, lying in bed with her, he couldn't sleep. Some brotherly instinct told him to go home.

When he finally got there around midnight, Lacey was out. He plugged his cell phone into the charger and after a moment the voicemail icon popped up. The first message was from Lacey, who seemed to be having trouble catching her breath: "Paul, call me as soon as possible. This is urgent." The second one was a calmer but equally urgent version of the same message. Paul braced himself as the third message began.

"Hansen, you there?" Terry's voice was dazed and happy. "This is the Puma. Jesus, what a day. Where to begin? Morphine is *not* overrated. Anyway, I'm in the hospital. The Falcon tried to kill me. Puma out."

After a potent brownie and a disappointing *Pet Medium,* Betty walked out to her mailbox on the gravel shoulder of the road. Along with the usual bills was an unstamped envelope. She opened it on the way back to her house. As she unfolded the single sheet of paper, a handful of minimarshmallows fell out. The letter's two sentences were typed:

Tell Lacy to let sleeping ducks lie.
Or she's next.

---

[25]Or solitaire.

NOTES:

Lisa,

Okay, I played it as straight as I could. As for Terry's comeback, please don't take it the wrong way. I think it had to be done for the reader's sake. I hope you'll agree. Next time you feel the need to kill someone off, how about, say, Deputy Doug?

Add *Sleeping Ducks* to the list of potential titles.

      Dave

Dave,

I suppose I should have been more specific when I suggested that Paul do some investigating of his own. I meant he should investigate Hart's murder. But it's my own fault for not spelling it out. If you are going to delve into the suspicious death of the Hansen parents, I'm actually fine with it, but it needs to lead somewhere. And if you don't know what that means, ask.

I guess I never realized the extent of your love for Terry. Hmm, what to do? Well, at least we're back to work. I'm going to take the Epictetus approach: "Make the best use of what is in your power, and take the rest as it happens."

In response to your previous note, please forgive me for forgetting about your 1996 publication of that great poem "Davy Cricket" in *Harper's*. I don't know how I could have forgotten that. I now present a very special Lutz's Index:

Number of times Dave has mentioned being published in *Harper's*: 90

Number of times Dave was published in *Harper's*: 1

Sorry, I couldn't resist.

Lisa

CHAPTER 17

Lacey and Paul stood beside Terry's hospital bed. Terry's face and body were mottled with bruises. He was hooked up to an assortment of monitors, tubes, and receptacles. His right leg, broken in four different places, hung in traction. His left arm, from shoulder to wrist, was also set in a cast that was so far unblemished by any friendly signatures. Paul was the first to get his hand on a Sharpie: *To the Puma, until the end, your friend, Paul.*

"I really thought you were dead," Lacey said.

"You and me both," Terry replied.

"No. I mean, like, I really, really, thought you were dead. In fact, there was no doubt in my mind that you were dead. Like totally and completely, never coming back, dead."

"Miracles can happen," Terry said in his blithely morphined state.

"Uh-huh," Lacey replied. "Only they usually don't."

"Just be happy for the man," Paul said, elbowing his sister, knocking her off balance.

"I'm happy for you," Lacey said.

When visiting hours ended, Terry's nurses ushered Lacey and Paul out of the room. The man needed his rest.

That night Lacey and Paul both dreamed about houses. In Lacey's dream, their rambler crumbled on top of them. In Paul's, he was trying to get out of the house, but the doors were locked and he didn't have the key. The morning following an unusually vivid dream, the siblings would often compare notes. But that morning, they were mostly silent over coffee and cereal. Lacey was the one to break the silence.

"So, I read an interesting article about Los Chungos the other day."

"Really?" asked Paul.

"Yeah. Seems they all moved to Florida in the late nineties. They haven't had a West Coast presence since then."

"Interesting," said Paul. "I guess that's the official story they want us to believe."

"'They'?"

"El Consorcio," Paul said solemnly.

No response.

"La Mano Invisible."

"Of course. The Invisible Hand," Lacey said, holding up a trembling hand and staring at it in mock terror.

Paul didn't have much fight in him that morning. He poured himself another bowl of cornflakes.

"Got any plans today?" Lacey asked.

"The usual," Paul replied.

"Making deliveries, getting stoned, and watching a full day's shift of television?"

"And what are your plans, Lace?"

"You know. The usual."

"Would that be going to work or fighting crime?"

"Don't see why I can't do both."

Lacey left her dirty mug and cereal bowl in the sink. Paul could clean up after her for once.

It was business as usual at the Tarpit. Until Betty arrived, that is.

"We need to talk," Betty said.

The morning rush was over, so Lacey made her friend a hot chocolate with extra marshmallows and poured a cup of straight coffee for herself.

"What's up?"

"This came for you yesterday," Betty said, sliding the note across the table.

Lacey read the terse message.

"You have any idea who sent this?" Lacey asked, her heart beating out of her chest.

"No. I found it in my mailbox, just that one sheet of paper. When I opened it up a bunch of mini-marshmallows fell out."

"Marshmallows?"

"Strange, huh?"

"Did you eat them?"

"Of course not."

"You know what this means?" Lacey asked.

"It means whoever left the note is a dimwit. The phrase is 'let sleeping *dogs* lie,'" Betty replied. "How could you confuse dogs with ducks?"

Lacey opted against enlightening Betty on the note's subject matter. This was her investigation and she'd deal with it.

"Should I be scared?" Betty asked. "The note writer knows some things, like where I live and that I like marshmallows."

"Don't worry about it. Whoever sent this is after me," Lacey replied, pocketing the piece of paper.

After Betty departed, Lacey continued to wonder who'd sent the warning. The question kept sticking in her head like a lousy old record. Big Marv was an obvious candidate, but hadn't he already made himself abundantly clear, both physically and verbally? It couldn't be Doc Holland, for too many reasons to list. For one, how would he know she was on to him? Secondly, if he was trying to keep a low profile, this was hardly the way to do it. Also, he knew where the Hansens lived—there was no reason to leave the note with Betty. Could somebody else besides the old non-doc have a stake in this matter? Lacey had no idea where to go with this lead, but she had to go somewhere.

After closing up the Tarpit, Lacey drove to her newly minted mailbox depot and opened the tiny door. She'd mailed the letter to Holland only two days earlier and hardly expected such a timely response. But there it was, an envelope addressed to "The Mallard" from "HH" with a San Francisco postmark. She returned to her car before cracking the seal. The script was pure Doc Holland.

From the Desk of
HERMAN HOLLAND, M.D.

Sook,

I thought we said our good-byes.
You've been shaking me down for five years. We're done now.
I'm retired and so are you.
It's time you and your "silent partner" find some other sheep to fleece.

HH

Lacey swung onto the road and broke every speed limit sign she passed. In ten minutes flat, she was inside Mapleshade and knocking on Sook's door.

"Lacey," Sook said as he invited her into his walk-in-closet-sized room. "What a pleasant surprise."

Lacey smacked the note into Sook's chest.

"Old man, you've got some explaining to do."

Sook took a few steps back under the pressure of Lacey's light shove. He unfolded the note, but couldn't read a thing without his glasses.

"Who are you?" Lacey asked.

Sook appeared confused and feeble, hardly the crafty extortionist she'd discovered him to be.

"I need my glasses," he replied.

Lacey scoured the room and found them atop the dresser.

"Read," she intoned as she passed him his spectacles.

Sook read the note, took a deep breath, and sat down on his bed, a sudden exhaustion setting in.

"Where did this come from?" Sook asked.

"I found it in your old mailbox. The Mallard Corp. headquarters. You remember that, don't you?"

"But I closed that box. I haven't written to Holland in weeks. I didn't even know how to track him down."

"I wrote to him," Lacey replied. "I wanted to find out what happened to the old doc and maybe flush out his blackmailer. Did *not* expect my plan to work so smoothly. You know what else I didn't expect?"

"I can explain."

"Really?"

"I needed money. My Social Security check goes straight to Mapleshade. I never had more than a few dollars to spend. I have grandchildren and sometimes I like to send them a little something on their birthday."

"Sook, you're a geriatric marijuana dealer. Don't you make enough pocket money with your first part-time job?"

"Who's to say what enough is?" Sook replied.

"You're a blackmailer, Sook."

"You know what blackmail is, Lacey? It's a business deal, plain and simple. I promised not to do something that I could legally do, in exchange for money. That, my dear, is a verbal contract, recognized by the law."

"Only, you knew something about Holland that the rest of the town should have known. If he wasn't a real doctor, he shouldn't have been treating patients."

"Well now. You have a point there," Sook conceded. "But I did what I had to do."

Lacey sat down in the crappy mesh chair Sook had pinched from Mapleshade's waiting room. She had so many questions for Sook, but only one was relevant to her case.

"Tell me the truth, Sook. Who is your silent partner?"

"Was," Sook corrected.

"Excuse me?"

"It was Hart."

As she drove home, Lacey went over the rest of her conversation with Sook. The old man had figured out during his first visit with Holland that he was no doctor. He could treat a flesh wound and do basic triage, but for any complicated concerns, he referred patients to the local emergency room. Holland knew what tests to run, but had only limited knowledge of the treatment protocol. Holland told Sook he was a Vietnam vet. On a hunch, Sook phoned up one of his Army connections and learned that there was no record of a Herman Holland as a physician in the Vietnam War. In fact, no Herman Holland had worked as even a medic. Sook then contacted the AMA and found that there was no Herman Holland in the doc's age range.

Sook couldn't believe that Holland had practiced in Mercer for twenty years without anyone noticing. He saw an opportunity and seized it. He rented out a mailbox and opened a bank account under the name Mallard Corp. Then he made his demands. It didn't take Holland long to figure out the identity of his blackmailer. Sook was the only Mapleshade resident who refused to visit his offices, even during that brutal strep throat outbreak.

How Sook's silent partner came into the picture was another story. Sook had once asked Hart to drive him to his mailbox store. They ate lunch at Diner afterward. Hart asked him about the letter. Sook's reply was cagey. Hart could always spot a liar, being such an adept one himself. He got curious and picked Sook's pocket when he dropped him off at the home.

As soon as Sook realized his check was missing, he got a phone call from Hart. He wanted a cut. Sure, Hart could blackmail Holland himself, but the fake doc could only afford so much hush money. If pushed, he would leave town, as he eventually did. Hart opened a bank account in the name of Merganser, Inc., and Mallard Corp. wrote him a check every month. Lacey's final question was one she never thought she'd ask Sook.

"Did you kill Hart?"

Of course, Sook denied killing Hart. And Lacey believed him. Unless the old man had an accomplice, it was a physical impossibility, considering all the variables involved in the aftermath of Hart's death. Still, Lacey was no longer sure what Sook was capable of. She decided to steer clear of him for a while.

She drove straight home, took a shot of whiskey, and sat down on the couch next to Paul. They watched a rerun of *The Littlest Catch*, about the perils of Canadian shrimp fishing. During a commercial break, Paul hit the mute.

"You know, Lace, maybe this is rock bottom," he said. "Maybe it's time I quit watching this stuff."

Lacey was stunned for a moment, but quickly recovered. "Or even ever mentioning it again?" she asked.

"Deal," said Paul.

It was the first thing they'd agreed on in days.[26]

The shock of the telephone ringing jarred them out of their shared moment of clarity. Lacey jumped for the phone.

"Give us ten minutes. We'll be right there," Lacey said into the receiver, and then hung up the phone.

"Who was that?"

"Deena. She's at the Timberline. Smashed. Needs a ride to the hospital."

"Why?"

"Terry took a turn for the worse."

---

[26]Agreed.

———————

When the trio arrived at Terry Jakes's hospital room, a sheet was pulled over his head.

"What happened?" Deena asked the nurse.

"Pulmonary embolism," the nurse replied. "I'm afraid it's very common with these types of injuries."

"A pulmonary what? I was just talking to him this morning. He was fine," Deena said as tears began rolling down her ruddy cheeks.

"It's a blood clot in the lungs. Most likely it traveled from his leg. A lot of damage was done there."

"So he's dead?" Lacey asked.

"Yes."

"Are you sure?"

"Um, yes."

"Because I thought he was dead the other day and he wasn't. So let's just—"

"Lacey!" Paul interrupted. "That's enough."

"Do you want to say good-bye?" the nurse asked.

Deena nodded her head. The nurse pulled the sheet down and there was Terry Jakes, looking bruised and battered and most definitely dead.

NOTES:

Dave,

Once again, please accept my condolences. I consulted my friend Dr. Pedram Navab and he assures me that a pulmonary embolism is a very common complication with these types of injuries. There was no foul play involved in Terry's second demise, if that makes you feel better. And he wasn't in pain. At least not too much, although he did have some difficulty breathing. My point being, don't delve into any hospital conspiracy. There is none.

As a friendly reminder, let's not forget that there's still one primary mystery to solve here: Hart's death.

     Lisa

P.S. If you bring Terry back again, I'm putting him through a woodchipper.

Lisa,

Greetings from the high road. Guess I should be pleased with small victories, like the fact that you didn't send Terry's gurney down an elevator shaft, or have him whisked away by a highly concentrated tornado. Putting a medical gloss on your *deus ex machina* doesn't make it any less clunky. You keep harping on keeping the mystery going; maybe you should focus on the characters' vendettas, rather than your own.

Sorry you were bored by my last chapter. Maybe, like Terry, I've learned that burning too brightly can be dangerous. If the *Fop* experience taught me anything, it's that Bordeaux and Twinkies don't mix.

     Dave

CHAPTER 18

On their way out of the hospital, Paul and Lacey were approached by another nurse. "Paul Hansen?" she asked. "I'm not supposed to do this, but Mr. Jakes asked me to let you know that his will is on a videotape in his bedroom closet. He said to show it to everyone at the same time." In his mind, Paul was already on the way to Terry's. He'd already postponed grieving for his friend—right now he had to get his plants back home just in case Sheriff Ed wanted to take this opportunity to start poking around Terry's place.

Lacey was silent on the drive home. She'd never seemed to appreciate Terry while he was alive, but apparently seeing him die twice in two days was more than she could take.

"Get some rest, Lace," Paul said as he dropped her off at home. "I'll take care of the plants."

She dropped out of the truck and somnambulated into the house.

At Terry's, Paul loaded his plants back into his truck, covered them with a tarp he found in the garage, and then went looking for the video will. Terry had a massive collection of tapes, both Beta and VHS, and Paul doubted it included one clearly marked "Terry's Will." Paul dreaded the prospect of enduring untold hours of dharma talks, bargain-bin porn, and metal concerts, but it had to be done.

After sampling a dozen tapes in front of Terry's nineteen-inch console TV, he played a hunch and inserted one marked "Intermediate Levitation." When Terry came on screen with a solemn look on his face and announced, "This is Terrence Leotis Jakes," Paul knew it was the one. Terry's forehead was smudged with the remnants of tribal war paint—he must have taped the will after one of his *Survivor* application sessions a few years back. Paul ejected the tape, honoring Terry's wishes. He stuffed it in his bag and drove his plants home.

Paul was up first the next morning, despite having been up late re-establishing the plants in the basement. "Happy anniversary," he said as Lacey trudged into the kitchen.

"A year since we found the body?" Lacey deadpanned.

"Close. A week."

"What did you get me?"

"A basement full of high-yield pot plants."

"Aw, you shouldn't have."

"It was my pleasure," said Paul, raising his coffee. "Here's to a less eventful week two."

"Whatever."

Lacey poured herself a cup to go and headed out the door. She worked full eight-hour Tarpit shifts on Thursdays and Fridays, and for once she seemed content to have two days of mindless work ahead of her. Paul noticed that her inquisitiveness seemed to have waned since Terry's death.

Paul called Deena just to check in on her. Several of Terry's friends and relatives had converged on Mercer as soon as they'd heard about the tower collapse. It seemed like a good idea to have some kind of memorial service while they were still in town. Deena said she'd put the word out. She was glad to have something to do other than, as she put it, "sittin' around thinkin' about old shoulda-beens and usedta-coulds." The coroner wasn't ready to release the body, but why should that hold things up? She agreed to arrange things with Tate. That afternoon, Deena's friends put signs up around town: "Timberline. Friday 6pm. JAKES' WAKE. All friends and family of Terry Jakes welcome."

With those details sorted out, Paul couldn't help wondering how a tower stands firm for decades and then spontaneously collapses. Maybe it had been on the brink for years, and Terry was as suitable a last straw as any. Stranger things had happened, including several in the past week. In any case, Paul wasn't about to go poking around the place, which was no doubt being scrutinized by Mercer's finest.

Paul's thoughts turned back to the list of WINO names from the cabin. If he couldn't begin to untangle the mystery that seemed to have Mercer by the neck, maybe he could tie up a loose string from the past. Or at the least get some reassurance that the two weren't parts of the same thread. He took out the list: Blakeys, Collaspos, Sundstroms. The Sundstroms were the only couple Paul thought he could picture, but their address was way out in Easternville. He decided to start with the closest address: Grace and Victor Collaspo, who apparently lived on the north end of town—or did when the list was made.

As he walked up to the house, he could see a small, plump woman washing dishes, her head barely visible in the window. She came out to her porch and hugged him. "Paul Hansen. You look just like your mom." She embraced him as though his parents' death had happened last week. Paul didn't recognize her. "Come in, come in," she said.

Sitting with Paul at her dining room table, she didn't ask how he'd found her or what he was looking for. Paul hadn't planned what to say, so he winged it. "I was just wondering about the time, you know, with my parents' accident. My, uh, therapist thought it would help me get some closure on it."

"Well, that's just great. Good for you," said Grace. "I don't know if I can help you, though. I hadn't seen your folks for a while when the accident happened. Victor and I were going through a rough patch at the time."

"Sorry to hear it."

"Don't be. We split up a good three years ago. And I do mean a *good* three years. Are you married, Paul?"

"Nope."

"That's fantastic. What's the rush, right?"

"So where's Victor now?" Paul asked.

"Florida, I think. He went off with Jas Blakey. All I can say about that is they deserve each other."

"Ah. She was part of WINO, too, right? Is her . . . is Walter Blakey still around?"

"Wow, I'm surprised you remember his name. Yeah, he's in the same house up in Emery. I think he even still uses the cabin."

Back in his truck, the reality of Terry's death started to hit Paul. He'd visit Walter Blakey when he had time. For now, he had some deliveries to make, some soil amendments to buy, a plot of young plants to check on, and a friend to mourn.

On Friday evening the Timberline was already starting to fill up when Paul and Brandy arrived. It felt like half of Mercer was there, along with lots of Terry's out-of-town friends and relatives. Someone had put together a decent buffet, and everyone had made at least a gesture toward funeral attire. Even Darryl was wearing black jeans. Paul said hello to Terry's goth teenage niece, Melinda, who actually looked a little perkier than usual.

Lito showed up just after Paul, and the two shook hands and made small talk. Betty and Wanda hung around the buffet table with Rafael. There were plenty of other locals in attendance. Paul wondered how many of them had known Terry, how many were just there for the free booze, and how many straddled that line. Then again, Terry was not one to deny anyone their rightful share of free booze. The question itself was what Terry would have called a "mute point."

Tate rang the "Last call for alcohol" bell to get everyone's attention. "Okay folks, thank you all for coming," he said stiffly. "We are here to celebrate and remember our friend Terry Jakes. I will now turn it over to Terry's cousin, Martin Jakes. Martin?"

Martin took Tate's place behind the bar, which would serve as the evening's podium. Judging from the eulogy, Martin was a devout Christian and hardly knew Terry. Next up, the goth niece delivered a poem that rhymed "incendiary" with "Uncle Terry." It wasn't until Wanda delivered a reminiscence about Terry as a misfit high school kid that the crowd started to choke up. Terry's old parole officer was up last. He started to say a few words but was too emotional to finish. His wife came up and hugged him around the neck. Tate announced the end of the speaker portion of the evening. It was time for the will.

Paul and Brandy stood together at the back of the bar, with Lacey teetering next to them. All three were bleary-eyed. As Tate popped the videotape into the VCR, Paul just hoped Terry didn't use the will to send the whole town on a wild-goose chase, like in *It's a Mad, Mad, Mad, Mad World,* one of Terry's favorite movies. After the static cleared and the crowd hushed, Terry's image appeared on the TV above the bar.

"This is Terrence Leotis Jakes," he said solemnly, and then slowly panned the room, as though examining everyone in the crowd. "The killer," he proclaimed, "*is among you.*" The Timberline went silent. Then Terry burst out laughing.

"Naw, I'm playin'. Chances are I died doing some dumb shit. Hope you all at least got a good laugh out of it, and that somebody caught it on tape. Maybe I'm a YouTube celebrity already. Okay, down to business." He raised his hand, Boy Scout style.

"This hereby is my final will and testament. It shall taketh precedent over all other documents. Forthwith I disclose my postmortem wishes and intentions as to the disbursement of my earthly possessions and whatnot." He cleared his throat.

"First, a word of warning. My body may remain in a state of *samadhi* for five days after my death. Do not be alarmed. This is normal for enlightened ones of the *yeshe chölwa.* That means crazy wisdom, for those of you who don't know." Paul thought he could feel the crowd roll its collective eyes.[27]

---

[27]Can he feel my eyes rolling too?

"After such period, I wish to be cremated. Whereupon, at the earliest convenience, my remains shall be scattered upon Mount Fuji, preferably by helicopter. Until such time, my ashes shall be maintained in a container of highest quality above the bar at the Timberline. Up near the good stuff."

Everyone started to choke up again.

"Okay, let's get down to who gets the goodies. To Deena Jake . . . er, Dixon," he stammered. "Girl, we almost made it. You are still my angel. I'll always love ya."

Terry cleared his throat and assumed a more officious tone: "Conditional upon the assumption that you are not in jail for killing my ass . . ."

"*I tried!*" Deena shouted from the back of the bar. The crowd erupted in laughter.

"I leave you my life savings," Terry continued, "as well as any and all other monetary assets. Seemed like it was all headed in your direction anyway. No hard feelings, babe. Don't spend it all in one place.

"And to my dear second wife, Christina Mackey: I know we had our disagreements, but after careful consideration, I leave you with one of my most profoundly cherished possessions . . . *bupkis!*"

As the laughs died down, Lacey said, to no one in particular, "What's a bupkis?"

Brandy blurted, "It's Yiddish for 'nothing.' Actually, the earlier Eastern European Yiddish term was *bobke*—the diminutive of *bob,* a type of bean. So, interestingly, *bupkis* is related to other legume-based expressions of worthlessness, such as 'not worth a hill of beans.'"

Brandy covered her mouth, realizing what she'd done. "I mean, like, I think that might be what it means . . . I had a Jewish . . . uncle?"

Paul put his arm around her and gave her a long, knowing look.

"How long have you known?" she asked.

"Pretty much since the Kierkegaard incident."

"Are you mad?"

"Splenetic," said Paul.

True to form, Terry's will went on for a while. He left Darryl, "my brother from another mother," his truck and his Bobcat mini-excavator.

"And to my cousin Harry," Terry continued, "I leave my house in Mercer."

Everyone turned to look for Cousin Harry, who apparently wasn't in attendance.

The tape played on. "As to my property on the Mercer–Emery line, the magnificent Shady Acres, I bequeath it to its previous owners—the Hansen family, Paul and Lacey."

Paul's eyes welled up as he absorbed Terry's gesture. All Lacey could think about was how it could hasten her escape from Mercer.

"Oh yeah, I almost forgot," Terry said. "To my buddy Hart, I leave my extensive library of spiritual literature. Be careful, brother. Don't take life so serious. I'll see you around the bend."

Lacey gasped when she heard Hart's name. She'd never known Terry and Hart to be anything more than distant acquaintances.

Then Terry reached off screen and brought a white bass guitar into the picture. "One last thing in closing," he said. He plugged it in, causing a loud pop, and lurched into a slow bass line. Paul had forgotten about Terry's bass phase. He recognized the tune immediately, though he hadn't heard it in years. It was a Terry Jakes original, "Travelin' On." Terry sang in a high and delicate voice:

> Girl I know you think it's over
> And you know I got to fly
> But I'll come find you some cold mornin'
> And we'll start a new good-bye

By the third verse everyone was crying, even Tate. Not content to let the vocal sentiment of the song stand as his final statement, Terry proceeded to improvise a four-minute slap-bass solo. It was terrible, and great. Pure Terry.

He reached out to turn the camera off, succeeding after a couple of tries. Tate turned off the VCR and the memorial abruptly shifted gears into raucous party mode. Someone set up a karaoke machine with Terry's favorite songs, and pot smoke seemed to rise up out of the floor. Terry should have been there.

NOTES:

Lisa,

I tried to nudge things along without turning Paul into Magnum P.I. Hope you're okay with Lacey's lack of activity here. Poor girl seemed like she needed a breather, what with all the redundant-death witnessing.

I realize the video-will takes a while, but I figure you won't begrudge me my last few moments with Terry. I thought he deserved a fitting send-off. I present it in the spirit of reconciliation, not provocation. Terry would have wanted it that way.

Dave

Dave,

Now that you've said a proper good-bye to Terry, I do hope you can get back to murder-solving. Let me rephrase that: Maybe you can get started on some murder-solving, now that we have not one but two bodies to worry about. And if you keep that shit up with Brandy, I wouldn't be surprised if a third person met an untimely end.

There's no way in hell Lacey hasn't heard the word "bupkis."

Lisa

CHAPTER 19

Lacey awoke in the kitchen with her head resting on her murder notebook and the smell of burnt coffee wafting through the room. She turned off the coffeemaker and scrubbed out the stale brew that had congealed on the bottom. Her head throbbed and her mouth tasted like Irish coffee, beer, and something else. Oh yes, Jägermeister. That was the salve for the group sing-along. At least that part of the evening would forever remain foggy.

Lacey chugged a pint glass of tap water and then searched the bathroom for aspirin. In the mirror she saw something on the side of her face that resembled a primitive starburst. It looked familiar, but she couldn't quite recall its origin. She scrubbed her face, brushed her teeth, and swallowed three aspirin, hoping that more coffee would give her the energy she needed to get to work. Her real work, that is—solving Hart's murder.

Paul's bedroom door was open, which meant he'd spent the night at Brandy's. Something about that woman never sat right with Lacey. If she was so smart, why did she waste that gift on stripping? And what kind of genius lives in Tulac? Besides, that whole "pole-dancing injury" always sounded like a chapter in a white trash fairy tale.

Over fresh coffee, Lacey revisited her notebook, where she drew lines linking Hart to every one of Mercer's citizens who had ever had anything to do with the man. The ink starburst on her face, she realized, had transferred when she slept on her notebook. Lacey decided to start from scratch and deepen her suspect pool—Big Marv and Jay Babalato, Doc Holland, Darryl Cleveland, Sheriff Ed, Deputy Doug, Rafael, Tate, Lito, and Sook, although she had a hard time writing down that last name.

She also had Terry on the list. Just because he was dead didn't mean he couldn't have murdered someone before he died.

Lacey decided to pay another visit to the sheriff to see if he was making any headway in his investigation. She watched Deputy Doug devour a bearclaw through the office window. He stuffed the remaining pastry in his desk drawer, brushed the crumbs off his shirt, combed his hair, and checked his teeth in the reflection of his screensaver. When she entered the office, Doug got to his feet as if she were a four-star general.

"Lacey. What a pleasant surprise."

"I'm here to talk about murder, so I'm not sure how pleasant it will be."

"I see. What can I do for you?"

"You? Nothing. I'm here to see Sheriff Ed."

Doug, disappointed, sat back down at his desk and picked up the phone.

"I'll see if he's in."

"He's in," Lacey said. "His car is parked out front."

Lacey strode down the hall to the door marked SHERIFF ED WICKFIELD. She knocked twice and waited. Inside she could hear the sheriff say, "I told you, no interruptions this morning."

Lacey knocked again. A moment passed and eventually Ed opened his door.

"Lacey," he said, wearily. His uniform, usually a specimen of military discipline, was wrinkled and spotted and had the odor of at least two days' wear. Perhaps Sheriff Ed was in fact burning the midnight oil on Hart's murder. Lacey decided to give him the benefit of the doubt.

"Morning, Sheriff," Lacey said, brushing past him and taking a seat.

The sheriff returned to his desk and summoned a smile.

"What can I do for you, Lacey?"

"I just thought I'd check in and see how the investigations are going."

"Investigations?" Sheriff Ed asked, emphasizing that final *s*.

"Yes. The Hart murder and the possible homicide of Terry Jakes."

"As for Hart, I have nothing to report. Unfortunately, without a head, we can't pin down cause of death, and without that, we're looking for diamonds in a manure heap.[28] And frankly, no one seems to know what he's been up to these last six months, but I can assure you, Lacey, that I'm working every lead."

"I have a theory," Lacey said.

"I'm sure you do."

"Terry Jakes's murder—"

"It could just have been an accident."

"For argument's sake, let's say it wasn't."

"What makes you so sure?"

"Well, for one, they were friends. Two, they happened within ten days of each other. Mercer hasn't had a murder in fifteen years. What are the odds?"

"Lacey, investigating ain't horseracing. We're not playing odds. We're looking for evidence. That's how police work is done."

"Have you found incriminating evidence at the fire tower site?"

"An architectural consultant is coming in next week to investigate."

"Next week?"

"That's as soon as we could get him. Anything else I can help you with?"

"I didn't do it," Lacey said.

"Do what?" Sheriff Ed asked.

"I didn't kill Hart and I didn't kill Terry, in case you were wondering."

"Lacey, I don't suspect you."

"Well you should," Lacey said.

---

[28]This would actually be pretty easy—they'd stand out. On a separate note, why does this process sound familiar?

"Excuse me?"

"It's obvious, isn't it? Objectively, I benefit from both of their deaths. There's that life insurance policy from Hart, which I didn't know about, but still. And then Terry bequeathed that land back to us. Plus, I was the only witness to the collapse. So, I could see how I would be a suspect, but I'd really like to save you the trouble of investigating me. Because, seriously, Ed, I didn't do it."

"Of course you didn't," Ed replied.

"How do you know?" Lacey replied.

Sheriff Ed sighed and sank back in his chair. "Because, Lacey, I've known you since you were in diapers. You never had a violent streak or even much of a temper against anyone besides that brother of yours. Also, in my experience, women don't usually chop off heads."

"That's very sexist of you, Ed."

"I knew you were going to say something like that."

"Since you've ruled me out as a suspect," Lacey said, "I'd look at Big Marv if I were you. He wanted Terry's land, and Deena is a notoriously bad negotiator. I'm sure he thought Terry was going to leave everything to her."

The sheriff's intercom buzzed. Deputy Doug's voiced boomed into the office.

"The missis is here."

"Send her in," Sheriff Ed replied.

Lacey got to her feet. "I'll be in touch," she said.

"Remember, Lacey. We all have our jobs to do. While I appreciate your assistance, I've got this investigation under control."

"Have a nice day, Sheriff."

Lacey passed Ed's wife, Lila, in the hall. They had the kind of acquaintance that required only a smile and the nod of a head. Lila left a scent in the air that Lacey found strangely familiar—some specific floral fragrance she couldn't name. As Lacey passed the front desk, Doug got to his feet again. Lacey didn't even look at him this time as she aimed for the door.

"So . . . uh, Lacey," Doug said, "I guess I'll be seeing you around."

Lacey turned around and looked at Doug. "It's a small town. We can't escape each other."

Lacey didn't notice the look of hope vanish from Doug's face. She was about to turn around again, but that scent stuck in her nose.

"Do you smell that?" Lacey asked.

"Smell what?" Doug replied, fighting the urge to check his armpits.

"Her perfume. What is it?"

"Oh that," Doug said. "It's lilacs. She always wears it. I guess 'cause her name is Lila. Although, it's not exactly the same . . ."

Lacey was out the door before Doug could finish his sentence.

Knowing that the sheriff and his deputy were safely ensconced in head-quarters, Lacey broke several traffic laws on her way to Betty's place. If anyone was clued in to the Mercer gossip mill, it was Betty. Lacey double-parked in her friend's driveway, ran up the steps, and rapped her knuckles on the door until they stung.

"Good Lord, Lacey. Do you have to pee?" Betty asked, when she finally answered the door.

"Excuse me?"

"I thought a woodpecker was trying to break in."

"Who smells like lilacs?" Lacey asked.

"Would you like to come inside?" Betty asked.

"No. I just want to know who smells like lilacs all the time."

"Lila Wickfield."

"Did you know?"

"I heard rumors."

"Why didn't you tell me?"

"Because there were so many rumors about Hart, I didn't know where they began or ended and whether it was true or false."

"You think the sheriff heard these rumors?"

"Maybe," Betty replied.

"Interesting," Lacey said, letting these facts unscramble in her head.

"You don't honestly think that Ed had anything to do with Hart's murder."

"I don't know," Lacey replied, "but he just moved a few notches up my list."

Lacey returned home and tried to sleep off her investigative hangover. The phone woke her just as she was nodding off.

"Lacey?"

"Yes."

"It's Matthew."

"Who?"

"Matthew Egan."

"Not ringing a bell," Lacey replied.

"Doctor Egan?"

"Why didn't you say so in the first place?" Lacey replied. "What can I do for you?"

"I've been expecting you to drop by."

"To get my stitches out?"

"No. You still have another two days. There's a delivery you're supposed to make."

"What kind of delivery?"

"Um, don't you remember?"

"Nope."

"You have something that I would like to purchase."

"You mean *the weed*?" Lacey asked.

"I mean the thing we talked about the other day."

"We're not being recorded, Doc. I can promise you that. Sorry. I forgot about that. I'll be right over with the *marijuana*. Make sure you have cash. Bye."

———————

The whine of a table saw emanated from Doc Egan's garage.

When Egan spotted her, he shut down the saw and lifted his plastic goggles. Lacey held out a paper bag.

"I have your drugs!" Lacey shouted at full volume.

Doc Egan rolled his eyes. He handed her a wad of bills.

"As we discussed," he said.

"Thank you."

The doctor was building bookshelves, which didn't look half bad. She was impressed that the doctor had a garage full of tools that he seemed to know how to use.

"So, you like to build things?" Lacey asked.

"Evidently," Egan replied.

"What's the most complicated thing you've ever built?"

"When I was in high school, my dad and I built a cabin near Lake Tahoe."

"Huh."

"Why do you ask?"

"If I were to show you a building that collapsed, would you be able to tell whether it collapsed accidentally or if there was some tampering going on?"

"Like a fire tower, for example?"

"You know about it?"

"I live here now. I hear things," Egan replied. "Aren't the police investigating?"

"They're waiting for a specialist. He won't come into town until next week. Do you want to see it?" Lacey asked.

"Yeah. I think I do."

On the drive out of town, Egan and Lacey passed the airstrip. Some of the debris from the explosion still lingered on the landscape.

"Did they ever find out what happened with the plane crash?" Egan asked.

"Nope," Lacey replied.

"A plane crashes and nobody knows who it was or why?"

"As far as I know, it's still a mystery."

"Isn't that strange?"

"Yes, it is," Lacey replied. "It doesn't make a damn bit of sense."

Their conversation ended there because nothing else could be said. Lacey pulled the car off the main road and she and Egan hiked down to the site of the old fire tower.

"This looks like a game of Jenga gone bad," he said, after slipping under the police tape and taking in the site of Terry Jakes's almost-demise.

"I saw it happen," Lacey said. "It crumbled in like five seconds. There was almost no warning. Just a squeaking sound. The tower tilted and that was it."

Egan trudged through the wreckage, studying the planks of oak on the ground. Lacey stood back and waited. There was a moment when she could have sworn she saw Terry's bright red long johns beneath the rubble. After about forty minutes, Egan had collected five pieces of oak, which he separated from the rest of the scraps. He approached Lacey and dropped the lumber to the ground. Then he joined two pieces that fit together like a puzzle and showed them to her.

"This plank? Was sawed down to about one inch," Egan said. "You can see where it snapped."

A distinct saw mark led to a splintered edge. Egan found another matching set with the same pattern.

"See—another one sawed down and then snapped."

"What are you saying?" Lacey asked.

"This was definitely not an accident."

Lacey and Egan hauled the evidence back to her car and returned to the main road. When the cell towers kicked in again, the message light blinked on Lacey's phone. There was only one call:

"Lacey, this is Yolanda at Mapleshade. It appears that Sook has taken ill. If you want to see him, I suggest you get over here as soon as possible."

Matthew noticed the shift in Lacey's expression as she listened to the message.

"You okay?" he asked, when she put down the phone.

"Do you mind if we take a detour? I need to check on Sook."

"Where is he?" Lacey asked.

"In his room," Yolanda said, avoiding eye contact.

"Why didn't you call an ambulance?" Lacey asked.

"He asked me not to," Yolanda said, still averting her gaze.

Lacey stormed into Sook's room with Doc Egan right behind her. She found Sook in bed with one of those old-time sleep caps on. He not-so-stealthily stuffed something under the covers and then hooded his eyes, trying to appear as if he'd just woken up. Lacey felt his forehead. It was baked-potato hot. She felt his neck. It was normal temperature.[29] His complexion appeared pale, but she noted something chalky about it. She rubbed his cheek. Powder came off on her finger.

Lacey yanked the bedcovers back and found Sook in a pajama top and blue jeans with a heating pad and face powder in the shade of "Ivory Doll" tucked next to him.

"I actually thought you were dying," Lacey said.

"Well, I am," Sook indignantly replied. "I'm dying more than you are or he is or Yolanda. Maybe not more than Gladys next door. But still, my days are numbered. You gonna waste them being mad at me?"

"Why don't I give you two a minute," Egan said, closing the door behind him.

Sook and Lacey entered into an embarrassingly long stare-off. Sook

[29]Funny how there's a doctor in the room yet Lacey's doing the examination.

eventually called a forfeit when Yolanda reminded him that it was time for his eye drops. Lacey sat down in Sook's stolen chair and waited for him to beg for forgiveness. But Sook was more the rationalizing sort.

"You're a drug pusher; I'm a blackmailer. You're younger and prettier, but are we really all that different?"

Truth was, Lacey's indignation had faded as soon as she'd seen her old friend on his sickbed. When she thought Sook might truly be ill, she realized how much she missed him. She also needed him—Sook was her only true ally in her galaxy of investigations.

"No more secrets, Sook. Are we clear on that?"

"Crystal."

"Have you ever met Lila Wickfield?" Lacey asked.

"Lilac Lila?" Sook said.

"She always smells like that, right?"

"As far as I know."

Lacey looked Sook dead in the eye. "Was she stepping out on the sheriff?"

Sook didn't like where this conversation was heading, but he answered, "Yes."

"With?"

"I think you already know," Sook replied.

"Just say it."

"Hart."

"Was she the only one?"

"Probably not."

"How many?"

"Couldn't give you a number. Most of it was just rumor," Sook replied.

"Wow," Lacey said, feeling the room spinning. Then she recalled something. "Was that why you gave me the safe-sex talk that one time?"

"Why else?" Sook replied.

"That was awkward."

"Agreed."

"Aside from Lila, who else?"

"Hmm, I'd have to think about it," Sook replied. He got out of bed and began making it in his precise military fashion.

"Who, Sook?"

"For a while he was spending time with this gimpy stripper from Tulac."

NOTES:

Dave,

I'm remembering now that you are virtually incapable of taking any kind of instruction from me—case in point that haircut fourteen years ago. How hard is it to take half an inch off the bottom? I looked like a prison inmate after a lice scare.

If you ever want to finish this project, you'll have to take at least one piece of advice: Please start tying up loose ends and figuring out who our murderer or murderers are.

One more thing: I would like to preempt any thoughts of bringing Los Chungos back to California. Como se dice "mass murder"? The first kill is always the hardest. It gets sooo much easier after that.

Lisa

P.S. If you want to quit I'll understand. I'll just continue the project with a different writer.

Lisa,

Who remembers a haircut from 1996? You hang on to resentments like a lint trap. If you wanted a real haircut, you should have gone to a salon, not to a grad student halfway through a twelve-pack. Likewise, if you wanted a standard mystery, you should have chosen a mystery writer.

As for your latest chapter, I enjoyed Sook's shenanigans, but I wonder whether you've made him adorable enough. The old-timey sleeping cap is nice, but I feel like there might be more cuteness out there, just waiting to be harvested. "Waste not, want not" is what I say.

On a separate note, who would have suspected Doc Egan was an expert on architectural forensics? It's comforting to know that if I ever need, for example, Big Marv to be an expert on, say, ikebana, the Japanese art of flower arrangement, I can simply make him into one. I guess that's what fiction is all about. I'm always learning!

Dave

P.S. Why would I quit when I'm winning? And who would agree to work with you on an almost-finished novel anyway?

CHAPTER 20

By Sunday morning Paul and Brandy were nearly laughed out, having spent Saturday going over what was true and what was part of her act. Her actual musical taste ran more Bach than rock, it turned out. On the other hand, *Blazing Saddles* really was her favorite movie. As for money, Brandy said she'd been getting by with online poker and some math tutoring on the side. Paul had joined in the confessional mood, revealing that he'd fallen a few units shy of his college degree. She promised not to hold it against him.

They were still in bed. "Maybe we could live on the property Terry left Lacey and me,"[30] Paul speculated to the ceiling. "I could get out of the business and raise heirloom turkeys or something. You could, I don't know, mastermind a global financial heist online."

"Or we could move up to Eugene," said Brandy, giving him a squeeze. "You could be the professor's hot young husband."

Mostly Paul was enjoying not thinking about Terry, Hart, or Mercer. After they got up she put on the *Goldberg Variations* and heated up the previous night's macaroni and cheese. As they ate, he beat her at Stratego, running his string to four straight. He was 85 percent sure she wasn't letting him win. And if she was, he could live with it.

"While we're clearing the air, there's one last thing I need to tell you," Brandy announced.

"Gulp," Paul pronounced.

"I gotta run. Every Sunday I babysit my friend Candi's kids. We used

---

[30]Wow. Paul sure got over his grief quickly. Show some respect. A man just died.

to dance together, before we both got hurt—different pole, same song. She decided to sue the place and lost. Went broke paying her lawyer. So now she deals blackjack at Spirit Rock on weekends. Sweet girl, but not the coldest beer in the fridge. She keeps making terrible choices with men, too."

"I'm glad you don't have that problem," Paul said, and kissed her good-bye.

Walter Blakey's backyard in Emery smelled like some specific flower Paul couldn't name.

"Fucking Raiders," Walter said.

The first game of the season was playing on an old portable black-and-white TV on the railing of his back porch. The Broncos had just returned an interception for a touchdown.

"I just keep coming back, year after year. Ever feel like the thing that really kills you is hope?" Walter asked.

"Never quite looked at it that way," said Paul. "But I guess I know what you mean." He'd stopped by and introduced himself on the way back down from Tulac.

After the extra point, Paul said, "So anyway, you're probably wondering what I'm doing here."

"I figured you'd get around to it."

"I wanted to ask you about the WINO days," said Paul.

"Shoot."

"Do you remember anything weird happening around the time of my parents' death?"

"Weird like how?"

"Like anything that made you wonder if the whole thing might not have been an accident?"

"Wow. Oh, man. . . . That period is a little blurry. We called ourselves WINO for a reason," Walter said with a chuckle, then stopped himself. "Sorry. It's terrible what happened to your folks."

"That's okay."

"Actually, Jas—Jasmine, my ex-wife—was more into the whole WINO thing than I was. She was kind of the secretary or treasurer of the group. You probably know this already, but another couple was originally scheduled to be there that weekend. That's what she told me, anyway."

"Mal and Mel Sundstrom?" Paul asked.

"Sundstrom, right," said Walter. "Me and Jas used to call them the Malmels. We could never remember which one was Mal and which was Mel. Was it Melanie or Melvin? Mallory or Malcolm? We used to crack each other up over that." He smiled at the memory. "Anyway, I never heard from them after the accident. I guess the party was just *over*, you know? They lived out in Easternville, I think."

"Yeah, that's what I heard."

Walter looked at him for a while. Then he said, "Look, Paul, I'd say you should probably just let it go, but that's what everyone says. The part they leave out is that it doesn't mean shit if the thing you let go of isn't ready to let go of *you*."

They sat for a moment, watching the game.

"Spoken like a true Raider fan," Paul said.

Walter laughed. He pointed to the overgrown jasmine in the corner of the yard. "Smell that? Every night the breeze comes right through that thing and I'm just transported."

"They say the sense of smell bypasses the rational part of the brain," said Paul.

"It definitely bypasses the part of the brain that would allow me to cut that fucker down."

"Do you ever hear from Jasmine or . . . Victor?" Paul asked.

"Not since she sent the divorce papers."

"Where are they now?"

"I try not to give it much thought," he said, staring at the unruly bush. "I mean, what are the odds?"

"Of what?" Paul asked.

"Her name was Jasmine, and that's exactly how she smelled."[31]

Paul had no answer for that. The Broncos waltzed in for another score.

Paul stopped at the Timberline to collect his thoughts. The place was lively for a Sunday night. He figured the regulars had finally recovered from Terry's wake and were ready to resume, as Terry would say, "fightin' that bear."

Paul was surprised to see Rafael running the pool table. It was unusual for him to be here on a Sunday night. Paul sat in the corner and put his name up on the chalkboard. In fifteen minutes Rafael had dispatched a couple of players, bringing Paul's turn up.

"Not a bad send-off, huh?" Rafael said, seeming a little tense as they shook hands.

"What's that?"

"Terry's party."

"Yeah. He would have been pleased."

Raf made two solids on the break, sunk another, and then missed a bank shot. Paul chalked his cue and asked, "So . . . did you know Terry well?"

"Tell you the truth, I only met him a few times. Great dude, though. My buddy Brice was friends with him. Anyway, I kind of figured Terry wouldn't mind a couple of freeloaders looking for free booze."

Paul laughed. "You got that right. So what brings you up here on a Sunday night?"

Instead of answering the question, Rafael asked, "What do you think happened to Terry?"

"No idea," Paul said, losing his smile. "Why?"

Rafael shrugged as he prepared for his next shot. "I haven't heard from Brice in a couple of weeks. He didn't show up at Terry's wake. Normally

---

[31]Shut up and write.

I'd be cool with it. Now that the whole random-violent-death thing is looking more chronic than acute, I'm not so cool with it." He sank the shot with unnecessary force.

"Nice shot," said Paul. "Tough leave, though."

Rafael gave him a cool look, then missed.

"Don't take this the wrong way," Paul said. "But is a week out of touch really so bizarre for your friend? Mercer isn't exactly known for its reliable nine-to-five types. I mean, Terry used to disappear all the time."

"Point taken," Rafael said. "Brice isn't the most predictable dude in the world. But we're tight—he should have at least texted me. All I'm sayin' is, whoever killed Hart and Terry might know at least something about Brice, too."

"Who says someone killed Terry?"

"Come on, man."

"Shit happens," said Paul. "Some towers just collapse. Some planes just explode. A lot of stuff goes on that we never understand. Seems to me that people don't really go off the rails until they try to assign meaning to things that are just random."

"Okay. But once you figure out one death, what if everything else starts making sense? Then maybe we could all stop worrying about where the hammer's gonna fall next."

Rafael crouched down to size up the eight ball. "I'm on your side, man," he said quietly. "Looks like we both lost our best friend."

Paul was already returning his cue to the rack when the eight clicked into the pocket. He didn't feel like they were on the same side. His best friend was dead; Rafael's had just become suspect number one. Or would have, if Paul were investigating.

On the way to his truck, Paul noticed Lito sitting in his car, talking on his cell phone. Paul gave him a casual wave as he passed. Lito kept talking into his phone as he hopped out of the Tercel, calling after Paul.

"Lito. How's it goin'?"

"Hey, man. Hangin' in there, I guess," Lito said, giving him a weary fist bump. "Look, my dad's on the line. He wants to say hello. Make peace, you know? He feels bad about Marv and everything." He handed Paul the phone.

"Hello?" said Paul.

"Paul. Jay Babalato. Look, I just wanted to say how sorry I am about your loss. Terry was a good man. We're going to miss him a lot around here."

"Okay, thanks."

"Also, I want to personally apologize for my brother's actions. He was way out of line. He gets a little passionate sometimes. He doesn't mean any harm."

"I appreciate that. Thanks."

"Look, I'd really like to buy you lunch. How about noon tomorrow at Verducci's?"

"Uh . . ."

"It'll be worth your time, I promise. Just you and me, no Marv, no strings attached. I have an opportunity that might interest you. If not, no harm done."

"Okay."

"Perfect. See you then, Paul."

Paul handed the phone back to Lito. "Dad?" Lito said into the phone, but Jay had already hung up.

"Thanks, bro," Lito said as he started toward the Timberline's entrance.

"Hang on a sec," said Paul.

"Yeah?"

"I was just thinking. You know what's weird? We saw that plane explode and then we never talked about it again."

Lito shrugged. "Shit happens," he said, and entered the bar.

On the drive home Paul called Brandy to tell her about the lunch with Jay so he'd at least have a witness if something went wrong.

"Just be careful, baby," she said.

When Paul finally pulled into his driveway, Irving came running up to the truck without the usual beak or squirrel elbow. Instead he gave Paul a blank look. Lacey's car was gone, but that wasn't so strange.

The front door was locked, and inside the house everything looked fine. Paul went downstairs to check on the plants. When he opened the sealed door to the grow room, he was blasted with light. Paul checked his watch in a panic. It should have been dark in there.

One of the first things Terry had taught him was that too much light during the plants' dark cycle would cause them to hermaphroditize, rendering them useless. *"Dude looks like a lay-day,"* Terry had sung, by way of explanation. "Sometimes 'she's got it all' ain't a compliment." Paul checked the timer. The settings had been reversed. A quick examination of the plants confirmed that it was too late.

Paul unplugged the lights and sat in his newly decorative herb garden. He was a man in the dark. In a few weeks, when the last of the finished product was sold, he'd be a man without an income. He wondered how Lacey would take the news. Then he had an ugly thought.

NOTES:

Lisa,

    I'll be brief. If you can continue to resist your murderous urges, I can keep playing nice.

       Dave

P.S. I hope Paul's admission about his college degree didn't touch a nerve.

Dave,

    So nice to see Irving again. That's one smart cat. I wonder if *he* turned on the lights.

    Amusing dig about my absent bachelor's degree. With an MFA in creative writing I can't imagine how many books I'd have published by now. Maybe zero.

    I'll play nice, too. I think I like what you're doing with Paul's investigation into his parents' death. It's a little off-point, but at least he's doing something other than listening to Bach with Brandy.

       Lisa

P.S. To answer your previous note, I suspect there are a few people who would work with me. I wouldn't have them start from scratch—we'd just excise your chapters and they'd figure out how to fill in the gaps.

CHAPTER 21

When Lacey returned home that night, the house was aglow, but not in the usual TV blue. Paul stared at the flames in the fireplace in stony silence.

"Paul," Lacey said. "Are you all right?"

"Check the grow room," he replied without turning away from the flames.

Lacey headed down to the basement, opened the door, and was blinded by the glare of the lights. Once her eyes adjusted, she recognized the sabotage at once. As she cycled through the possible suspects, she also felt relief. With most of their income gone, wasn't this a good time to get out?

"I'm sorry," Lacey said.

In the glow of the fire, Lacey could see Paul's eyes watering.

"Forgive me for saying this," she said, "but you seem more broken up about the loss of your plants than the loss of your best friend."

"People grieve in different ways."

"Do you know who did this?" Lacey asked.

"If I did, do you think I'd be sitting here doing nothing?"

"Probably." She regretted the response the moment it escaped her lips. But it was the truth. Even as children, Paul's response to a crisis was inertia. For some reason, Lacey remembered what she would later refer to as The Pop-Tart Incident. Paul's breakfast caught fire in the toaster when he was ten. Lacey came into the kitchen and saw Paul staring at the flames as they ignited a dishrag. There was a fire extinguisher under the sink. Lacey put out the flames as Paul watched.

And here he was again. Just staring at the fire.

"What now?" Lacey asked.

"I don't know."

"I have some things to tell you," Lacey said.

"Can they wait?"

"You're just watching a fire burn."

"It's peaceful, Lace. Just let me have this."

Tiny bursts of glowing embers breathed their last breath. All that was left was spent lumber and ash. Lacey broke the silence just as the final flicker of light died.

"Terry was murdered," she said.

"I figured as much," Paul replied.

"Whoever murdered him probably wanted the land."

"Maybe."

"Probably."

"That's debatable," Paul said. He was already thinking about his meeting with Jay Babalato the next day. If he believed Jay was a murderer, he'd feel like an accomplice.

"What else do you need to tell me, Lacey?"

The news about Brandy was on the tip of her tongue, but she decided there was a better way to handle it.

"Nothing," she replied.

"You said you had *things* to tell me," said Paul. "That implies there was at least one more thing."

"Oh right. Uh, I think the porch light needs changing."

"I'll get to it tomorrow," Paul replied.

That light had been out for six months. He knew Lacey was holding out on him. That night he went to bed wondering how well he really knew his own sister.

The next morning, Lacey slipped out of the house while Paul was still in bed. She drove past the police station, spotting Sheriff Ed's cruiser in the parking lot. Then she moved on to her real destination: the Wickfield residence on the Emery city line. Lacey rang the doorbell, which chimed a few bars of the *William Tell* Overture. She thought it was the height of tackiness. Then she noticed that the doormat had a photo of Charlton Heston—in the spirit of honor, not debasement—and next to that was a gnome lawn jockey.[32]

Lila answered the door in a floral silk bathrobe. She had on full eye makeup, but her lips were bare, which meant Lacey had woken her. She cut to the chase.

"How long were you seeing Hart?" Lacey asked.

"Who?"

"Hart, my ex-fiancé, the headless guy who showed up on my driveway. Your memory coming back yet?"

"Lacey, I don't want any trouble."

"Too late for that. Listen, Lila, be straight with me and I'll keep the sheriff out of it, but if you keep telling lies, I might have to pay him another visit. How long were you seeing Hart?"

"Only a few months."

"When?"

"After you broke up with him."

"The truth, Lila."

"Okay, there was some overlap."

"Did the sheriff know?"

"He was suspicious, but he didn't know who. And he had no hard evidence."

"You sure?"

"We were careful."

"Who else was he seeing?" Lacey asked.

"What's the point in dredging all this up?"

---

[32]Really a combination of these two very different things? Was there a sale at Wal-Mart?

"Because it might have something to do with his murder. Who else?"

"I think he was spending time with that gimpy stripper from Tulac. You know which one?"

"There's only one," Lacey replied.

"That's what I thought," said Lila. "But there are, in fact, two strippers who got bum legs from freak pole-dancing accidents."

"What are the odds of that?" Lacey replied.

"Just don't go confronting the wrong stripper. You're looking for the blond one, Brandy, not her friend Candi, who's a brunette."

"I guess that's all," Lacey said as she turned to walk away.

"I'm sure it doesn't mean anything now," Lila said, "but I think he loved you. I really do."

"Yeah," Lacey replied, not looking back. "Then why was he screwing anyone who'd have him?"

"It's Mercer," said Lila. "What else is there to do?"

Brandy was pulling out of her driveway in her canary-yellow VW Bug as Lacey pulled up. For lack of a better idea, Lacey followed her all the way back to Mercer and, oddly enough, to We Care Gardens. While Brandy pulled into the driveway, Lacey drifted past the entrance and parked her car in a shady turnaround by the side of the road. Then she threaded back through the dense woods that bordered the neglected facility.

A two-room bungalow that served as the administrative office was surrounded on three sides by woods. Lacey concealed herself behind a patch of pine trees that offered a direct view of the only entrance to the office. She assumed Brandy was inside and decided to wait her out. After twenty minutes, her cell phone rang. It was Paul. She pressed the mute button and then listened to the message as she continued her vigil. He was checking in, wondering what she was up to that day since she wasn't scheduled to work. She could hear the suspicion in his voice.

What Lacey saw next genuinely took her by surprise, which is saying something for a person who'd found a headless body on her property twice in the past ten days. Brandy and Big Marv exited the office. As Brandy limped to her car, Marv lumbered right behind her.

"I'll be in touch," Marv said.

Brandy looked at her watch. "You better hurry. Verducci's is at least a forty-minute drive."

Lacey couldn't fathom the connection between Big Marv and Brandy, but she decided that Big Marv's appointment held a little more intrigue than the rest of Brandy's day. Lacey waited until both cars were out of sight, ran to her Toyota, and headed after Big Marv, who was on his way to Birkton, home of Al's gas station, the $1 to $5 store, and Verducci's, the best Italian restaurant in a fifty-mile radius.

Exactly forty-two minutes later, Lacey was parked in the lot of the $1 to $5 store, which offered a decent view of Verducci's parking lot. A few spots down from Big Marv's Mercedes was her brother's truck. Paul's secret gimpy stripper girlfriend was one thing; a secret meeting with Big Marv was an entirely different monster. And now that the two were somehow linked, Lacey had to get to the bottom of it.

Lacey ducked into the store and purchased a ten-dollar lumberjack shirt, a two-dollar trucker's cap, and a one-dollar pair of sunglasses. She tucked her hair inside the cap and donned the rest of the outfit. She looked like a wimpy serial killer. In Birkton, she'd blend right in.

Lacey crossed the road and circled the establishment. The windows were dark on the outside, so she had to get her face right up to one to see inside. She scanned the room and in a back booth saw her brother sitting across from the Babalato brothers. It clearly hadn't been a table for three. Only Jay and Paul had plates of pasta in front of them.

A waitress taking a smoke break exited the building. She turned to Lacey and said, "Can I help you, sir?"

Startled, Lacey stepped back from the window.

"How's the food here?" Lacey asked.

"It's okay," the waitress replied. "A hell of a lot better if you go inside."

"Good to know," Lacey said.

Lacey dialed Paul's cell phone to see if he'd pick up.

"What's up?" Paul said.

"It's Lacey," Lacey replied. She hadn't expected Paul to pick up.

"Yeah, I know that."

"What are you up to?" Lacey asked.

"Just . . . uh . . . running a few errands."

"What kind of errands?"

"The kind that involve buying things in stores. What are you up to?"

"Nothing much."

"You sure got out of the house early," said Paul.

Lacey aimed for a better alibi than her brother.

"Just got my stitches out. Might run a few errands of my own and then head home."

"See you later," Paul said.

"Not if I see you first."

The line was a standard part of their banter, but she noticed an edge in her voice as she said it. She'd already begun to wonder if she really knew her brother at all.

Lacey headed back to Mercer, intending to stop by Mapleshade. But when she arrived, Mapleshade was in lockdown—someone had pinched every last penny from the petty-cash box. The prime suspect was Sook. While the staff was searching his room, he snuck out the back. Lacey caught sight of him slipping into the woods and decided to follow. Sook was easy to trail; years of hunting without earplugs had rendered him half deaf, and his path was marked by tiny bits of ribbon hanging from trees. Eventually she caught him crouching down, unearthing a rock.

"*Now* what are you doing?" Lacey asked, exasperated.

Sook grabbed his heart and sat back on his heels.

"Damn, Lacey, at my age startling a man is tantamount to attempted murder."

Lacey watched Sook slip a wad of bills into his pocket.

"I saw that, Sook."

"Then I will ask you to keep your silence. They've got a three-strikes policy here at Mapleshade and I am not about to get kicked down to We Care."

"So you've done this before?"

"Do the math."

"You've stolen the petty cash three times?"

"You have no business judging me for illegal behavior."

"What's your plan?" Lacey asked. "Since clearly they're onto you."

"I'm going to slip these bills into Martha's underwear drawer."

"Martha doesn't even know how to wear underwear anymore," Lacey replied.

"Exactly," said Sook. "They'll forgive her. Probably won't even count it as a first strike."

Lacey followed Sook back to Mapleshade. As they approached, Yolanda was exiting the building, clearly on a Sook hunt.

"I told you to stay put, Sook," she shouted.

Sook slipped the wad of bills into Lacey's coat pocket and replied, "I needed some fresh air after the Spanish Inquisition."

Yolanda shook her head in disappointment. She returned to the building followed by Lacey and Sook. In the lobby, all eyes were on the guilty party. Lacey sat down on the couch and stuffed the wad of bills under the cushion.

"Just tell us where the money is, Sook, and we'll let it slide this time," Yolanda said.

Lacey could tell she was lying.

"Yolanda," Lacey said, "I'm sure it's all an innocent misunderstanding. I bet the money will turn up any day now. You'll find it just like loose

change, under a couch cushion or something silly like that. In the mean-
time, while tensions are high, why don't I take Sook off your hands this
evening?"

"You want him?" Yolanda said. "You can have him, sweetheart."

Yolanda then did the oddest thing. She approached Lacey and
embraced her. Lacey was disarmed by the warm gesture until she felt
Yolanda's hands patting her down. Lacey pushed Yolanda away, pulled her
pockets inside out for emphasis, and said, "I got nothing on me except
my wallet and car keys. Now, if you don't mind, Sook and I will be on our
way."

On the car ride back to the Hansen home, Lacey debriefed Sook on
her day's adventure with Brandy and Big Marv. While they agreed the
new evidence was certainly incriminating, neither of them could name
the precise crime.

Lacey made Sook a grilled cheese sandwich, which he called the best
meal he'd had in months. Lacey felt a twinge of guilt for not having
invited him over before.

"You keeping the gun in a safe place?" Sook asked.

"In my nightstand, like your average American."

"Good girl," Sook replied.

"I need a shower," Lacey replied. "Can I get you anything else?"

"I wouldn't turn down a glass of whiskey," Sook replied.

Lacey pulled the bottle from their meager liquor cabinet. She poured
Sook a stingy glass, trying to be responsible, and then started to put the
bottle away.

"Leave it," Sook said. "There's no booze at Mapleshade. I'm on vacation today."

Lacey nodded and left the room.

In the shower, she remembered her lie. The stitches had to come out
before Paul got home. She dried off and doused a pair of nail clippers
with rubbing alcohol. She cut the first stitch and tugged it out of her arm.
She wished she had taken a slug of whiskey beforehand, but continued.

By the time she heard Paul's truck in the driveway, her arm looked as good as an arm with a fresh five-inch scar can look.

Paul entered his home to find Sook sitting at the kitchen table, cleaning his gun and drinking whiskey.

"Sook, what are you doing here?" Paul asked suspiciously.

Sook served Paul a drink and refilled his own glass.

"Sit down. Drink with me," Sook said, snaking a cloth through the barrel.

Paul sat down and took a tentative sip. Sook checked the clip of the gun and stuck it in the revolver. He smiled in a way Paul had never seen before. It made the younger man uncomfortable.

"What's new?" Paul asked.

"Why don't you tell me?" Sook replied.

NOTES:

Dave,

This book isn't big enough for two gimpy strippers, so forget about Candi. She's dead to you and me. And if you don't think she's dead, she will be.

While I'm on the subject of death, I should point out that taking my creative advice now and again wouldn't kill you. In fact, my advice in general often contains life-preserving properties. Case in point: Thanksgiving 1998. Your refusal to put the turkey back in the oven risked not only our lives but also those of your ninety-year-old grandparents. Notice how I'm not mentioning another near-death experience that could have been avoided if you'd listened to me.

Let's not neglect the Babalatos. You came up with them, so let's use them. Ideally, incriminate them in Hart's murder. It's always good to have a few spare suspects in a murder mystery. And who knows, maybe they did it.

I hope Sook's not too cute for you in my chapter. Remember who's holding the gun.

　　　　Lisa

Lisa,

As I've explained repeatedly, after I've had salmonella once, I'll happily endure cardboard turkey every year. The real question is, what are we aiming to provide here? A surprisingly delicious bird bursting with flavor, or a safe, chalky-dry one?

We didn't die, did we?

Dave

P.S. I'm curious about all these other writers who are so eager to work with you. Specifically, I wonder why you didn't extend that opportunity to them in the first place. Or did you?

CHAPTER 22

"Heard you have a roomful of hermies," Sook said, shaking his head.

"News travels fast," said Paul from the easy chair across from him. The two had already settled in for some leisurely commiseration.

"Well, that just about tears it for me," said Sook. "Maybe the Army will take me back. Or maybe We Care wouldn't be so bad."

"I don't know, man, do you really want Big Marv breathing down your neck?"

"Just trying to see the bright side."

Paul took a drink. "Speaking of the Babalatos, I saw them today. I was supposed to meet with Jay, but then Marv busted in."

"Lacey didn't mention that," said Sook. "Please describe the conversation in detail. Really. Don't leave anything out."

"I had a lunch meeting with Jay, but before we really got talking Marv came tearing into Verducci's. He sat down and said, 'Jay, baby, let's not lowball the kid.'"

Sook laughed at Paul's Big Marv impression, a hybrid of Orson Welles and Hulk Hogan. "Lowball the kid on what?"

"Jay wants to buy Shady Acres from me. They both do."

"How much?"

"We didn't even get to that. Marv said, 'Whatever my brother offers you, add twenty percent. My way of putting the other night's incident behind us.'" Paul pointed to his forehead bruise, which had settled down into a pretty amaranthine color.

"You didn't agree to anything, did you?" Sook asked.

"Hell no. For one, why is Shady Acres so valuable to start with? Two, why wouldn't they go in on it together? They own other stuff jointly. And c, whoever sabotaged my plants put me in a spot where I'd be more likely to accept an offer. The timing is suspicious, to say the least."

"Unless the timing's *too* suspicious," Sook offered, ignoring the botched outline. "They wouldn't be so bold as to ruin your plants and make you an offer the next day, would they?"

"Unless they were counting on me to assume that," Paul countered. "And five, while I'm sitting across from them, outside the other end of the restaurant I see some effete weirdo in Lou Reed sunglasses come stumbling through the shrubs and smash his face up against the glass." Paul made a pig nose with his thumb to illustrate the effect. "That's, what, four types of weirdness too many for me to even think about making a deal."

"So what'd you do?"

"Excused myself to the restroom. But I hung a right through the kitchen, came out the other side, and hid where I could hear them. Jay told Marv he was fucking everything up again, just like with Hart.

"I went back around through the kitchen and came back from the bathroom. By the time I got to the table—literally a minute later—they were gone."

"What about this . . . Louie Reed creep?" asked Sook.

"Also gone."

"Great. One more suspect for Lacey's list."

"Let's keep him to ourselves," said Paul.

"Agreed," Sook said, and drained his glass. "Now if you'll excuse me, I'm off to bed. I'm on the second-to-last chapter of *Mascara Mayhem*. It looks like Detective Nikki Maxwell may have finally met her match."

Lacey woke up to an empty house, running late for her shift at the Tarpit. On her way to her car, she stopped, went back into the house, and took a quick look around. No gun. She called Paul's cell phone, got his voice-mail, and didn't know what to say. She hung up.

———

"Ever hear of Mal and Mel Sundstrom?" Paul said to his new bodyguard as they eased off the highway onto the West Easternville exit.

"Doesn't ring a bell, but I'm guessing they live in Easternville," said Sook.

"You're a natural," said Paul.

"Been hanging out with your sister."

Paul found the house number, pulled over, shut off the ignition, and turned to Sook. "Leave the gun, Hardcastle," he said.[33]

"Who?"

"Just leave the gun."

Sook slipped it into the glove compartment and they exited the vehicle.

On the front wall of the house were hand-carved wooden letters spelling out "The Sundstroms." "Looks like this is the place," Sook observed.

"Again, nicely deduced," said Paul.

A tall blond woman in her late twenties answered the doorbell, two kids hanging onto her legs.

"Hi, I'm Paul Hansen, and this is my friend Sook."

"I'm Ilsa," the woman said cautiously through the black wrought-iron screen door.

"We're looking for some of my parents' old friends, Mal and Mel Sundstrom. Are they home?"

The woman looked defensive. "What's this about?"

"My parents shared a cabin with your . . . with the Sundstroms."

"I'm sorry, I can't help you."

"Wait," said Paul. "My parents are dead. I'm just trying to figure out what happened to them."

———

[33]Are you referring to Judge Milton C. "Hardcastle" from the 1980s television series *Hardcastle and McCormick*? How many people do you think are going to get this reference?

Ilsa shot him a hurt look. "Hang on," she said. She closed the door and parked the kids somewhere in the house.

When she opened the door again, her tone had turned frosty. "I'm sorry for your loss, but I can't help you. My parents had their problems, but they didn't kill anyone." She started to close the door.

Sook perked up. "*Had* their problems?" he asked.

"Halloween 1999," she said. "They drove off a cliff. Freak accident."

"Jesus," said Paul. "So that means—"

"That we're both orphans," said Ilsa matter-of-factly. "Anything else I can do for you?"

"Listen. I just found out that the night my parents died at the cabin, *your* parents were supposed to be there instead. And the car crash was only, what, two months later."

"What are you saying?" Ilsa stammered.

"I mean, are you sure your parents' death was an accident?" said Paul. Ilsa's face went stiff.

Sook chimed in again. "What if someone was trying to kill your folks, but killed Paul's by mistake?"

"This conversation is over," Ilsa said, her voice trembling as she closed the door.

Paul and Sook were silent on the drive back to Mercer. Paul had forgotten all about getting Sook's take on Lacey's recent behavior, his initial motivation for bringing him along. While he still wasn't quite ready to clear her as a suspect in the plant sabotage, now she was just his sister again. Paul was starting to feel that maybe everything that had happened since they found Hart *was* connected somehow—maybe Rafael was right. Maybe Lacey was right. In any event, their parents might have been accidentally murdered. And the murderer could still be out there, wondering if anyone would ever find out.

"Drop me at the Tarpit," said Sook when they reached town. "I could use some coffee—and some time to figure out what the hell I'm going to do with myself."

"Sure," Paul said. "But don't tell Lacey about the Sundstrom stuff, okay? She doesn't know anything. I'll tell her when I know for sure what happened. Or maybe she's better off not ever knowing. I'll figure it out later."

"Your secret's safe with me," said Sook.

As he drove the few blocks from the Tarpit to the Timberline to look for Rafael, Paul's phone rang—"American Woman," Terry's ringtone.

Paul pulled over, startled. "Hello?"

"Paul, my brother. Harry Lakes, Esq., at your service." The man pronounced it "esk."

"Uh . . ."

"Terry's cousin. The one he left his house to."

"Oh, hey, Harry . . . I take it you're out at Terry's already?"

"Yep. His phone ain't been cut off yet and I been meaning to call you since I got in yesterday. I'm havin' a bit of a private send-off over here since I missed the official memorial."

"I actually was just on my way to meet a—"

"You sound a little shaken up, my friend," said Harry. "You okay?"

"It's just . . . you sound *exactly* like Terry."

"Man, we been getting that since we were fifteen. I used to make dirty phone calls to all the moms of Terry's friends, acting like I was him. One of them called him back. That's actually how he lost his cherry. If you don't count hookers."

Paul didn't know whether he counted them or not.

"Come on, brother. Terry would have wanted us to get together mano y mano. He told me you were the smartest dude he knew. Other than himself and me, of course."

"Okay," Paul said. "I'll stop by."

Outside Terry's place, the air was thick with the strong, sour smell of healthy plants. Nepalese Kush, maybe, Paul thought. Harry must have brought his own plants to his new estate. Paul heard singing from inside the house, in a high voice like Terry's:

> *I'm leavin' everything I hoped for*
> *Cause the road has called my name*

Paul knocked on the door for a while, but the singing didn't stop. It was impossible not to picture Terry in there.

Harry finally came to the door, pointing to his ear. "Sorry, man, hearing aid on the fritz," he explained. Harry was wearing overalls ripe with resin, ladies' white après-ski boots, and a purple mustache. Paul recognized the boots as Terry's. Harry wasn't quite a dead ringer for Terry, but he carried himself the same way and had the same rickety frame, uneven walk, and ragged teeth. He embraced Paul and invited him in.

"Mi casa is su casa," Harry said. "I mean literally."

"Thanks, man," said Paul. "Wish we could have met under better circumstances."

They sat down at the kitchen table and Harry poured a couple of Winner's-Cup-and-grape-sodas, no ice.

"So, how you holdin' up, man?" Harry asked.

"Not so great, actually. On top of Terry and everything, somebody hermaphroditized my plants."

"I had some plants go Herm Edwards on me once," said Harry. "Wiped me out. I gave up on everything and went to Thailand. Turned out to be the best five years of my life. One door hits you in the face, another one opens."

"Right," Paul said.

"Look, man, what we have here is a case of fortune smiling on us in our darkest hour. I need your help. For starters, I need to get Terry's old Air Scrubber up and running. As you probably noticed outside, it ain't scrubbin' shit. You help me get things up and running, I'll get you back in business. We'll be partners."

It was the best offer Paul had heard in a long time. They shook on it, and Harry raised his cup.

"Opportunities multiply as they are seized," Harry said.

"Sun Tzu?" Paul asked.

"Ted Nugent."

Paul couldn't wait to tell Brandy about his day. In a strange way it was almost comforting to think that there might have been some intention behind his parents' death, rather than utter chance.

When he got to her place, Brandy was tense and cool.

Paul tried to defuse the tension with a joke. "Look, I've known for months that you're a DEA agent. I'm willing to work around it."

Brandy wasn't laughing. "Something's been eating at me and it's better to just say it. I knew Hart."

"Okay," Paul said. "And?"

Brandy took a moment to compose her response.

Then Paul panicked. "Wait a minute, *knew him* knew him?"

"God, no," said Brandy. "Actually, it's not so much about Hart as it is about his dad . . . and my dad."

"What about them?"

Brandy unconsciously twirled her finger through her hair, lapsing into ditz mode. "They were, like, kind of the same guy," she said.

Paul swayed for a moment, then found his balance. "Hart was your *brother?*"

Brandy took a deep breath and snapped back to her normal self. "Half," she said.

"When were you planning on letting me in on this?"

"I don't know—as soon as possible? I didn't want to drop everything on you at once. You were so sweet about the other stuff."

Paul sat down for the rest of the story.

"After Hart's dad left the Drexel's ranch down south, he lived up here

for a while. That's why Hart's mom moved back up here with Hart—
she was still hoping to bring the family back together. Anyway, he met
my mom, swept her off her feet, and voilà: Brandy. He didn't even stick
around for my debut. Now he's a cattle baron in Argentina. I've never met
him."

"How'd Hart get in touch with you?"

"His mom found out about me and told him. He was sweet to me, you
know? We'd just get together for lunch and stuff like that. He always said
his plans were on the brink of paying off, and he loved to talk about putting me through school. Then he started getting weird. He became more
and more obsessed with Lacey. The way he talked about her, it was like
they were still together."

"I can't believe I'm hearing this," said Paul.

"I'm sorry, Paul. But this has been hard on me, too. You know what,
Hart really liked you. In fact, that's how I first learned about you. The way
he described you, you sounded like a great guy. When I met you, I felt like
I already knew you."

"Jesus. Is that everything? What else do you know about Hart? Did he
ever talk about the Babalatos or . . . Doc Holland or Tate?"

"He kept the specifics to himself. One thing always stuck with me,
though."

"What's that?" Paul said, bracing himself.

"He always said he wasn't going down without a fight."

NOTES:

Lisa,

Okay, I have a confession to make. After spending a little time with Sook, it's hard not to make him a little bit cute. It just feels like that's how the character wants to be. Just like Brandy has a heart of gold, no matter what you say about her. After thwarting your latest attempt to sully her name, I'm hoping you'll finally accept her for who she is.

Overall, I'm feeling good about how things are going. I even put one of those workplace-safety signs up on my bulletin board: ___ DAYS WITHOUT A GRATUITOUS MURDER BY LISA. For the record, we're now at six days (in Mercer time), and I do appreciate your restraint.

Another note in the spirit of harmony: I'd just like to confirm that, since you wrote the first chapter, I'll be writing the last one. I'm trusting that you'll acknowledge the logic and fairness of this.

       Dave

Dave,

Please don't take this the wrong way, but I think it would be unwise for you to write the last chapter. It's one thing to end a TV season with a vague and unsatisfying cliffhanger, but readers generally like some closure with their crime novels. At least if I write last, I'll have a chance to tie in all the wayward clues. Plus, I have more experience.

Interesting chapter, by the way. I wouldn't have pegged you as a telenovela fan, but clearly that's the plotting school you attended.

I'm looking forward to spending some quality time with Harry Lakes.

Lisa

CHAPTER 23

The sharp ringing of the telephone woke Lacey from a restless sleep. She stumbled through the house, searching for the cordless. She yelled at Paul for not putting it back in the cradle until she realized that he wasn't home. He was with Brandy, of course, which left Lacey with a queasy feeling in her gut.

The phone rang until the answering machine picked up.

Paul's voice said, "You know what to do."

Lacey shook her head. It would be her turn to record the message in another week.

"Hi, Paul. It's Ilsa. We met yesterday. I thought of something. It might be connected to their deaths. Or . . . murders. Give me a call when you get a chance. My number is . . ."

Lacey raced around the house for a pen. She found one just in time. She stared at the scrap of paper with Ilsa's number on it and tried to connect all the dots that had formed in the last few days. Paul's suspicious behavior was reaching epic proportions. Secret meetings with the Babalatos, buddying up with Sook, and now a mysterious woman named Ilsa calling him. Was Paul investigating Hart's murder and not telling her about it? Lacey didn't wait around to confront Paul herself. She called Ilsa right back.

"Hello?"

"Ilsa?"

"Yes."

"This is Lacey Hansen. I'm Paul's sister."

"Oh, hello."

"Paul's gone for the day. He asked me to call you. Is there any chance we could meet in person? I really need to talk to you."

"I guess so. Where?"

"Diner in Emery work for you?" Lacey asked.

Two hours later, Ilsa and Lacey were sitting in a back booth with a basket of fries and two chocolate shakes in front of them.

Lacey treaded carefully, since she had no idea what Paul and Ilsa had discussed.

"How did my brother find you, by the way?"

"He got in touch with someone from WINO."

Hearing the name again sent a shiver through Lacey. It also threw her off her game. She thought she was meeting Ilsa to discuss the Hart and Terry murders. How was WINO, her parent's timeshare, connected to that? Lacey sucked down half her shake to buy some time.

"You must be thirsty."

"Haven't had one of these in a while," Lacey replied. "So, Paul was kind of busy yesterday. He got in a fight with his stripper girlfriend—don't get me started—and didn't fill me in on what you discussed. Do you mind giving me the brushstrokes?"

"As you know, while investigating your parents' death, he discovered that the week they were at the cabin, my parents were supposed to be there. They swapped for some reason. He wondered if there was a connection and came to speak to me. I told him that my parents had died in a car accident two months later. Some old guy was with him. He has a funny name."

"Sook?"

"Yeah, that was it. Sook said that maybe someone set out to kill my parents, and your parents just happened to be in the wrong place at the wrong time. I always thought the car crash was an accident, but now I'm not so sure. It's quite a coincidence. . . . You okay?"

Lacey's eyes were watering. She clasped her hands under the table so Ilsa couldn't see her shaking.

"I drank that too fast. I don't feel so good."

"Have some fries. They'll warm you up. Maybe a cup of coffee?"

"Sorry," Lacey said. "It still gets to me."

"Me, too," Ilsa replied.

Lacey took a few deep breaths and it sank in that Paul had been looking into their parents' death, not Hart's or Terry's.

"So," Lacey said, still shaping her vague thoughts, "if our parents were both, in fact, murdered by the same person, that takes some conviction. Do you remember anything about that time? Were your folks having trouble with anyone?"

"They had just filed a lawsuit. After I saw Paul the other day, I remembered that. I couldn't recall the details, but then I went hunting through their old files and I found it. It seems unlikely that it's connected, but I thought I should mention it."

Ilsa pulled an aged manila folder from her bag.

"My folks found an attorney. He drafted a complaint, but as far as I can tell it was never filed with the court. I don't know why. When they died, no one thought to follow up on the case."

Lacey opened the file and read the caption page: *Malvina and Melton Sundstrom v. Herman Holland, M.D.*

A cursory look at the complaint confirmed Lacey's suspicion: It was a malpractice case.

"What happened?" Lacey asked.

"My mom had a spinal abscess that Holland diagnosed as a lumbar strain. He loaded her up on painkillers, but then a week later she got a really high fever and started stumbling around. My dad took her to the emergency room. She was diagnosed at the hospital. If they had waited another day or two, she could have been paralyzed. Still, she ended up with nerve damage."

"This lawyer who drafted the complaint. You know anything about him?"

"No. He was just a small-time ambulance chaser. From what I gathered, my father did most of the investigating, 'cause we were hard up on cash. I think he and Holland were trying to work something out on their own."

"Doc Holland and your father spoke after he consulted an attorney?" Lacey asked, knowing that any lawyer worth his salt would have discouraged such activity.

"I think so," Ilsa replied. "I remember driving to Holland's office one time while my mom was still in the hospital. I sat in the waiting room while he and my dad talked."

"Where was the lawyer?"

"He wasn't there."

Lacey searched through the file, page after page. She found a photocopy of a medical license under the name of Herman Holland and then looked at the doctor's date of birth: 1921. That would mean Doc Holland was pushing ninety. Despite his haggard appearance, the Doc Holland Lacey knew was no more than seventy.

"Your dad must have figured it out," Lacey mumbled.

"Figured what out?"

"Doc Holland wasn't a real doctor. In fact, he probably wasn't even a Herman Holland, as far as I can tell."

"He's a phony? He's been treating patients since I was a girl."

"And he was willing to do whatever it took to maintain his front."

"What are you saying?" Ilsa asked.

"I think he killed your parents to keep them quiet. My folks just got caught in the crossfire."

"But my father was trying to settle with him," Ilsa replied.

"I think that was your dad's only mistake. He must have decided not to file the attorney's complaint when he found out Holland wasn't really a doctor. An attorney would have had to file a report with the AMA. Your dad probably thought Holland would offer a better settlement if he kept quiet."

"Still. Was it worth killing over? Why didn't Holland just move?"

"It would have torn down everything he'd built up. If he wanted to practice medicine somewhere else, he would have had to create a whole new persona, including references. He also would have had to co-opt another medical license somehow. It must have seemed easier to just make the problem go away."[34]

"We have to turn him in," Ilsa said.

"We have to find him first. He's not here anymore. Doc Egan took over his practice last week."

"So how did he con an entire town for twenty years?"

"He didn't con everyone," Lacey replied.

After Lacey's meeting with Ilsa, she drove straight to Tulac to get to the bottom of another equally mysterious matter. She rang the bell.

"Who's there?" Brandy shouted from the other side of the door.

"Lacey."

"You alone?"

"I'm alone."

Brandy opened the door and invited Lacey inside. She was wearing a pink bathrobe and the smell of bleach was in the air, which made sense since a strip of it was covering her upper lip. A shower cap covered her head, beneath which, Lacey could only assume, chemicals were performing their magic.

"Please excuse my appearance," Brandy said. "I swear if it weren't for bleach and silicone, I'd look like a twelve-year-old boy."

Lacey refrained from comment.

---

[34] A response to adversity that sounds a lot like a certain coauthor's.

"I take it Paul told you," Brandy said.

"Uh . . . right," Lacey replied.

"I don't know why Hart made me keep it a secret."

"That seems obvious to me," Lacey said.

"Why? Was he ashamed of me?"

"Where I come from, a man doesn't tell his fiancée that he's dating a stripper on the side. That's just common sense. Of course, not dating the stripper in the first place is even more common sense."

"Dating?" Brandy said, raising a well-plucked eyebrow.

"Whatever you want to call it," Lacey replied.

"Good lord, you're just a blind pickle in a jar of information."[35]

"Which Brandy am I talking to now? Dim-bulb-stripper or genius-too-smart-for-MIT?"

"Which one do you want to talk to?"

"The one that's going to tell me the truth. How long were you and Hart . . . *seeing* each other?"

"Do you and Paul even talk anymore?" Brandy asked.

"Not so much."

"Hart was my half brother, not my *boyfriend*. Yuck."

"What?"

"We have the same father."

"No."

"I even have DNA documentation to prove we were related."

"Huh," was Lacey's response. She supposed it was good news, but then realized that it was another case of the stars lining up to make Brandy Chester her sister-in-law, one way or another. The thought of it sent a wave of nausea through her.

---

[35]Where'd you pick this up, *Farmer John's Almanac of Baffling Non Sequiturs*? Do yourself a favor and leave the homespun wisdom to me. Or I'll be as ornery as a polecat in a bucket of thumbtacks.

"Is that all, Lacey? Because this bleach is starting to burn."

"No. One more thing," Lacey replied. "What business do you have with Big Marv? I saw him slip you some money outside of We Care Gardens."

Brandy sighed and said, "Excuse me." She walked back to the bathroom and washed off her mustache bleach. She returned to the living room with her upper lip shaded an irritated pink. Lacey desperately wanted to take a photo for Paul, but refrained.

"Paul told me about his meeting with Jay. Those brothers have been after Shady Acres for years, which means it's worth something. There's something special in that land."

"Like what?" Lacey asked.

"It could be a number of things. For starters, there are these rare earth elements with high-tech applications, like magnets, batteries, and bombs. Dozens of them with names you probably haven't heard of, like yttrium, tantalum, and niobium. They haven't been mined in the U.S. since 1959, but there could be a resurgence. Hell, that land could even have uranium. There hasn't been a boom since the fifties, but the value is coming back. Or it could be as simple as oil or gold. This was Gold Rush territory, after all. It's not like they found it all."

"So why did you tell Big Marv?"

"So he'd bid against his brother and drive up the price. Don't you want out of this town, Lacey?"

"Until these murders started, it was all I ever thought about."

"Between Hart's insurance settlement and what you could get for that land, you could set up house in a new city, sock some money in long-term, tax-free investments, get a boob job, and still have money to spare," Brandy said.

"So you're looking out for me now?"

"No. I'm looking out for Paul. But the money gets split fifty-fifty." Brandy looked at her watch. "Anything else? My hair is about to fry."

"That's all for now."

Brandy walked Lacey to the door. "Do me a favor," she said. "Don't tell Paul."

"About Big Marv?"

"*No*," Brandy replied, rolling her eyes. "About the bleach."

"Your secret is safe with me," Lacey replied.

Paul's car was parked in the driveway when Lacey returned home. She found him in the basement sweeping up the last debris from the hermie plants.

"Where are they?" Lacey asked.

"Darryl helped me take them out to Tulac. We had a burn day.[36] Then I checked on a few grow sites and harvested what I could."

"Where's Sook hiding?"

"Betty said she'd take him for a few days. Then Deena, then maybe Darryl, then maybe back to us for a few days. We're hoping Yolanda cools off and lets him back in. We just got to give her some time. Maybe when the money turns up—"

"Why didn't you tell me about Brandy?" Lacey asked.

"Tell you what?"

"That she's Hart's sister."

"Half sister."

"Still."

"I would have gotten around to it eventually."

"When?" Lacey pressed.

"We haven't been in the same place at the same time."

"They have these things now called telephones. It's news, Paul. I deserved to know."

"Communication isn't our strong suit these days," Paul replied.

---

[36]Not a bad title: *Burn Day.*

"Was it ever?" Lacey asked.

Paul just shrugged.

On cue, the telephone rang. In unison both siblings said, "I'll get it." But Lacey beat him up the stairs and found the phone on the fireplace mantle.

"Hello?"

"This must be Miss Hansen," said an eerily familiar male voice.

"Maybe. Who is this?"

"Harry Lakes, Esk."

"Right. Terry's cousin."

"May he rest in peace," said Harry.

"Funny how your names rhyme," Lacey said, not actually thinking it was funny. "Terry Jakes. Harry Lakes. What are the odds of that?"

"I'm the older one. Terry was rhymed after me."

"Good to know," Lacey replied.

"Your brother around?" Lakes asked.

Lacey passed the phone to Paul.

"This is Paul."

"Harry Lakes, Esk, at your service."

"What can I do for you, Harry?"

"It's what I can do for you. I've been looking through some of my cousin's papers and there's something here that you need to see. What are you doing right now?"

"Give me thirty minutes," Paul replied, and hung up the phone.

Paul knocked on Terry's, now Harry's, front door. There was no answer, so he knocked again. He waited another minute and then tried the door. It was unlocked, so he let himself in.

"Harry," Paul said. "I'm here. Where are you?"

Paul traveled through the house until he reached Terry's old office. He pushed the door open and found Harry Lakes, slumped back in a chair with a single bullet through his head. Paul shook him, just to be sure. Harry's entire body crumpled over to the side and fell to the floor.

While there have been cases of people surviving bullet wounds to the head, this was not one of them. Harry Lakes, Esq., was undeniably, irreversibly, irreparably dead.

NOTES:

Dave,

Harry Lakes, R.I.P. This is like the pumpernickel from *The Fop* all over again. Should a Jerry Gates, third cousin twice removed from Terry Jakes, turn up in the next chapter, I swear to you, another of your beloved characters will be fish chum.

Let's recap: We are nowhere near solving the Hart and Terry Jakes murders. If we follow the assumption that all the murders were committed by the same individual, then we only need to solve one. Harry Lakes gives us a clear window of time when the murder occurred and therefore the simplest way to check an alibi.

Let's say Harry was murdered between 1:15 and 1:45 p.m. on Wednesday. All we have to do now is interview the town folk and find out where they were during that half-hour. You can handle that, right?

I mean, you want this to end eventually, don't you? I know I do.

      Lisa

Lisa,

Can I get you anything else while I'm up? Compelling plot developments for you to commandeer? Essential backstory to ridicule? Another painstakingly crafted character to assassinate?

I guess I was hoping success might have helped you get your need for control under control. Your insistence on having the last chapter suggests otherwise. I wonder if you'd be so bold with any of the alternative coauthors you're so reticent about.

How about we flip for it, just like Paul and Lacey?

      Dave

CHAPTER 24

Paul's gut told him to run, but he didn't make it to the front door. Harry Lakes had called him only a half-hour earlier, so he was already a person of interest. The longer he waited to call, the more suspicious it'd look. And the way his career was going, he had less to hide every day. He called 911. He figured he'd still have twenty minutes or so to look for whatever it was that Harry had wanted to show him.

The place was a mess, but it didn't look ransacked. The giant oak desk was piled with article printouts, Terry's cheap journals, hideous vintage porn magazines, handwritten letters from friends, and plenty of documents that were unclassifiable at first glance. It was hard to see where Terry's stuff left off and Harry's began, except for a few pieces of mail addressed to Harry in Jirsa, CA. Paul grabbed a couple of paper towels from the kitchen and wrapped his hands in them to go through the papers without leaving prints.

The journals were standard Terry stuff: diatribes, poems, sketches for inventions. Paul checked the last few pages of each and came up empty. He turned to Harry's mail. The first piece was a brochure from a Belarusian mail-order bride outfit. The next was from an ex-wife looking for palimony. The third and last was a month-old letter from the State Department of Parole, citing Harry Lakes for failure to appear and notifying him that another violation would make him, officially, a fugitive.

Paul figured Harry might not have left the document (or whatever it was) out in the open. He opened a desk drawer. Sticking out of a book of haiku was an obituary page from the *San Francisco Chronicle*, dated three months back. Before he could study it, Paul heard a car coming up the driveway. He bolted for the kitchen, pocketing the obit page and the paper towels on the way. He sat down at the table and tried to look composed. Then it occurred to him how fast the response had been—what, five minutes, tops? He eyed the back door. If the killer was back to tidy up, Paul's only option would be hauling ass into the forest. For the first time in his life, Paul prayed for the company of Sheriff Ed.

Then he heard the front door open. A voice called his name. It was Deputy Doug.

"In here," said Paul. "The kitchen."

Doug looked a little shaken up himself. He told Paul to wait while he checked out the crime scene. When he came back to the kitchen, he questioned Paul about his day. Paul told him about the phone call from Harry, as well as their meeting the previous day. He described both as social calls, leaving out the business partnership they'd informally launched, as well as the mysterious item Harry had mentioned. "Reminiscing about Terry, that kind of stuff," Paul said.

As Doug filled out his report, Paul noticed that the deputy didn't seem like himself. A confident glint in his eye made for a striking change from his usual look, which fluctuated between confused determination and determined confusion.

"So how's the investigation going?" Paul asked.

"That's official business."

"Come on, man," said Paul, "I just want to help out. What's going on?"

Doug thought for a moment, then looked around as though making sure no one was listening. He stared Paul down and announced, "With all due respect to Mr. Lakes, we just got a whole lot closer to our killer."

"What, you think I did it?" said Paul.

"Not necessarily, although the general vicinity of you and your sister does seem to be a dangerous place to be as of late. What it means is that we finally have what we in the investigative field call a *fi-nite window.*"

"Help me out with the argot," said Paul.

"Argot?" said Doug.

"The lingo."

Doug rolled his eyes. "Let me put it in layperson terms. Unless you're lying about the phone call—which the phone records will show—we now have a murder that we know was done at a definite time and place," said Doug.

Paul gave him a confused look.

"Allow me to review," said Doug. "Crime number one, the killing of Hart Drexel. Without the head we can't pin down the event. We don't know when or where it happened, which significantly impairs our ability to narrow down the pool of suspects. Which, I might add, you and your sister are still in the deep end of." He smiled at his turn of phrase.

Paul nodded solemnly.

"Crime number two," said Doug, making the peace sign, "Terry Jakes and the tower collapse. I am not at liberty to divulge the latest findings of the . . . crime-scene guy, but let's say for the sake of argument that we know somebody rigged the thing to collapse. Once again, no clear time frame. Could have happened anytime before Terry went up there."

Paul raised an eyebrow as Doug continued.

"What we have here with Mr. Lakes is quite simply a different animal. We know that the crime happened right here in this house *and* that it happened between the times of approximately one-fifteen p.m. and one forty-five p.m. Bang. Finite window."[37] Doug snapped his hands into a rectangular shape to illustrate the window.

When Paul's expression didn't change, Doug sighed. "Think about it. Most people will have alibis for such a specific time of day. Anyone who doesn't moves to the top of the suspect list. And I don't think I have to tell you that whoever killed Harry must have killed Hart and Terry, too. Unless you believe that three murders in two weeks, after zero murders in twenty years, is just a coincidence."

---

[37] Why, thank you.

Paul held his tongue. In a way, he envied people who viewed the world so simply.[38] It wasn't an optimal trait for police work, however. Finite window or not, Harry Lakes was a wild card. No one knew the kind of connections he had, or the enemies he'd accumulated over the course of a wide-ranging life, or even why, if he and Terry had been so close, Paul had never met him.

While the murders were almost surely connected in some way, Paul thought, to assume that all three killings were done by the same person closed off all kinds of plausible scenarios. For example, what if the second and third killings represented a *response* to the first, not continuations of it? Or what if someone had wanted to kill Harry for years, and recognized his move to Mercer as a chance to tie the killing into the previous local murders? It was like Doug was stuck in the first half-hour of *Nightcrimes,* just before the obvious scenarios get shot full of holes.

The sound of another car in the driveway drained all the confidence out of Doug. Paul stayed in the kitchen as Doug went to the front door.

Paul overheard Sheriff Ed: "Jesus H., Deputy, what are you doing in here?"

"I was protecting the—" Doug said.

"We got a fresh murder here. Did you even secure the perimeter? No signs of AVD out front. Suspect could have come in on foot, still be nearby."

"AVD?" Paul interjected.

"Abrupt vehicular departure," Doug recited grimly.

Ed sent Doug out to case the woods. Then Ed reexamined the body and requestioned Paul, who repeated what he'd told Doug. After that, Paul was free to go.

Paul had left his phone on the seat of his truck. There was one new message: "Paul. Marv Babalato. I'm sorry about the confusion the other day.

---

[38] I take that back.

My brother and I have had a chance to talk things over and get our ducks in a row. We are prepared to make you a *very* generous offer, as well as an explanation of our interest in your property. Maximum transparency, no B.S. Give me a call."

Whatever had the Babalatos so hot to buy the property could wait. For now, he just wanted to get out of there. Then he remembered the newspaper page in his sweatshirt pocket. He uncrumpled it and read through the listings. One in particular caught his eye: an attractive thirty-three-year-old woman named Laura Loomis. No cause of death was mentioned, but the last line got Paul's full attention: *She is survived by her loving husband, Dr. Matthew Egan of San Francisco.*

Paul tried not to pull an AVD as he took off for the Tarpit to have a talk with his sister about her would-be boyfriend, who, if Paul remembered correctly, had told Lacey he was divorced, not grieving. At the coffee-house he found Sook playing checkers with a ten-year-old kid. "Paul, help me. I'm dying of boredom here. No offense, kid."

"King me," his opponent said. Sook did.

"Where's Lacey?" Paul asked.

"Lunch break," said Sook. "I wasn't invited. What's up?"

"Be right back," said Paul.

Paul went out to the sidewalk and called Lacey on his cell.

"Lace, it's me. What do you know about Doc Egan's wife?"

"Um, I think you have the wrong number."

"What? Lacey, it's Paul, your brother."

"Nope. No Mrs. Golaberry here. Okay, good luck," Lacey said, and hung up.

There was only one reason she'd respond that way. Paul ran to his truck and sped the half-mile to Doc Egan's home office, just enough time to review the doctor's recent bio: *a.* Lies about young wife's death of unknown causes. *b.* Takes over the business of another doctor, who was being blackmailed and has now disappeared. *c.* Arrives in peaceful mountain town just in time for string of homicides.

Lacey's car was parked outside Egan's office. *Don't bust in*, Paul told himself as he pulled up. Egan probably wasn't dangerous unless he knew someone was onto him.

The reception area was empty, so Paul knocked on the door to the examination room.

"Doc Egan? Paul Hansen here. I'm looking for my sister."

After a long moment, the door opened. Egan came into the waiting room, giving Paul a chipper look and a warm handshake. "Paul, good to see you. We're just finishing up here. What brings you to these parts?"

"It's Terry's cousin Harry Lakes. He's dead," Paul said with a tremor in his voice. "I found him at Terry's."

"Good God!" Egan exclaimed.

"Are they sure he's dead?" Lacey asked as she entered the waiting room.

"Bullet in the forehead," said Paul. "I'm sorry to interrupt, Lace. I'm just a little shaken up. Sook told me you were here. I just needed to talk."

After an awkward departure from the office, Paul and Lacey got into his truck. She let out a long exhale.

"What the hell's going on?" she demanded. "Why'd you call me about Matthew's wife?"

"I found something at Ter—Harry's. What do you know about her?"

"Not much," Lacey said with a shrug. "They split up recently. It was rough."

"That's one way of putting it," said Paul.

"What's that supposed to mean?"

"She died in June."

"Oh," said Lacey. After a pause, she added, "Are you sure?"

"Yes, I'm sure she's dead. What is it with you and death verification, anyway?"

She ignored the question. "So what's he supposed to do? Tell people, 'Hi, I'm Matthew, I'm new in town and my wife just died?' And shouldn't we be talking about Harry Lakes right now?"

Paul just stared at her.

"Maybe Egan's not ready to deal with her death," Lacey offered. "So he tells people they got divorced instead. He's in the five stages of grief or whatever."

"Something tells me you'd respond differently if he were, say, my girl-friend. For two weeks you've been treating everyone like a suspect. Doc-tor Dreamy bats his eyes at you and it's innocent until proven guilty?"

"Nice one, Paul," Lacey said, and opened the truck door. "I gotta go finish my shift."

Paul was glad to find Rafael at the Timberline, nursing a beer and a ciga-rette in a back booth.

"Any word from your buddy Brice?" Paul asked.

"Nope. Why don't you join me?"

A few pints later, Paul had told Rafael about the botched Babalato meeting, Harry's urgent call, Egan's dead wife, even the WINO findings. When he was done, the information that had been piling up around him seemed a little less threatening.

"First thing we gotta do," said Rafael, "is find out everything about Egan." He whipped out his smartphone and started typing "Matthew Egan" into his browser.

Paul felt a large, soft hand come to rest on his shoulder.

"Gentlemen," said Big Marv. "Forgive the interruption. I wonder if I could borrow five minutes of Paul's time."

Paul thought for a moment. "Okay, but he stays," he said, gesturing to Rafael. From now on, any Babalato meetings would be witnessed by a third party.

Marv squeezed in next to Rafael, vivifying the verb *to dwarf*.

"Okay. Let me break it down," said Marv. "I have business ties with a group of investors based in Tokyo. Long story short, they're buying up northern properties all over the world. It's all done with computers—they got all kinds of maps, weather patterns. Basically, they're making a bet on global warming. They say that when it warms up, the whole climate will change, the, what's the word . . . terror of the land."

"Terroir?" Paul offered.[39]

"Yeah, the terroir. They're buying up what they think will be primo wine-growing regions in thirty, forty years. They even have spots lined up in Finland, no joke. You ask me, the global warming thing . . . I mean, it's fucking September, right? Last night I step out for a pee and my dick nearly breaks off in my hand. But what matters to me about these guys is they keep their word and they have deep pockets. I'm putting together a package of local properties—they're not interested in buying fifteen acres at a time. This is the most I can pay and still do the deal." Marv stopped and took a pen out of his pocket, flipped over a round Timberline coaster, and wrote down a figure. It took a long time to write, Paul noted. Marv slid it across the table.

Paul flipped it over. *$600,000.*

"That's five zeroes, right?" said Rafael. Paul was still catching his breath.

"Five zeroes," said Marv.

---

[39]Remember my rule: If the spell-check doesn't recognize it, don't use it. And when did Paul's vocabulary get so big?

NOTES:

Lisa,

I'm not enough of a dreamer to ask you to read this chapter objectively, but I'm hoping you'll suspend your stubbornness long enough to absorb it on its own terms. Sometimes giving up the fight is the best thing that can happen to you. Like on the road trip, when we found that hot spring in the snow because we didn't stay at the safe motel like you wanted.

    Dave

P.S. You never answered my question. Was I the first writer you asked?

Dave,

Somehow I don't think almost freezing to death is the best thing that can happen to me. "I'm sure we can make the next gas station," you said. We were stranded in the car overnight during a snowstorm and your main memory of that trip is the fucking hot spring?

I could go on, but let me keep my criticism constructive and objective. Please don't make up phony argot. AVD? Not a real term, if Google counts for anything.

    Lisa

P.S. If you must know, I asked a few established authors before contacting you.

CHAPTER 25

Lacey stifled a chuckle. Exhaustion, stress, and nerves tore through her system and suddenly that muffled chuckle transformed into hysterical laughter. About a minute later, under Paul's impatient scowl, she was able to speak. Barely.

The words came out in hiccups. *"Glo-glo-bal war-ming? Real-ly?"*

"Is it so impossible to believe?"

Lacey responded with more laughter. She held up the piece of paper with five zeros on it as if to make a point. Paul realized then that he should have consulted his genius girlfriend before bringing the news to his sister.

"So," Lacey said, still choking with mirth, "you think Big Marv wants to pay us six hundred thousand dollars for a property that *might* be worth something in thirty years? Look at the man! He won't be around another fifteen."

"He said it was his final offer," Paul said.

"It's not," Lacey replied. "You know what you should do, since the Babalato brothers clearly prefer negotiating with you over me? You should call Jay and thank him for the offer and tell him you're thinking it over."

"Don't tell me what to do," Paul said.

"I didn't," Lacey replied. "I was merely making a suggestion."

As soon as Lacey departed, Paul called Jay Babalato and left a message.

Lacey had quite a to-do list for the day and she wasted no time getting started. She drove directly to Doc Egan's office and got straight to the point.

"Why did you tell me you got a divorce when your wife died?"

"I didn't want to talk about it."

"That's suspicious behavior, don't you think?"

"I suppose so. But I never thought it would come up."

"What happened?" Lacey asked.

"She was hit by a bus," Egan replied.

"My condolences."

"Thank you."

"Were you with her at the time?"

"Excuse me?" Egan replied.

"Were you with your wife when it happened?"

"No."

"So, it's not like you could have pushed her in front of the bus, right?"

"Right," Egan replied, clearly startled by Lacey's lack of delicacy.

"And it's not like you could have paid off a bus driver to do it. That would be almost impossible to arrange. Especially since they're never on time and stuff."

"What are you getting at, Lacey?"

"I'm just thinking out loud. With all the murders happening around me, I want to make sure that I can dispense with some vague suspicions and get on with the real business."

"I see."

"Shit happens, right?"

"I guess so," said Egan. "Do you need something?"

"Yes," Lacey quickly replied. "You need to make a face-to-face appointment with Doc Holland."

She departed without saying another word.

On each of the three days since he'd been expelled from Mapleshade, Sook had made a habit of pickling himself at the Timberline. Lacey decided an afternoon excursion would be good for his health.

"You're coming with me," she said.

Sook was tanked enough to be agreeable. He finished his well whiskey and followed Lacey out of the bar.

Twenty minutes later, Lacey parked just down the road from We Care Gardens. "Here's the plan," Lacey said. "You play drunk."

"I am drunk," Sook replied.

"Then it should be a piece of cake. I need you to keep Big Marv busy while I search his office."

"For what?"

"I don't know yet. He wants to buy our property. Bad. I just have to figure out why. It's a long shot, but I need to see if there's anything he's keeping in his paperwork that would help me negotiate."[40]

"What should we talk about?"

"I don't know, Sook. Tell him what it was like during the Civil War. No, tell him your days are numbered at Mapleshade and you're thinking about a move to We Care."

"Bite your tongue."

Lacey ignored his protest. "Keep him occupied and out of his office as long as you can. Try to get him to give you an official tour. Can you handle it?"

"I've always considered myself a formidable raconteur. I accept your challenge," Sook said, slurring his words.

While Lacey circled the building, Sook entered through the front door and rang the bell at reception. Lacey watched Big Marv hoist himself out of his chair and lumber into the front office.

Lacey raised the window to Marv's office halfway and vaguely overheard the conversation in the front room.

"Sook. You get lost or something?" Big Marv asked.

---

[40]Sounds a little similar to my night-vision chapter, but I'll take it as an homage.

"No, sir. I am exactly where I am supposed to be."

"Something I can do for you?"

"I assume you've heard about my difficulties at Mapleshade," Sook said.

"I heard you were accused of stealing from the petty-cash box. Third time in a row."

"A man is innocent until proven guilty."

"Maybe in a court of law. Not in these parts," Marv replied.

Lacey quietly somersaulted through the window. She gingerly paged through the paperwork on Marv's desk. All patient-related, mostly Medicare billing. She tried the file drawer on the bottom left side of the desk and it was locked. She checked for a key in the center drawer, but found only pens and a variety bag of mini Hershey's chocolate bars.

"I've been thinking of finding a new home," Sook said, just on the other side of the wall.

"Well, good luck with that. Thanks for dropping by."

Lacey froze, thinking their conversation might be coming to an end. She'd either have to throw herself out the window or slip into the closet, but Sook's raconteuring gave her a short reprieve.

"I got two options," Sook said, "We Care Gardens, or find another town. I'm liking the first choice better."

"You want to become a resident of We Care?" Marv asked.

"I'd consider it," Sook replied.

"No offense, Sook, but we like our residents to be a bit more . . . how do I put it."

"Comatose?" Sook suggested.

"Cooperative," Marv replied.

Next to the desk was a three-drawer file cabinet labeled "active." The top drawer was slightly ajar. Lacey opened it, hoping the noise wouldn't disturb Marv. Inside was a collection of resident files. Lacey didn't know what she was looking for, but it wasn't that. She closed the top drawer and tried the second one.

Sook continued to hold his own in the front room, but Lacey knew she was running out of time.

"I'd be willing to provide a security retainer if you thought that was necessary," said Sook.

"Interesting proposition," Marv replied.

"Now how about the official tour," Sook said.

"Let me check my calendar in the office and we can schedule one."

Lacey ducked behind the file cabinet, holding her breath.

"Who am I kidding," Sook said. "I know this property like the back of my hand. How about you and me take a little stroll and hammer out the details."

"I'm kind of busy right now, Sook."

"Just give me five minutes to plead my case."

"Five minutes."

Lacey opened the second drawer in the file cabinet as she heard Sook's and Marv's voices fade as they left the building.

"Marv, did I ever tell you about the time I was shot in the ass during the Korean War?"

"No, Sook, I don't believe you have," Big Marv wearily replied.

"*Shot in the ass*. It was friendly fire, too. I always hated that phrase. *Friendly fire*. There's nothing friendly about it."

Lacey opened the second drawer and found more patient files. She was about to close it when a name on one file caught her eye: "Moak- ler, Eldridge." A glaucoma patient, among other things. The Hansens used to sell to him—Lacey remembered bringing him brownies around Christmastime—but then he had a stroke and could barely feed himself. He'd died sometime in the spring. This presumably relevant medical fact appeared nowhere in the file. And it wasn't that the file was out of date— in fact, it contained a Medicare claim from just last week.

Just then she heard Sook's voice booming in the office. He was warn- ing her that her time was up.

"You can't sit down. That's the worst part," Sook said.

"You don't say," Marv replied.

"I tell you, we take sitting for granted."

"Sook, we'll be in touch," Big Marv said.

"Try not sitting for a whole day. I challenge you. Just give it a try and see what it does to your whole worldview."

"I'll give it some thought," Big Marv replied.

Lacey tossed the file out the window and then somersaulted out after it. She circled the building and met Sook in the adjacent woods.

With Sook back in her custody, Lacey drove to the Tarpit to sober him up and review the file.

"This is big," Lacey said when she was done. "Looks like Big Marv and company were billing Medicare and receiving Social Security benefits for dead residents."

"I knew something was fishy about that place. And you're welcome, by the way," Sook replied, drinking his cappuccino and eating a bran muffin.

"What should I do with this?" Lacey asked.

"Shouldn't you wait until you've closed the deal with the Babalatos before you start nosing into their business?"

"I guess," Lacey replied.

"Don't take this the wrong way," said Sook, "but you seem to be getting distracted, just like your brother. I thought you were looking into Hart's murder. Isn't that what you're really after?"

Sook had a point. If she started poking around every unpunished crime, this saga would go on forever and she'd never get out of Mercer. She had a murder to solve, plain and simple, and she was going to do it. She decided to put the Babalatos on the back burner—at least until there was reason to think their scam was related to the killings.

Lacey turned her thoughts back to the death of Harry Lakes. She wasn't the only sibling who was aware of the finite window. In fact, she'd thought of it on her own ages ago. But now she realized there were *two* finite windows that could eliminate suspects. Suddenly, solving the murder seemed as simple as conducting a survey of all their acquaintances. She started with the person sitting right in front of her.

"Sook, where were you yesterday between one-fifteen and one forty-five p.m.?"

"Why are you asking?"

"Just answer the question, Sook."

"I was at Betty's place. Don't you remember? You dropped me off?"

"Right," Lacey replied. "And Betty can confirm you were with her?"

"We were playing pinochle."

"So you can confirm Betty's whereabouts. Correct?"

"That's usually how it works when two people are together," Sook replied. The cappuccino was sharpening him up.

"Congratulations," Lacey said.

"For what?" Sook replied.

"I've just cleared you on the Harry Lakes murder. Now tell me, where were you last Sunday between two and three a.m.?"

Lacey drove to Tulac and made a copy of the Moakler file on the ancient Xerox machine at the Slow and Easy convenience store. She'd have to figure out how to sneak the file back into Big Marv's office, but she figured he wouldn't notice its absence for a day or two.

At home, Lacey drafted a list of all the persons of interest who lived in Mercer, Emery, and Tulac, which basically consisted of all of Paul and Lacey's friends and acquaintances. Lacey scratched Sook off the list and Doc Egan, since he had no motive; she also eliminated a few obvious non-suspects, like anyone legally blind or immobile, which included a large majority of the We Care and Mapleshade residents. At the top of the list she wrote *Doc Holland* in quotes. As far as Lacey was concerned, he was suspect number one. Although she couldn't figure out how he could lug a grown man (minus head) on and off their property. But maybe he had a sidekick, some brain-dead local short on cash.

When Paul came home, he entered the kitchen and, against his better judgment, asked Lacey what she had been up to. Lacey split the piece of paper in half and handed it to Paul.

"You want this thing to end, don't you?"

"What thing?"

"Living with your sister in a nowhere town, looking over your shoulder for killers. Maybe you even want to break up with that gimpy stripper and find a genius with a good leg and less history."

"I love Brandy."

"It was worth a shot," Lacey replied. "Still, you want this investigation to come to end, right?"

"Most definitely," Paul replied.

"I'm not telling you what to do. I'm merely suggesting you help me with this investigation. We do that, we're free to move on. This here is a list of suspects. We've got a finite window now. All we have to do is ask a few questions, exonerate one suspect at a time, and eventually our suspect pool will be a puddle and the killer should be obvious."

"I see," Paul said, studying the list. "I'm on board. But can you do me one favor?"

"What's that?" Lacey replied.

"Scratch me off the list."

"Sorry about that," Lacey said, striking a pen across Paul's name. "Clerical error."

The siblings sat in silence until the telephone broke it. Paul picked up on the second ring.

"Hello," he said. "Hmm. Interesting. Well, I'll have to discuss it with my sister and get back to you. Good-bye."

"Who was that?" Lacey asked.

"Jay Babalato."

"Did you call him like I told you to? I mean, like I casually suggested."

"Yes."

"What did he say?"

"He just upped the offer to eight hundred thousand dollars."

NOTES:

Dave,

I hope you don't mind me fleshing out the criminal activities of your Babalatos. Remember that suspicious interview with Mr. Portis? I thought our readers might like to be clued in about what was going on. I could trust that you would eventually handle the matter, but there's still an unexplained plane crash haunting Mercer, so my trust is in the wind.

Since you're committed to seeing this thing through, let's try to see it through as quickly as possible. Quick refresher on murder mysteries: By the end, we know who killed everyone.

Lisa

Lisa,

Eureka. We've finally found our common purpose. Let's finish this up so I can move on. Only one thing: You never responded to my coin-toss suggestion for who gets the last chapter. Until I hear otherwise, I'll interpret your silence as assent. You name the time and place; I bring the coin.

Dave

CHAPTER 26

Perched on her stool in Mercer Airport's radio booth, Wanda slid the little window back. Through the opening, Paul made the usual joke about the booth's resemblance to a snack bar.

"I'll have a corndog and a small Mr. Pibb," he said.

"Good one," said Wanda. "Haven't heard it since yesterday." She had sunken eyes.

He handed her a big cup of Tarpit coffee. The sun was halfway up.

"Rough night?"

"Online poker tournament. Around three a.m. I flopped a set and went all in. Some maniac caught runner-runner for the straight."

"Bad beat," said Paul, demonstrating a large percentage of his poker vocabulary.

"You too—I heard about your plants," said Wanda.

"I didn't know you played," said Paul, re-changing the subject. "I should get back into that."

"Oh yeah. In fact, I host a game every other Saturday night."

"*Every* other Saturday?" Paul asked, perking up.

"Yep. Usually we're done by four, but sometimes we go almost till six. You should join us sometime."

"Save me a seat," Paul said. "So do you remember who played last time?"

"The night after the plane crash? Sure. Let's see. It was mostly ladies' night. Deena was the first to show up. Then some cute brunette from Tulac, walked with a cane. She really owned it, though. Made it sexy.

Who else? Oh yeah, Betty. One brownie too many—she folded a gut flush and then crashed on the couch."

"My bad," said Paul, reconsidering the optimal pot/chocolate ratio and feeling a little sad about the craft he might be leaving behind.

"Then a little after two, Tate from the Timberline showed up," Wanda continued.

"Weird assortment of people," Paul remarked.

"Weird town."

"So who won?" he asked.

"Yolanda from Mapleshade. She came with Betty. Her first time. Had quite a few bills on her for a nurse's aide. All small denominations. If she was built a little different, I'd say she was stripping on the side. Hey, why are you so curious? Sorry I haven't invited you, but you said you didn't like to socialize too much with your customers . . . "

"Just scoping the competition. I should go home and start practicing. You heard about Harry Lakes, right?" he asked as he stood up from the stool.

"Terry's cousin? I hear he's just like Terry."

"Was," Paul corrected.

"Aw, no way," she said. "When?"

"Yesterday afternoon. Bullet in the head."

"Shit, no one tells me nothin' out here. This shift is killing me. Six in the a-goddamn-m to two in the afternoon every day."

"Stay safe," said Paul. He started for his truck, then stopped and turned. "Hey, about that plane—" he started.

"No idea," said Wanda.

Back in his truck, he took a look at the suspect list Lacey had assigned him, then crumpled it. He wasn't doing this just for Lacey. He was also doing it so he could start his new life—just him, Brandy, Irving, and either a valuable new property or a suitcase full of Babalato cash. In a pocket notebook, he made his own list of the poker players:

POKER NIGHT
Betty
Candi
Deena
Tate
Wanda*
Yolanda

The poker game gave all six a strong alibi for the night Hart's body was moved back to their property. The star after Wanda's name indicated an additional alibi, for Wednesday's Harry Lakes shooting, during which she would have been at the airport. It wasn't exactly watertight, but he reminded himself that he only had to satisfy his sister's *Scooby-Doo–* caliber investigative standards, not his own.[41]

And by anyone's standards, all the women on the list were extreme long shots anyway. Only Wanda would be strong enough to move a large body on her own, and none of them, with the possible exception of Candi, had a shady past or an imaginable reason to mess with him or Lacey. They also lacked a motive to kill Hart, Terry, or Harry (though that trio was hardly known for smooth relations with women). His friend and colleague Rafael also seemed beyond suspicion.

Among the poker players, that left only Tate for the Jakes–Lakes killings. Paul had arrived at the Timberline around four p.m. on Wednesday, just as Tate was getting off his shift. That meant Tate had been on the afternoon shift and would have been seen by at least a few customers. So Tate, too, was in the clear for both finite windows. The sky was still brightening, and Paul had already knocked off a half-dozen suspects. Maybe this wouldn't be so hard after all.

---

[41]And yet, he's being the perfect Shaggy.

———————

Paul drove back home to pick up his remaining stash. It was Senior Circuit Friday, and he still had bills to pay.

Irving came jogging up to his truck with a sorrowful look on his face and, as usual, something in his mouth. When Paul got out of the truck, Irving dropped the grisly item at his feet. Paul picked him up.

"What's the matter, mister?" he asked.

Irving meowed.

"Senior Circuit today. Want to come?"

No response.

"Suit yourself, but it might be the last one ever."

Paul looked down at the stringy offering.

"What's that boy, a clue?" he said, his standard Lassie joke.

The bloody little pile didn't look like something Irving had brought him before. The digestive tract of a bird, maybe? Did birds even have digestive tracts? Paul put Irving down and poked it with a twig. It wasn't animal at all. It was medical thread and blood-soaked gauze.

Two thoughts crossed Paul's mind: 1. Lacey had lied about her stitches. She'd removed them here, not at Doctor Egan's office. Which made her visit to his office Wednesday afternoon suspicious. 2. Irving had brought him the one item on their property that was tied to Doc Egan.

Paul didn't believe in assigning human traits to animals, but Irving was a highly intuitive cat. And didn't all animals have incredibly sensitive mechanisms for sensing danger? As Terry liked to point out, almost no wild animals had drowned in that massive flood in Indonesia a few years back. They'd all headed to higher ground. Maybe Irving was just trying to help Paul do the same.

"Good boy," said Paul. [42]

————————

[42]We both know you're doing this just because I hate cat mysteries.

———

Paul called Rafael and explained his alibi project. Rafael promptly offered up his Wednesday whereabouts.

"For lunch I had a burrito up at Taco Bout Delicious in Emery. Hang on a sec," he said. "Yep, I still have the receipt in my wallet. Buck-fifty for extra guacamole. Time stamp says 13:12."

"Awesome," said Paul. "So how about late Saturday night two weeks ago, say two to three a.m.?"

A long moment passed.

"Shit," Rafael finally said. "I hate to kiss and tell."

"Who is she?" said Paul.

"Oh boy," said Rafael. "This is just between you and me, okay?"

"Of course," Paul said.

"All right, think MILF."

It took Paul about two seconds. "Lila Wickfield."

"Uh, a little higher up the age range."

"Wow. Deena Jakes?"

"Higher up, in every way."

Paul was stumped. "Come on, man. Who?"

Paul heard Rafael exhale before he gave the answer: "Marybeth Monroe."

"Jesus," Paul exclaimed. "Hart's mom?"

"I went up there looking for Hart to see if he'd seen Brice. She was having some wine and I joined her. It got weird. Afterward she wanted to make me a sandwich and stuff. Not my finest hour, okay?"

"Did you at least find out anything about Hart?"

"Just that his mom—"

"Okay, okay," Paul interrupted. "Want to help me out later?"

"Sure. What do you need?"

"A ride. Egan knows my truck."

———

Back in his room at Mapleshade, Sook was grateful to get his usual package, and Paul let him defer payment. The old man had been reinstated the previous night, and he'd need every bit of juice he could get to stay out of trouble, including the special services he provided to certain staff members and residents. Paul didn't bother giving Sook the alibi quiz since Lacey said she'd already cleared him.

Down the street at We Care, Lito was trimming some bushes on the side of the main house. Before Paul had even left his truck, Lito called out, "I don't know anything. My dad and uncle aren't here."

"Take it easy. I'm here on business," said Paul, patting his pocket. He was fine with the wait-and-see approach with the Babalato deal. At the current rate, their offer could hit seven figures before the weekend was out. He and Lito went back to a tool shed and made their customary transaction. Mr. Skittles watched them sleepily from a corner.

"I do need to ask you one favor," Paul said afterward. "I'm trying to help my sister get through her fear and start living a normal life again. So I'm just asking everyone where they were during a couple of recent time periods."

"She always seemed a little high-strung," said Lito.

"So how about two weeks ago, late Saturday night—between two and three a.m.? The night before I called you from Diner."

"I was playing Crystal Orc online. That was the final battle for the realm. We took on some punks from New Zealand. The whole thing's on YouTube if you want to check it out."

"'We?'" said Paul.

"The Shattered Legion," said Lito. "My guild."

"Anybody else I'd know in your guild?" Paul asked with a straight face.

"Uh, not unless you've been hanging out with high school kids," said Lito.

"Okay, what about this past Wednesday afternoon from around one to two?"

"Just here, working in the garden. In plain sight."

"Good enough. Thanks, man."

"No problem."

After a pause, Paul asked, "How about your dad and your uncle?"

Lito's face turned hard. "No idea," he said.

On the way back to his truck, Paul saw Mr. Portis being wheeled out to the central patio by a nurse.

"None for me, thank you!" Mr. Portis shouted cheerfully, to no one in particular.

At dusk, Paul and Rafael sat in Rafael's truck a couple doors down from Egan's home office. It was a warm night; the windows were rolled down. They'd both read the reports online about Egan's wife and the bus accident, but it hardly eased their suspicions. Egan seemed like the type who'd hire someone to give her a push rather than get his own hands dirty.

"Something about him is just *too* vanilla," Paul said from the passenger seat. "Lacey wants me to interrogate all my friends when the rational suspect is grinning right in her face with those anchorman teeth."

"Why do men constantly get shit for thinking with their dicks, but women never get called on it when they do the same thing?" Rafael asked. "Uh, no offense to your sister."

"None taken. They're supposed to have this intuition, but you know what's better than intuition? A strong, logical mind. Like Brandy's."

"Your girl's quite a catch, I gotta say," said Rafael.

"But a little young for your tastes, right?" asked Paul.

"Hey, it was *one night*, okay?"

Egan came out his front door and hopped down the stairs. He was wearing a shiny tan leather jacket and smoking a cigarette.

"What the?" said Rafael. "Is that him?"

Egan got into his Audi and peeled out.

Rafael waited a few seconds, then followed.

"Smell that?" Paul asked as they passed his driveway.

Rafael inhaled. "Whoa, menthols? Who *is* this guy?"

They tailed him onto the northbound highway. Halfway to Tulac, he pulled into a truckstop.

"Don't tell me it's date night for the doctor," said Rafael.

They pulled in behind an idling semi and they watched Egan get out and use the pay phone in front of the bathroom hut.

"A doctor who can't afford a cell phone?" said Rafael.

"Or can't afford to be triangulated," said Paul.

Judging by the way Egan slammed the receiver, the conversation wasn't a successful one. Egan walked in a huff back to his car and peeled out again, continuing north. He took the first Tulac exit and turned into a trailer park on the outskirts of town.

"Manzanita Meadows," said Rafael, reading the sign across the park's arched entryway. "Good stripper name. No offense."

"Again, none taken," said Paul.

They couldn't follow Egan into the trailer park without being seen, but from the street they could see him approach one of the trailers carrying a paper bag, go inside, and depart five minutes later, returning to the northbound highway. A few miles later he took the exit to Spirit Rock, the Indian casino.

Egan parked in a distant corner of the big parking lot, where there were plenty of empty spaces. Rafael found a spot a few rows away, facing the doctor's Audi. It was dark now; they could see the ember of Egan's cigarette behind his steering wheel.

After ten minutes the parking lot's fluorescent lights flickered on. A black Lincoln with tinted windows rolled up into the space next to Egan's. Egan got out of his car and into the Lincoln's driver-side rear door. After a few minutes, the opposite door opened and Egan came tumbling out.

His face was unmarked, but he was curled in fetal position, holding his sides.

"No smoking in their car, I guess," Rafael said.

"Lost his Kool," said Paul.

The Lincoln pulled away and left the parking lot. Still snickering, they discussed following it but decided to watch Egan's next move instead. He'd made it up to his knees by the time a security guard came over to investigate. Rafael and Paul watched Egan talk his way out of it, flashing a self-deprecating smile, probably making up a story about a jealous boyfriend or practical joke.

The guard let him go and they tailed him all the way back home.

"No more house calls tonight," said Paul.

They watched from across the street as he staggered up his steps.

"So much for vanilla," said Rafael.

"I don't know," Paul said. "For a menthol-smoking, truckstop-loitering, drug-dealing, casino-beatdown-taking doctor, he still seems kind of . . . blah."

NOTES:

Lisa,

Now that you're getting the final chapter, I thought I should accelerate things a bit.

Sorry about your beloved Dr. Egan. That's what happens when you create a character about as compelling as a collar stay. Note, however, that I didn't feel the need to *kill* him. One more difference between you and me.

Dave

P.S. I'd love to see the supposed list of authors you approached for my role. I feel like I took a bullet for every one of them.

Dave,

When I came up with the idea, the obvious choice was to go with a crime novelist, specifically a published one. But then I thought of you and figured this might be a way to mend some fences. If it makes you feel any better, you were only number 4 on the list. David Corbett claimed to be too busy, Tim Maleeny really was too busy, and Domenic Stansberry said he'd get back to me after he read one of my books. I'm still waiting. To be honest, if I had it to do over again, you'd be number 5. I should have asked John Vorhaus. He totally owes me. Satisfied? I'm sure you haven't heard of any of these people, since the last time you picked up a genre novel was Ellroy in the nineties, but they're all well respected and published and understand that when you start with a dead body, you eventually reveal the killer.

I'm sorry about the coin toss, but it was fair—I even let you call it.

In the interest of productivity, I should remind you that it's time to start sewing up loose ends. I'll try to steer things in the right direction for you, but if you decide to take the wheel and run us off the cliff, well, there's nothing I can do about that.

That said, I hope you don't. I used to think that writing half a book would be easier than a whole one. I was dead wrong. Then again, if any of my top four had said yes, who knows?

Lisa

CHAPTER 27

That night, both Paul and Lacey dreamed about the land deal. In Paul's dream, he was paid with Monopoly money; in Lacey's, Big Marv kept passing her the check and then pulling it away at the last minute. Over coffee, neither sibling mentioned their dream. Trust had waned to the point that sharing even their subconscious seemed like a risky undertaking. When they were kids, they had the world in common. After their parents' death, they drifted in different directions. And now, though they were living together again, they were worlds apart. Lacey wanted justice; Paul wanted to bury his head in the ground, run off with a maimed stripper, and live happily ever after.

"Have you seen Irving?" Paul asked, noticing that the cat's food remained untouched.

"Not since yesterday," Lacey replied.

"I'm worried," Paul replied. "He never misses breakfast."

"Relax," said Lacey. "He's a cat. They go missing all the time. Sometimes they find a new home and never come back. Sometimes they fall out of tall buildings and live. Sometimes they get hit by a car and die."

"Don't say that."

"I'm not saying that Irving has come to an untimely end, I'm just saying he might."

Lacey cleared the table and grabbed her car keys. "Have you called Big Marv to see if he's going to counter Jay's offer?"

"Not yet."

"Well, if you have any spare time today, it might be something to consider," Lacey said, knowing that her brother had only time to spare.

"I'll get on it. Where are you headed?"

"I have a shift at the Tarpit," Lacey replied, pulling the directory of suspects from her pocket. "I figure I can scratch a few names off the list while I'm at it."

"The list just got shorter," Paul said, taking the crumpled piece of paper from his sister and striking it several times over with a pen. "Wanda hosted a poker night. Six people can vouch for each other. Also, forget about Rafael, for both the Harry Lakes murder and the night the body was dumped for the second time."

Paul returned the list to Lacey.

"Thank you," she said. "What's Rafael's alibi?"

"Last Wednesday during the Harry Lakes murder he was getting a burrito."

"Did anyone see him?" Lacey asked.

"I can go one better. He gave me the receipt."

"Huh," Lacey replied. "That's preposterous. Why would anyone hang on to a burrito receipt?"[43]

"I don't know," Paul replied.

Lacey's suspicion remained intact. "What was he doing the Saturday night of the body dump?"

"You won't believe it," Paul replied.

"I'm sure I won't," Lacey deadpanned.

"He was, um, having a romantic interlude with a certain older woman."

"Do we know her?"

"Yes."

"Spill it."

"I think he'd like to keep it quiet."

"Unless I know who it is, we have to consider Raf a suspect."

"He's not a suspect, Lace."

"Then tell me."

---

[43]Taxes? He's an orderly dude.

"Marybeth Monroe."

"I think I'm going to be sick."

"I warned you. Now you're not gonna go verifying an alibi with Marybeth, are you?"

"Of course not," Lacey replied. "Who'd make that shit up?" Lacey checked her watch. "I better go."

"Wait, Lace. Are you planning on seeing Egan today?"

"Maybe. He's supposed to set up a meeting with Doc Holland."

"You should know something," Paul said. "Egan isn't who he says he is."

"None of us are," Lacey replied.

While Lacey was steaming milk and making shots of espresso, Sheriff Ed dropped in for his usual, only this time he ordered two shots of espresso in his regular old cup of coffee.

"You okay, Ed?" Lacey asked.

"Better than ever," Ed replied, unconvincingly.

"You look tired."

"If the Mercer crime rate holds steady, we'll have to start a local police academy."

"Any new developments?" Lacey asked.

"Still hitting dead ends on the Drexel murder. Sorry, Lace. But I finally got a preliminary report on the plane crash investigation."

"There was an investigation?" Lacey asked.

Ed responded with a quizzical glance and said, "Of course, Lacey. You think planes just crash and the FAA doesn't insist on an investigation?"

"I've never crashed a plane before, so I wouldn't know. My brother seems to think a plane can crash and become a distant memory in two weeks."

Sheriff Ed seemed lost in thought until Lacey handed him his turbo-charged coffee. "They got some DNA from the crime scene," he said. "Testing it right now. But if there's nothing to compare it to, a lot of good it does us."

"Think it was just a random crash?"

"That's not what my gut tells me."

"What does your gut tell you?"

"That Holland was in the plane," Sheriff Ed replied. "Unfortunately, we got no DNA to test it against."

"I hate to argue with your gut, Sheriff, but there's no way Holland was flying that plane."

"What makes you so sure?"

"I got a letter from him almost a week after the crash."

"A letter from Doc Holland?"

"The man previously known as Doc Holland."

"How come you never mentioned this before?"

"Must have slipped my mind."

"What was in the letter?"

If the letter had mentioned only Hart, she would have told the sheriff the truth, but she couldn't implicate Sook in a blackmail scheme.

"Oh, nothing important. Just a past-due notice on a bill."

She wasn't sure Ed bought that, but he didn't press her further.

"Bring it by the office tomorrow, Lacey. That's evidence."

"Sure thing."

"Take care of yourself, sweetheart."

The sheriff was almost out the door when Lacey stopped him. She couldn't figure out a delicate way to clear him in the Drexel murder, so she just spat it out. "Where were you between two and three a.m. the Sunday before last?"

"Are you hunting for my alibi, Lacey?"

"Just being thorough, Sheriff," Lacey innocently replied.

Ed sighed. "The wife and I were driving home from our vacation lodge in the Sierras. You can call Lila and verify."

As soon as Ed was out the door, Lacey called Lila to confirm, which she did after consulting her calendar. Lacey crossed Sheriff Ed and Lila off her list.

During the mid-morning lull, Darryl Cleveland showed up. It seemed like ages since Lacey had spied on him while he watched TV, but it was only two weeks ago. The scar on her arm would always make her think of that sad sight of Darryl sitting alone, watching a repeat of *Cudgel*. It would also make her think of slicing her arm open.

"What can I get you, Darryl?"

"Decaf double espresso," Darryl replied.

"Are you sure?" Lacey asked.

"Yes," Darryl sad.

Lacey couldn't figure half of the town's beverage choices. While Lacey firmly believed in freedom of choice, more often than not she wanted to tell them that they were ordering wrong.

"Long time no see," Lacey said as she prepped Darryl's drink. "Where you been?"

"Turtling."

Lacey held her tongue again. She served Darryl his beverage and got to the point.

"So, Darryl, do you remember where you were the Sunday before last between two and three a.m.?"

"Why are you asking?"

"I'm helping the sheriff with his investigation of Hart Drexel's murder."

"Why would I kill Hart?"

"Not interested in motive right now. Can you provide an alibi?"

"My stepmom," Darryl mumbled.

"She'll corroborate?" Lacey asked.

"Uh-huh. Do me a favor, Lacey."

"What?"

"Keep it to yourself."

"Why?"

"Because I don't need the whole town knowing that I spend my Saturday nights watching TV with my stepmom."

———

A few hours later, Lacey's cell phone rang.

"Hello?"

"It's Brandy."

"What can I do for you?"

"We need to talk."

"About what?"

"In person. The Timberline. Two o'clock," Brandy said.

The next thing Lacey heard was a dial tone.

Lacey arrived early. Rafael was drinking a beer and doing a crossword puzzle. Lacey sat a few barstools away from him, hoping to avoid any kind of conversation. Just seeing Raf made her think of him with Hart's mom, and there wasn't enough booze in the world to erase that image.

"Tate, can I get a drink?" Lacey asked, hoping to at least blur it.

"What'll it be?" Tate asked.

"Whiskey with a beer back," Lacey replied.

"At two in the afternoon, Lacey?" Tate asked.

"How are you planning on staying in business with an attitude like that?"

Tate poured the shot and pulled the pint. Rafael looked up from his crossword and nodded at Lacey.

"How are you doing, Lace?"

"Okay," Lacey replied, without making eye contact.

Rafael slid over to the stool next to hers and rolled up his sleeve. "Your fomenting trick worked," he said.

"Good," Lacey said, downing her shot. "Can I get another?"

"Sure you're okay?" Rafael asked.

"Uh-huh. Just got a lot on my mind."

"He told you, didn't he?"

"Rafael, I don't know what you're talking about."

"I swear, nobody in this town can keep a secret."

Lacey was thinking he got it all wrong. Everyone was keeping secrets. That was the problem with this town.

Rafael finished his beer in one swift gulp and headed for the door. A triangle of daylight entered the Timberline and left with him. When the light returned, Lacey swiveled on her barstool and saw Brandy's unmistakable silhouette limping in her direction. Brandy hooked her cane on the edge of the bar and seated herself next to Lacey.

"What can I get you, Brandy?" Tate asked.

"Easy Jesus," Brandy replied.

"Refresh my memory," said Tate.

"Brandy and Dr Pepper."

"You got it, sweetheart."

Lacey waited until Brandy's drink was served and Tate was out of earshot before she launched into her usual questioning.

"So, Brandy, where were you the Sunday before last, between two and three a.m.?"

"You mean the night before your brother asked me to serve as his alibi?" Brandy asked, looking a little too smug for Lacey's liking.

"Yeah, that night."

"I was home all evening. Doing my nails, I think."

"No one can verify your whereabouts?"

"Nope," Brandy replied. "You're just going to have to take my word for it."

Lacey finished her whiskey and looked Brandy in the eye.

"So what are we doing here?" Lacey asked.

"Big Marv just upped his offer to one million."

"How do you know this and I don't?" Lacey asked.

"Paul will tell you when you get home."

"Then why trouble with this secret meeting?"

"You need to take the offer. Now," Brandy said.

"Well, if he's up to a million, who says Jay won't go higher?"

"When you're buying land, you have to pay cash. Jay can't access more than that. Neither can Marv. They won't work together and pool their funds. It's their final offer."

"So maybe someone else will join the bidding war."

"You don't want any professional surveying that land."

"Why?"

"Because it's worth *nothing*, Lacey."

"What?"

"It's worth about a hundred grand, in a good economy. There's nothing valuable on the property besides the potential for development and, let's be frank, that urban sprawl isn't happening anytime soon."

"So why do the Babalatos think it's worth something?"

"Terry was playing a long con on them. He hired a phony surveyor, mocked up official-looking documents that made it look like the soil was loaded with rare minerals. Then he outbid them when your parents were selling and they were low on cash. Jakes always planned to sell to the brothers, but chickened out. Too afraid of what the Babalatos would do when they learned the truth. He knew if he sold, he'd have to skip town right away. And he was never ready to leave. I think part of him always hoped he and Deena would get back together."

"Why didn't you tell me about this the last time we talked?" Lacey asked.

"This stuff is strictly need-to-know. You didn't need to know. No offense," Brandy said.

"So how did you even get involved?" Lacey asked.

"I hacked into Terry's computer."

"Of course. So why didn't you tell Paul?"

"He needed to believe he was holding all the cards. You ever see him play poker? He's got a tell for every Shady Acre of land."

"You sure about this?" Lacey asked. Suddenly, the Babalatos shot to the top of her suspect list.

"Yes," Brandy replied. "Close the deal tonight and sign those papers as soon as possible."

Lacey dropped by Doc Egan's office on her way home from the Timber-line. The new doc was sitting on his stoop, wearing some lame leather jacket from the eighties, and smoking a cigarette.

"I didn't know you smoked," Lacey said.

"I bet there are a lot of things about me you don't know."

"Menthols, really?"

"They're refreshing," Egan replied, blowing out a minty stream.

"You make contact with Holland yet?"

"Yeah. I just got an e-mail from him. He wants to meet day after tomor-row at some Italian restaurant in Birkton."

"Verducci's? That's a bit of a drive."

"Yep. What's in it for me, Lacey?"

Lacey pulled a dime bag from her purse and tossed it on the stoop next to Egan.

"That work for you?"

"For now," Egan replied.

"I wouldn't smoke it all at once," Lacey said. "We're closing up shop soon."

"What's new?" Lacey asked Paul the second she walked through the door.

"Irving is still missing," Paul said.

"Sorry to hear that. Anything else new?"

"Yeah, Big Marv upped the offer again."

"To what?"

"One million."

"He sure wants that land," Lacey said.

"Enough to kill for?" Paul asked.

"Don't know," Lacey replied. "I wouldn't put it past him."

"You think he killed our folks?"

"Maybe. But I'm gambling on another suspect," Lacey replied.

"What are you talking about, Lace?"

"There's something I should tell you."

"More secrets. That's just what we need."

"Ilsa Sundstrom called a few days ago."

"Why didn't you tell me?"

"I met with her. Did you know her parents were filing a malpractice suit against Doc Holland? But then her father started negotiating with Holland without an attorney. I think Holland tried to kill them because he couldn't risk being exposed and he had no other place to go."

"And you think he accidentally killed our parents?"

"It makes sense. The Sundstroms were supposed to be at the cabin that night and then two months later they die in a car accident."

"Then why did Big Marv say something to you at the bar?" Paul asked. "What would he know about it?"

"Maybe he was just trying to scare me. I'm not saying Marv's innocent. I'm just not sure what crime he's committed," Lacey replied.

"So do we take his offer?"

"I don't know. Do we?" Lacey asked. She knew better than to tell Paul what to do. Somehow it had to seem like his idea.

"I don't want the land. Do you?"

"No."

"If they'll pay a million, they'll probably pay more," Paul said.

"Maybe. But how long do you want to strategize against the Babalatos?"

"Just the other day you were pushing for more. What's changed?" Paul asked.

"Five hundred thousand is enough for me," Lacey casually replied.

"Just remember that the offer is only good as long as both brothers are alive. People seem to be developing a habit of getting themselves murdered lately. Either way, the decision is yours."

"Really?" Paul skeptically replied.

"Really."

The next morning, Paul took the deal. Irving was still nowhere to be found.

On Monday afternoon, Lacey reprised her Verducci's disguise and followed Egan to Birkton. She parked across the street at the $1 to $5 store and then scoped the Verducci's lot for Doc Holland's Oldsmobile, a tan clunker from the early nineties. It wasn't there.

Instead of waiting outside and raising suspicion, Lacey sat at a table in the corner where she could spy on Egan's booth in the glass mirror that crossed the length of the restaurant. She figured if her own brother couldn't recognize her, how would old Holland?

Egan ordered a soda and waited. Lacey chose a burger, trying to stay in character with her trucker disguise.

An hour passed and boredom set in. Egan eventually ordered a sandwich and Lacey was on her third refill of Coke. She picked up the *Birkton Bee*, a flyer-sized newspaper, and dove into their crime blotter. Birkton had a little more action than Mercer. Just last week there was a hit and run, a nude drunk-and-disorderly, and a UFO sighting by three separate individuals. In fact, the UFO sighting also made the front page.

When Lacey glanced up from her paper, she noticed that Egan was gone from his booth. She figured he was in the restroom and waited. When fifteen minutes passed and he didn't return, she checked the parking lot for his car. It was still there.

Lacey approached a waitress and asked if she had seen the man who'd been sitting in the corner. The waitress said she thought he had gone to the restroom. Lacey waited another minute and knocked on the men's room door. She knocked again. She shouted Egan's name. Then she checked the handle. The door was open, so she entered.

Inside, Egan was sprawled out on the floor in a thick pool of his own blood. His throat had been slashed; his lips were already blue; his eyes stared frozen at the ceiling.

Lacey screamed for help, but no one could help Matthew Egan. He was most definitely dead.

NOTES:

Hi Dave,

I bet that was a surprise. I'd like to say that I was planning on killing him all along, but we both know that's not true. You put the idea in my head, so I guess I should thank you. I'm assuming Egan got beat up in the casino parking lot because of a gambling situation. But now we'll never know. Let's be honest, even if I let him live, we'd still never know.

Lisa

P.S. Keep Irving missing, if you know what's good for him.

Lisa,

You're right; I am surprised. I never thought you'd sacrifice one of your own. But I guess when you find one tool that feels good—in your case, killing anything that presents a problem—there's no impetus to consider other tactics. What happened to you? Your previous books didn't hint at this brutality. But I'm done complaining. If you really want to become the Pol Pot of mystery writing, I can't stop you.

As for the reasons behind Egan's casino beatdown, let's just say your predictable assumption is nowhere near what I had in store. But as you noted, you'll never know.

Dave

P.S. About your stable of would-be collaborators, I don't doubt that all of those authors are adept at building and resolving intricate mysteries. But I'd argue that bringing a psycho to justice on the page and cowriting a book with one require different skill sets.

CHAPTER 28

Sheriff Cole Staley, head of the Birkton branch of the county sheriff's office, looked around at the swarm of crime-scene workers in Verducci's and shook his head in disbelief. Four murders in sixteen days, and the mayhem now seemed to be spreading geographically. His fear wasn't great enough, however, to completely blot out an irritating thought, which he related to one of his deputies: "Great. Now I gotta call Ed."

A few years back, when Sheriff Ed Wickfield was painstakingly building the case for a major coke bust in the area, Staley had run some smaller raids that yielded some minor convictions but also ruined Ed's chances of nabbing the region's main supplier. Relations between the two offices had been chilly ever since. Nevertheless, standing in Verducci's, Sheriff Staley called Ed out of professional courtesy, politely declining any help from Mercer in the investigation, saying the crime scene was busy enough as it was.

Ed didn't fight him to get involved in the new killing because he knew once the FBI came barging in—and if this last killing didn't guarantee that, nothing would—both of them would be lapdogs for the Feds. Instead he called Paul and asked him to drop by the station immediately.

Halfway through the short drive to the station, Paul found himself suddenly nauseated and pulled over to the shoulder. It hadn't occurred to him right away, but now he was sure of it. He'd failed to protect his sister again, and she was gone. Why else would Ed call him in so urgently? He should have packed up with Lacey and left at the first sign of trouble. Or the second or third one. He opened his door to throw up but nothing came.

Inside Sheriff Ed's office, Paul refused to sit down. Even after Ed had provided a summary of the afternoon's events, it took Paul a moment to realize his sister wasn't dead. Then he sat down.

"No one is accusing Lacey of murder," Ed said. "But she's sure tangled herself up in this. Until we untangle her, I think you're both in danger."

"Where is she now?" Paul asked.

"She's still at Verducci's. They'll keep her for a while until they secure the crime scene. Then they'll probably take her to the station to finish their interrogation."

"Can I call her?" Paul picked up his cell phone.

"You're welcome to try," Ed said. "I'm sure she'll pick up if she can."

Lacey answered on the third ring.

"Hello?"

"Hi, Lace . . . uh, it's good to hear your voice. What's going on?" he asked.

"Not much."

"You sure about that?"

"Uh-huh." She wasn't budging.

"Anything new?" Paul said. The relief he'd felt a few minutes before was being replaced by familiar irritation.

"We need more milk," Lacey said.

"Anything else?"

"Cereal," Lacey replied.

"Lace, are you in shock? I know where you are. I'm in Sheriff Ed's office right now."

Paul held up the phone awkwardly.

"Hi, Lacey," Sheriff Ed called out.

"What were you doing in Birkton with that creepy doc?" Paul asked.

"Investigating. Tell the sheriff I think Doc Holland is suspect number one right now."

"Lace, please. You're putting yourself in danger. This has to stop."

"It will stop when the murders stop," Lacey replied, disconnecting the call.

Paul stuffed his phone back in his pocket.

"I'd tell you to talk some sense into her," Ed said, "but that train has clearly left the station."

Paul didn't know how to respond to that. "Yep," he said.

"This keeps up, we're gonna have to change the population sign," Ed said, shaking his head. His attempt at a light tone didn't quite come off. He seemed shaken up.

"I guess so," said Paul.

He wasn't comfortable hanging around inside a law enforcement office, especially when it wasn't quite clear what was expected of him.

"So, can I go?" Paul finally said.

"Yep," Ed said, and stood up. He walked around the desk to Paul and took him by the shoulders, looking him in the eye. There was no sense of threat, only genuine concern. "Get some rest. And try to stay out of trouble. I'll make sure Lacey gets home safe."

For a second Paul forgot that he was a pot grower inside a sheriff's office.

As Paul started toward the door, Ed said, "Remind Lacey to bring that letter to me tomorrow."

"What letter?"

"From Doc Holland."

"Right," said Paul, like he knew what Ed was talking about. "Will do."

When Paul got back home, he saw a familiar shape in the rocking chair on the porch.

"Irving!"[44]

---

[44] If you really loved Irving, you would stop writing about him.

Paul picked him up and gave him a squeeze. His thick fur was tangled with thistles, burrs, and even part of a cigarette filter. He'd apparently been on quite an adventure. Paul took him inside for some milk and tuna, then cut the reunion short to start looking for the Doc Holland letter. It was for Lacey's own good. Keeping stuff to herself seemed to have a way of putting her in the vicinity of dead bodies.

He was about to lift Lacey's dresser when Brandy called his cell.

"You want to come over? I made mac 'n' cheese. Don't worry—it's from a box. I figure you could use some quote-unquote home cooking."

"That sounds delicious," Paul said.

"You sound distracted," Brandy said. "What are you doing?"

"Looking for a letter. Lacey has apparently heard from Doc Holland. Ed wants it. Not sure why. Maybe to test it for DNA or something. I just don't know where she'd be keeping it. For all I know she might be carrying it around with her."

"You've tried the obvious places, right?" Brandy asked.

"Probably. Like what?"

"Like between her mattress and box spring?" Brandy said.

Paul lifted the mattress. There it was, still in its envelope. He put the phone down and read the letter. He was surprised to find that it was addressed to Sook. He didn't know the old man had been involved in the whole blackmail scheme. Yet another one of Lacey's secrets.

"How'd you know?" Paul asked.

"Sometimes you have to dumb yourself down a little to find what you're looking for," Brandy said.

"I'll be over right after I drop the letter off at the station."

"I'm not sure that's the right move, Paul."

"Why?"

"Getting official DNA test results can take months around here. Bring the letter over with you."

"Why? What will you do?"

"Let's just say I know someone."

"Of course you do."

"See you in a bit, buttercup," Brandy said.

After their preliminary talk at Verducci's, Sheriff Staley took Lacey to the Birkton station for more questioning. At the restaurant, sipping stale coffee, she'd seemed barely capable of hearing his questions, but now she was coming out of her daze.

Since there were only a few drops of blood on Lacey's clothes and the waitresses could place her outside the men's restroom until the moment the body was discovered, Staley knew it would have been impossible for Lacey to have committed the crime. Besides, no weapon was found. But she was the closest thing he had to a witness. Lacey told Sheriff Staley about the missing Doc Holland and how Egan had arranged a meeting with him. While she hadn't seen Holland in the vicinity, she made it clear to Staley that she was certain Doc Holland was behind the murder.

Staley asked her why she seemed to be the common denominator in the murders.

"I wish I knew," said Lacey, her voice breaking. "You'd think someone at the center of the whole mess could figure out what tied it all together. But I just can't. And believe me, I've been trying."

With the letter in his pocket, Paul got into his truck and started toward the freeway and Brandy. But as he approached the on-ramp he veered toward downtown. An hour ago, he'd been seized by the certainty that his sister had been murdered—and the knowledge that he hadn't done anything to prevent it. Whatever she'd gotten herself entangled in, he thought, the only way he could protect her now was to risk entangling himself. No, that was bullshit. What he had to do was accept that he was already neck-deep in it, whether he liked it or not.

Paul realized he could no longer stand above the fray and hope things worked out. He also couldn't count on Lacey to share what she knew—or on anyone else to help him out. Who could he really trust when Sook was a blackmailer and Sheriff Ed was a pal? He had to finish the investigation of Doc Egan, and he had to do it alone.

He parked his truck around the corner from Egan's home and office. No sheriff's cruiser was out front, but he knew that would change soon. He got out and strolled down the leafy street toward Egan's driveway, and then hopped the fence into his backyard.

Paul opened the screen door and found a locked but not bolted back door. Terry had taught him how to do it when Paul was a teenager, but he'd never done it in real life. He took a credit card out of his wallet and slid the lock open. In a few seconds he was in a mauve kitchen littered with takeout cartons and menthol butts.

Paul headed to the bedroom first. He was looking for any clues about who this guy really was, and maybe what his connection was to Doc Holland. But mostly he had no idea what he was looking for. He just knew he had to do something.

He opened the closet door because he figured that's where most people hide things. On the top shelf he spotted an old shoebox. He pulled it over the shelf so it nearly came crashing down on him. It was just receipts and software manuals and office debris, but at the bottom was a single photo, facedown. He held it up. In faded purple cursive, it said "Dad & Matthew, Summer '75." He flipped it over. A smiling kid with a bowl cut stood on a pier. Behind him was a middle-aged man with a crooked smile who rested one hand playfully on the boy's head. A tiny fish hung from each of the boy's outstretched hands. The man's distinctive crooked smile looked familiar. After a moment Paul realized why. It was Doc Holland.

A heavy car door shut somewhere near the front of the house. Paul shoved the photo in his pocket, next to the letter, and went out the back. He peeked around the corner of the house. The front bumper of the cruiser was only a few feet away. Paul took off toward the back fence, hopped it, and ran through a lot covered in clover. He came out the other side and walked around the corner to his truck.

NOTES:

Lisa,

I thought it was time we had an actual revelation to balance out the bloodshed. If you can find it in yourself to just let things unfold naturally from here on, I think this book can still work. Of course, that'd be an unprecedented development for you, on or off the page.

    Dave

P.S. One last question about the authors who rejected you: Why all men?

Dave,

Yeah, Paul's convenient discovery of the photograph in the closet was totally natural. I'm starting to think you never took this project seriously. I'm also starting to think if a dead body turned up at your door, you'd step over it and go out for a burger. If we weren't so close to the end, I'd forfeit this "game," because that's what it's starting to feel like.

But in the interest of finishing what we've started, I have a gift for you: I'm going to let Irving live. You know why? So you have a character to jump-start your cat mystery series. It'll be awesome—bodies piling up on the streets and no man or feline giving it a second thought.

    Lisa

P.S. I wasn't rejected, I was politely declined. I asked men because I wanted my book jacket to use colors outside of the pastel palette for once. End of discussion.

CHAPTER 29

That night, Paul returned home still reeling from his discovery that Doc Holland was Doc Egan's father. He didn't want Lacey to be alone after discovering a corpse, but he certainly wasn't going to share the news with her. He still didn't know what to make of the connection, and after everything Lacey had survived that day, he figured she didn't need any more information to fuel her investigative urges.

"Mac 'n' cheese from a box," Paul explained, sliding the dish in front of her. "You should eat something."

"Who made it?"

"Brandy."

"No thanks."

"It's not poison. I had it for dinner."

"Well, I'll wait a few more hours to be sure."

"Cereal?" Paul asked.

"You never got the milk."

"Right."

Lacey took a beer from the fridge and sat back down at the table. "What if Big Marv was the killer?" Lacey asked.

"Of who?"

"One or all of the victims."

"Then he should go to prison for a very long time," Paul replied, not sure what answer Lacey was hunting for.

"Well, of course. But my question is, we've agreed to take this man's money. Should we take it if he's a murderer?"

"I'm *more* inclined to take it if he's a murderer," Paul replied. "If you think about it, we're swindling him."

"But he thinks he's swindling us."

"Right," said Paul. "When did our lives get so complicated? We used to grow plants. Now you're hunting a serial killer and we're engaged in shady million-dollar business deals."

"So, we're taking the money," Lacey said, ignoring Paul's comment. Her mind was crowded enough, she didn't need to worry herself about what was crowding his. She took her beer and went to bed.

In the morning Paul was gone. Sheriff Ed called Lacey and reminded her about the letter. She searched for three hours until she gave up. Was it possible that she'd hid it from herself? With all that had transpired, the idea crossed her mind, but then she figured something more sinister was going on. Mercer used to seem like a nice place, but the town had splintered into jagged shards right in front of her.

Up in Tulac, Paul lounged around Brandy's apartment all morning. He picked up that Wittgenstein biography, but lost interest after the introduction. He stuck a bookmark on page three and headed to the Timberline.

At 3:15 in the afternoon, Tate called Lacey's cell and said, "Your brother's drunk and out of cash."[45]

"We have iddall figged out," Paul slurred, when Lacey arrived and took a seat next to him and Rafael.

---

[45]How's Paul supposed to help solve the murder if you always incapacitate him in your chapters?

Apparently even just a sliver of a biography on a major philosophical thinker had gotten Paul's mind working in overdrive. Unfortunately,
none of Wittgenstein's intellect was passed on to Paul. He was as logic-
challenged as ever.

"What have you got figured out?" Lacey replied.

"The two docs were innit together."

"Oh yeah."

"Most def-in-ite-ly," Paul replied, forming the word as if for the first time.

"What's their connection?" Lacey asked.

Paul leaned in close and whispered Budweiser breath into his sister's
ear. "Doc Holland was Doc Egan's father."

"What?" Lacey asked, grabbing her brother by the shoulders.

"The fake doc was the father of the dead doc," Paul said.

"How do you know this?"

"I investigated. I have proof."

"Then prove it," Lacey replied.

Paul pulled the photo from his pocket and smacked it on the bar. Lacey
picked up the photo and studied the front and back.

"Where did you find this?" Lacey asked.

"In Egan's closet," Paul replied.

"Why didn't you tell me?"

"You don't need to know everything."

"What does it mean?" Lacey asked.

It was more of a rhetorical question, but Paul answered anyway.

"I think that the docs were plotting something."

"What were they plotting?" Lacey asked.

"Don't know, don't care. But now that Egan is dead there will be no
more murder."

"Think about it, Paul. That doesn't make any sense."

"Let me sleep on it," Paul replied. "Wake me in fifteen."

Paul then rested his head on the bar and within moments his distinct snore layered another sound track over the Steve Earle album playing in the background. Lacey ordered a beer and scowled at Rafael.

"How many has he had?" she asked.

"I lost count at eight," Rafael replied.

Musings on murder suspects now qualified as small talk in Mercer. Rafael proceeded to inform Lacey of all Paul's theories, both standing and debunked. As Rafael spoke, Lacey's suspicion of him grew—in part because he was spending too much time with Paul, nosing around their investigation, but also because she had not yet investigated him herself. But Paul insisted that Rafael had an airtight alibi. Or at least a receipt.

Paul's cell phone rang, which caused him to stir and changed the tone of his snore. But he didn't wake. Lacey pulled the cell from his pocket and answered.

"Paul's phone," she said.

"Lacey?"

"Who's asking?"

"Big Marv."

Lacey's heart skipped a beat when she heard his name. Ever since the verbal land agreement was struck, Lacey had feared the worst.

"What can I do for you?" she said, in an atypically polite tone.

"My lawyer has just drawn up the paperwork. When can you and Paul sign?"

Lacey glanced at her comatose brother.

"Give me an hour."

Rafael helped Lacey load Paul into the back of his pickup truck. Through-out the ride home, blasts of cold air and carefully targeted potholes jolted him awake. Paul managed to walk without too much assistance into their house, where Lacey plied him with half a pot of coffee and a quart of Gatorade, and then made him perform a round of calisthenics.

An intriguing phenomenon with Paul was that when he was stoned you couldn't get him to budge, but drunk he'd follow orders like a private in boot camp. Once, in high school, when their parents were out of town, Paul drank a six-pack of beer and Lacey dressed him in a jacket and bow tie and had him play her butler until he sobered up and lost interest. "Mr. Paul" made many cups of tea and sandwiches that afternoon.

After Paul had sweated out some of the booze, Lacey told him to take a cold shower, and by the time Paul was finished, he was still drunk but could walk on his own and sign his name. Lacey had him practice a few times to be sure.

On the drive to Marv's office, Paul started nodding off again. Lacey had brought along a spray bottle for that very eventuality. She used it unremittingly. Paul's anger proved to be the most sobering elixir yet.

When they entered Big Marv's office, the siblings were introduced to a bespectacled man named Franklin Fisher. Marv referred to him as his lawyer.

"That name rings a bell," Paul slurred. "How do I know that name?" The memory that eluded him was that he'd heard it during his night of surveillance with Terry, when Jay was asking for a fat check from his patient. Lacey, of course, hadn't heard the name—it was just one of many pieces of evidence her brother had withheld from her.

"Have we met?" Paul asked Mr. Fisher.

"I don't believe so," Fisher replied.

"That name sure rings a bell."

Lacey smacked Paul on the head. "Has the ringing stopped?"

At the very least, Paul stopped mentioning it.

Lacey waited until the bank confirmed two wire transfers in the amount of $500,000 before she agreed to pick up the pen.

"Sign here and here and here," Franklin Fisher said.

The siblings passed the gold fountain pen back and forth until they'd worked their way through the inch-thick pile of papers. When they were done, a series of handshakes followed, and some sighs of relief.

"See you around," Big Marv said with a Cheshire Cat grin.

"We'll see about that," Lacey replied, as she and her brother departed.

On the drive home, an awkward silence set in. So much had gone on in the last few weeks, so many ugly thoughts and images that would be forever imprinted in their minds. A deal like this was once in a lifetime, but they both felt empty. Lacey knew her time in Mercer was coming to an end, and yet, if pressed, she couldn't tell you where she was going.

"I don't want to go home," Paul said.

"Where do you want to go?" Lacey asked.

"Take me to Brandy's."

"Really?"

"Please, Lace."

Lacey spun a U-turn on the desolate road and headed up to Tulac. Paul didn't say a word as he got out of the car.

When Lacey returned home, she collapsed on the couch and fell fast asleep.

The next morning, she turned on her computer and checked her bank balance, as if everything that had happened the previous day had just been a dream. She breathed a sigh of relief as she saw her comical bank balance: $500,114.54.

She realized she could go anywhere. It was a soothing thought and yet she stayed put.

Lacey killed most of the morning watching bad television. While making a sandwich, she sorted through the collection of bills, catalogs, and coupons from distant towns until she noticed a blank white envelope in the mix. She cracked the seal and found a note inside, cut and pasted from newspaper and magazine print.

Get oUT *now* or NEver

Lacey's heart raced and within seconds her palms grew sweaty. She slipped on her shoes, grabbed her keys, and made a beeline for the door. She drove straight to the Mercer sheriff's station.

This time when Doug saw her, he remained seated.

"Lacey."

"Doug."

"What can I do for you?"

"I need to see the sheriff."

"I'll see if he's in."

"He's in," Lacey said, striding down the hall and straight into Ed's office.

The sheriff spun around when he heard the door creak. He put his hand over his heart and said, "You startled me."

"We need to talk," Lacey said, taking a seat across from his desk.

"You bring the letter?"

"No."

"Why not?"

"It's missing; at least I think it's missing, or maybe I misplaced it."

Ed leaned back in his chair and put his boots up on his desk. He closed his eyes for a long enough moment that Lacey thought he might have nodded off.

"Ed?"

"Yes?"

"You know why Egan was at Verducci's yesterday, right?"

"I do."

"He was meeting Doc Holland."

"He was meeting Doc Holland because *you* arranged for the meeting."

"I regret that now. But until we flush out Holland, these murders won't stop."

"What's his motive, Lacey?"

"I don't know."

"And why are you in the middle of every single one of these crimes? Your ex-fiancé dies, and lo and behold a life insurance policy turns up in your name. Terry Jakes is murdered and you and your brother inherit some land that turns out to be worth a pretty penny. Paul discovers the body of Harry Lakes. And you discover the corpse of Doc Egan. Remind me, Lacey, why aren't you my primary suspect?"

"After twenty-eight years, I cut off the head of my former fiancé and dump the rest of the body on my driveway? You don't really believe that now, do you, Ed?"

Ed sighed and brushed back the flap of thinning hair that covered his bald spot. "No, I know you're not a murderer, Lacey. But somehow all of this is connected to you."

"We need to find Doc Holland."

"*We* don't need to do anything. I'll handle the police work here. You just stay out of trouble. As for Doc Holland, he's a dead end for now."

"What do you mean?" Lacey replied.

"He's a ghost, Lacey. I wouldn't get your hopes up about finding him. He impersonated a doctor named Herman Holland for twenty years. Since we don't know who he really is, he could be anyone or anywhere right now. And while I agree he's suspicious, I'm not convinced he's behind these crimes. Remember, he lived among us for twenty years without murdering anyone."

"I wouldn't be so sure of that," Lacey said.

"Excuse me?"

"I think Doc Holland killed my parents."

Lacey sunk down in the leather chair and felt a sharp pain in her gut. She was out of theories other than the one that placed Doc Holland behind everything. And if Doc Holland couldn't be found, then how would the murders ever be solved? She explained to Ed everything she knew about the WINO killings. She couldn't tell if Ed believed her or not;

all she could see was another layer of exhaustion settling over his features. For the first time since all this murdering began, Lacey started to believe that justice would never be served.

Lacey got to her feet and was heading out the door when she heard Deputy Doug mumbling to himself. She closed the door for privacy and whispered.

"Sheriff, what about Doug?"

"What about him?"

"Does he have an alibi for the nights in question?"

"Lacey, Doug's not your killer."

"Does he have an alibi?" Lacey insisted.

The sheriff consulted the back of his brain and said, "Sweetheart, you're pulling at straws here. Doug was working. I bet we even got him on video surveillance."

"Then why is he acting so suspiciously?" Lacey asked.

"Because, and let's keep this between you and me, he's off his meds."

"Meds?" Lacey asked.

"Doug has some issues."

"Sheriff, do you think it's wise to hire an unstable man to carry a gun and act as town deputy?"

"I don't see anyone else applying for the job, do you?" the sheriff asked.

"What am I supposed to do now?" Lacey asked.

"Take your money and run?" Ed suggested.

Lacey was starting to think that was a good idea. She rushed out of the station, hoping to avoid engaging Doug in any conversation, but that was a fool's dream.

"Where's the fire?" Doug said.

"I have to get to the store before it closes."

"The store? Likely story."

"We're out of milk."

"What do you need milk for?" Doug asked.

"Um, coffee?" Lacey replied, backing toward the door.

"Save your lies for the amateurs," Doug said.

"Excuse me?" Lacey replied.

"You drink your coffee black."

"And cereal."

"Ever try orange juice? Works just fine in a pinch."

"Okay. See you later, Doug," Lacey said, practically racing out of the office.

When Lacey returned home, she started packing. If she couldn't find the murderer, she'd have to leave town soon. At least before Big Marv learned that his land was made of plain old dirt.

Later that evening, she heard the front door unlock and the sound of feet scuffling and unbridled laughter traveling through the house. Paul and Brandy entered with an open bottle of champagne.

Paul shouted Lacey's name. Then Brandy echoed him. Lacey sheepishly entered the living room.

"What's going on?" she asked.

Brandy chugged straight from the bottle, then passed it to Paul, who took another healthy gulp.

"We're celebrating," Paul said, offering the bottle to his sister.

"What are we celebrating?" Lacey asked.

"Show some manners," Brandy said to Paul as she scavenged the kitchen for a proper glass. There were no champagne flutes to be found, so she grabbed a coffee mug and drained the bottle into it.

Brandy passed the mug to Lacey.

"We're engaged," Paul said.

"Engaged?" Lacey asked, as if she didn't understand the meaning of the word.

"Yeah, we're gonna get hitched," Brandy replied.

"Show her the ring," Paul said.

Brandy flashed something that could only have come out of a gumball machine, made from plastic and an unidentifiable metal that would eventually turn her finger green.

"Nice ring," Lacey said.

"We have to go to Redding for the real thing," Paul replied, waiting for his sister to say something nice.

Lacey could feel all eyes on her, so she said the only thing she could. "Congratulations."

Lacey then downed the entire mug of champagne and brought out the whiskey. A bad mix, no doubt, but after the day she'd had, the only option.

That night, Lacey's mind kept working at the mystery even as her body slept. By morning a new theory had formed. She called Sook to confirm her worst fears.

"What happens if I die?" Lacey asked.

"I'd be heartbroken," Sook replied.

"I mean, what would happen to my money if I were to die suddenly."

"Do you have a will?"

"No."

"Then it would go to your closest relative. Paul."

"Say I die, Paul gets my money, and then Paul dies. What happens then?"

"I take it Paul doesn't have a will."

"No."

"I'm not sure what would happen then," Sook replied.

"What if Paul was married?"

"Then everything would go to his wife."

Lacey opened her nightstand drawer to make sure the gun was where she left it.

"You still there, Lacey?" Sook asked.

"I think I know who our killer is."

NOTES:

Dave,

I assure you there was nothing passive-aggressive in my incrimination of Brandy. It just fits, if you think about it.

I'm too tired to make threats, suggestions, or even to offer encouragement. I don't know what it is about us that makes working together so painful.

I'd like you to take this next chapter seriously and work within the confines of what we have already written. Of course, you'll do whatever you want. While you're thinking of ways to screw with me, remember this: Your next chapter is your last.

On a happy note, we're in the home stretch, Dave. Soon we will be free of each other.

      Lisa

Lisa,

Our troubles don't seem like such a mystery to me. We have different values and standards. For example, is an anonymous note composed of letters cut out of magazines and newspapers really the best we can do? What's next, THE KILLER WAS CALLING FROM INSIDE THE HOUSE?

Since you haven't taken up any of the leads I established in my last chapter, I guess I'll have to lay everything out myself. I may not have the luxury of the final word, but I have a feeling I'm not going to need it.

      Dave

CHAPTER 30

After the call from Sook, Lacey had realized that Paul wouldn't be in real danger until he married Brandy—or until Brandy found out he knew her secret. So she let the couple sleep off their champagne. She'd give Paul the news when his fiancée was at a safe distance.

Paul woke with a smile on his face and Irving purring on his chest. Next to him was a note from Brandy to come up to Tulac whenever he got up. They were supposed to spend the day planning their wedding. Hangover aside, he felt great, and he knew it wasn't just the engagement or the Babalato windfall. Lacey's half-packed suitcase meant she was finally ready to give up her investigations and skip town. He looked forward to the day he could stop worrying about her.

Marv Babalato might be a problem when he discovered the truth about the property, Paul thought, but that would take a while. And even then, what could Marv do? He'd bought the place under a fraudulent pretense. The more Paul dealt with him, the more he seemed like a garden-variety opportunist, not a homicidal avenger. Irving half opened his eyes, and after a while, Paul got up.

Brandy was out when he got to her place, so he used the key she'd given him the night before. A note on her TV said she'd be back by noon, but it was already almost one. He started worrying about her, and before long he was worrying about everything. Was he crazy to think everything was fine? Only a few weeks ago, she was pretending to be an entirely different person. Was he rushing into things? On an impulse he went into her bedroom and sat down at her computer. Her e-mail account was password-protected, but he nailed it on the third try, with *vonshtupp*, a reference to her favorite *Blazing Saddles* character.[46]

He opened her Sent folder and started scanning for the dates he'd been collecting alibis for, starting with the pre-dawn hours of September fourth. He ignored the e-mails from earlier that evening and found three after midnight. Around one a.m. there was one to her friend Candi about how tortured she was about deceiving him with the ditz routine. "I think he might be the one," it said. Paul felt queasy as he moved on to the next message Brandy had sent:

> Hey 0.5 bro,
>
> Where are you? Haven't heard from you in a while. I hope you know I'm not mad at you. Just let me know you're OK if you get a chance. Love, B

Paul checked the time stamp: 2:33 a.m. Brandy had been home when Hart's body was moved, and apparently had no idea he was already dead. Then the monitor's reflection darkened.

"Find what you were looking for?" Brandy said.

Paul swiveled on her chair to face her.

"I guess you're also wondering," she continued, "whether your fiancée also killed your best friend and his cousin. And then, just because she was getting a taste for it, took a knife to the new doctor."

"Brandy—"

"Let me break it down for you, Paul. The Wednesday when Harry Lakes was shot I was with your *sister*. Then this Monday, when Doc Egan was killed, I was at the monthly Quorum Group meeting over in Easternville."

---

[46] I like how you're conjuring your dream girl in Brandy. Key word "dream." You do understand that no real woman can live up to these obscure and outrageous expectations.

Quorum was her brainiac club—a fact Paul had discovered, he realized with shame, during an earlier snooping session.

She went to her desk and showed him the flyer.

"I can download the meeting minutes if you like," she continued coolly. "You can read all about my ideas on autopoiesis. As for Terry's tower, I have no alibi beyond my utter uselessness with tools. So I guess I must have done that one."

"I'm so sorry," Paul said. "I'm just . . . everything *might* be so perfect, I guess it almost feels too good to be true. Maybe I don't feel like I deserve all this."

"You do," Brandy said.

Paul had expected a more sustained tongue-lashing. "Uh, you're not mad?" he asked.

"Well, I did pretend to be a low-mental throughout the beginning of our relationship. Maybe now we can call it even?"

Paul wasn't buying it. "You're not miffed that your fiancé figured out your password and went through your e-mail?"

Brandy sat down on the bed and put her head in her hands.

"Oh shit," said Paul.

"I do have a confession to make," she said to the floor. Her voice was shaking. "I can't marry you until you know the truth. And you probably won't want to marry me after you do."

"What is it? We can work it out, no matter what it is. Please, talk to me."

"I want you to know I had the best possible reasons for killing them," she said. "You have to believe that."

Paul managed two words: "Killing who?"

She was sobbing now. "Your plants."

When he'd recovered, Paul got up and embraced her.

"I just want better things for you," she said into his chest. "I don't want us to have to lie to anyone about anything."

"Funny way to go about it," said Paul, trying to muster some indignation. He failed.

"It's just a job," he said. "We'll figure it out. We have plenty of time, plenty of money, plenty of options. For now, how about this: Next time you want me to do something, tell me."

"And the next time you want to know something about me," Brandy said, "ask me."

"Deal."

"You know, it's strange," Brandy said. "When Lacey was grilling me about my alibis, she didn't seem to realize that she and I were actually *together* during the Harry Lakes killing."

"She's not the investigator she thinks she is." Paul replied.

Later they went to work on the guest list for the wedding. It was shaping up to be a paltry collection of locals, some of whom were probably too freaked out by now to even leave their houses. Both Paul and Brandy started wondering whether a visit to a courthouse with a witness or two was a better idea. Their planning was interrupted by the telephone.

Brandy picked up. "Hello? That was fast. Give it to me. No, you don't need to explain variable number tandem repeats. Just give me the results. Really? Are you sure? No, I don't know what it means. Thanks, Max. I'll be in touch."

She hung up the phone and jotted down a sequence of numbers below their wedding list.

"Who was that?" Paul asked.

"Max," Brandy replied. "A friend from Quorum Group. He's the guy from the crime lab."

"What's going on?"

"Call Lacey. She's going to want to hear this."

An hour later, Lacey was sitting on Brandy's plush pink couch, tapping her foot silently on the shag carpet, waiting for Brandy and Paul to come out of Brandy's bedroom.

"You said you had a break in the case," Lacey finally called out. "Spill it."

Paul and Brandy were giggling when they entered the living room and squeezed into a loveseat across from Lacey.

"You do it," a beaming Paul told Brandy.

Brandy cleared her throat. "Paul said you got the envelope from Doc Holland, a.k.a. Doc Egan's father, just a week ago. But Sheriff Ed seems to believe Holland was the guy in the exploding plane. I knew both of those couldn't be true; I wanted to know if either one was. So I tested the envelope against the DNA from the crash site."

Lacey's foot stopped tapping and burrowed deep into the shag. She didn't know where to start—the stolen envelope or Brandy's sudden forensic expertise. She went with the latter. "How the hell did you get DNA from the crash site?" she finally said.

"I didn't. My friend Max works at the crime lab," Brandy replied.

"I see. How convenient," Lacey said.

"What can I say? He owed me a favor. So I gave Max the envelope you received from Holland. He just called with the results."

"I thought DNA testing took weeks," Lacey replied.

"I put a rush on it," Brandy replied.[47]

"Okay, assuming all this is true, what do we know?" Lacey asked.

"The DNA from the dead pilot and the envelope weren't an exact match, but they were close. In fact, they indicated paternity. Turns out the pilot was the *father* of the envelope-licker."

Lacey responded with a blank look.

Brandy spoke slowly, as though to a child. "That means it *was* Doc Holland who died in the plane crash. And it was his son, Doc Egan, who sent you the letter."

After a long pause, all Lacey could say was, "So much for my top suspect. But we still don't know who Doc Holland really was."

---

[47]What is this, Kinko's?

Brandy sighed. "This is the easy part. As you learned from Ilsa Sundstrom a week ago, the real Dr. Herman Holland was born in 1921. If you'd followed up, you'd know that he lived and practiced up in Orendale until his death in 1980."

"So?"

"So when Paul found out that the fake Holland was Egan's dad, I did some research, starting with anyone named Egan who'd lived in Orendale. I found a Roy Egan born in 1946. He served as a medic in Vietnam and then racked up a minor police record, mostly check fraud and failure to pay child support. From 1980 on, there are no traces of the man."

"So you're saying Roy Egan killed the real Herman Holland and took his name?" Lacey asked.

"Well done, Lacey. That's possible, but according to the coroner's report, the real doctor died of natural causes. That can be faked, of course, but my best guess is that Egan Senior just recognized an opportunity when Holland died. For twenty years he had a good thing going in Mercer. Then his past caught up with him."

"But how did Egan Junior find his father?" Lacey asked.

"No idea," said Brandy. "With both parties dead, we'll probably never get all the facts straight."[48]

"But I still don't get what the docs had to do with the killings of Hart, Terry, or Harry," Lacey said.

"Join the club," Paul replied. "Now you know everything we do." He put a consoling hand on Lacey's shoulder. "In terms of the investigation, at least."

"I need a drink," said Lacey. "I'll be at the Timberline."

"Are you sure that's a good idea, Lace?" Paul asked, but she was already out the door.

---

[48]You got that right.

On the drive back to Mercer, Lacey realized that what she needed, much more than a drink, was answers. Now that she knew "Doc Holland" had died even before Hart's body was returned to their property, the only remaining suspects she could think of were the Babalatos. She felt sick. Fat bank account or not, she had to know before she could break free of the town. She pulled into the sheriff's station.

Inside Sheriff Ed's office, he gave her a tentative but warm hug.

"Lacey, how you holdin' up today?" He looked pretty rattled himself.

"So far so good," Lacey lied.

"You here to tell me you've cracked the case?" he asked, trying for a gentle joke.

"Look, Ed. I know you don't want me poking around anymore. If you can just help me out with one little detail, I promise I'm done."

Ed didn't answer, so she continued. "What have you found out about the Babalato brothers?"

Ed took some time, apparently deciding whether to answer. "I don't know what the Babalatos were doing during Egan's murder. But they alibied up for Harry Lakes."

"Can I trouble you for the details? It'd help put my head to rest."

"Jay was at a class in Japanese tree trimming—icky somesuch."

"Ikebana?"

"That's it. And Marv was at bread-making class. He brought me a loaf of pumpernickel the next day. Not bad at all."

"Doesn't that sound a little suspicious to you?"

"Next time I hear something that *doesn't* sound suspicious, I'll let you know. Fact is, the alibis check out. Both brothers got sent to anger management a few months ago after they started a fight at a basketball game. The classes are part of their therapy. I talked to both of their course instructors personally. So there's no way either brother could have committed the Harry Lakes murder. And the night Hart's body turned up on your doorstep, the whole We Care staff was trying to track down a patient who was trying to break into Mapleshade. One of these days I'm going to have to look into that place."

"Yeah, well, I guess you've got a few other things on your plate right now."

"You could say that. We're starting to run low on suspects. Way it looks now, the killer might just end up being the last man standing."

Lacey had no answer for that.

The Holland–Egan revelations were having the opposite effect on Paul, reviving his belief that the murders could be solved—as well as his desire to find out who'd killed Terry. After Lacey had left, he'd told Brandy he had an important errand. The least he could do was check out his friend's house again, newly armed with the knowledge of the doctors' true identities.

Outside Terry's, a sagging X of police tape across the front door was the only sign of trouble. Paul slipped in through a back window. The room where Harry had been killed had been entirely cleared out. All the papers and journals and recordings were gone from the rest of the house, too. No more mysterious scribblings to puzzle over or clippings to decode. Still, Paul was glad he'd come. The Puma hadn't been forgotten. On his way back to his truck, Paul checked the mailbox in the driveway, just in case delivery to the address hadn't been canceled.

There were two envelopes inside, a big FedEx one curled around a standard-sized one. He opened the smaller one first. It was another "final" notice for Harry from the parole department, this one forwarded from his Jirsa address, up near the Oregon border. Establishing a forwarding address with the post office was a very strange move for a wanted man, Paul thought. He'd never been to Jirsa, but he was starting to feel like a road trip was in order.

The FedEx envelope was addressed to Terry and postmarked Los Angeles. Paul opened it and started reading.

Dear Mr. Jakes,
    We are pleased to inform you that you have been selected as a contestant on the upcoming Survivor: Tokelau. *We have been unable to reach you at the phone number you provided. Please call us at your earliest opportunity to discuss . . .*

Paul laughed and then started crying a little. He stuffed the letters into his jacket pocket and walked back to his truck. He had a killer to find.

NOTES:

Lisa,

While you've been occupying yourself with petty killings and misdirections, I've been laying out a precisely calibrated—yet surprisingly sturdy—solution just underneath the surface. Unfortunately, I've been prohibited from executing it to completion. I can't say I'm optimistic about *your* chances of doing so, now that I've removed all the obvious possibilities. Good luck writing your way out of this one.

I can't say it's a peace offering, but I do have a parting gift for you, too. The perfect title occurred to me back when I lost the coin toss: *Heads You Lose*.

Dave

Dave,

Heads You Lose sounds like the perfect title to me, too. Finally, you've made a substantive contribution to the book.

That was quite a chapter—maybe one of the most convoluted wrap-ups in the history of tertiary plot points. I know you think you've painted me into a corner by giving alibis to all the prime suspects, but I've been at this longer than you.

You've won a few battles, but I'm going to win the war.

Lisa

CHAPTER 31

The next day, Lacey returned to the sheriff's office with Paul and Brandy and they delivered all the evidence they had on the plane crash and the Holland–Egan connection. Sheriff Ed jotted down all the details and reluctantly complimented Brandy on her investigative acumen.

"What a bizarre series of far-fetched events," Sheriff Ed said. "Nothing in my career to date could have prepared me for anything more ridiculous. But at least we've got those minor matters sorted out."

"I don't mean to diminish the importance of uncovering a twenty-year-old conspiracy or identifying someone who died in a plane crash, but we do still have a murderer roaming free. I think it would be wise if we didn't forget that little detail," Lacey said, looking Brandy directly in the eye.

Brandy didn't seem to notice or didn't care. On the way out of the station, Lacey pulled Paul aside and said, "We need to talk. In private, please?"

"I'll meet you at Diner in an hour," Paul replied.

"So, what's your news?" Paul asked, over a Diner hamburger and fries.

"I'm pretty sure I know who our killer is, and you're not going to like it."

"Who?"

"Your fiancée."

Paul had quite a chuckle at his sister's expense when he informed her that she herself was Brandy's alibi for Harry Lake's murder. However, since Lacey was single-handedly solving these crimes, she could hardly be blamed for one tiny investigative slip. That certainly didn't clear Brandy of the other crimes. No, a computer alibi did that. How convenient.

As much as Lacey questioned Brandy's motives, taste, and general decency, she had to admit that it seemed less and less likely that she was the killer. With her limp, Brandy would have had a hard time moving a full-grown man over and over again. But that didn't mean she hadn't master-minded the whole plan.

"Just remember something, Paul: If you marry Brandy and you die, she gets all your money. And if she is such a genius, I sure bet she could make it look like an accident."

"You keep talking like that, Lace, and we won't invite you to the wedding."

The siblings parted in the Diner parking lot.

"I'll see you around," Paul said.

"Watch your back, okay?" Lacey replied.

Lacey decided to drop by Mapleshade on her way home. Sook was in his room reading a pink-covered tome about a woman who shops herself to death.

"You got to stop reading that crap," Lacey said.

"Is this good-bye?" Sook asked.

"No," Lacey replied. Although she wasn't sure. She knew it was time to leave, but she didn't know if she could get out of Mercer with the weight of unfinished business on her mind.

"Take some advice from an old man who knows a thing or two. You need to leave and never come back."

"Then I'll never see you again," Lacey said.

"Good," Sook replied. "I want you to remember me young and pretty. Listen, I was going for a stroll the other day over at We Care . . ."

"Why does that sound suspicious?"

"Pay attention. Big Marv has hired a geologist to do some studies on Shady Acres. He arrives in three days. You want to be long gone by then."

"It's funny," Lacey said. "There's a murderer loose in Mercer. Killed

Hart, Terry, Harry, the new doc, and probably the old fake doc. And you're telling me I should be worried about Big Marv?"

"Lacey, you got your whole life ahead of you. If you stopped worrying yourself about the dead, you might just get to live."

Sook had a good point there. Lacey didn't like leaving unfinished business, but maybe that was the only way to do what she had meant to do for the last ten years: Get out of this nowhere town.

"Say good-bye, Lacey," Sook said.

"Good-bye, Lacey," she replied, giving Sook a warm kiss on the cheek.

Lacey phoned Paul on her way home.

"Big Marv hired a geologist. He'll be here in a few days. Time to leave," she said.

"Shit. I didn't think it would be so fast. What do we do about the house?" The idea of a vengeful Marv had been acceptable as a future possibility—something he could make an outline for. As a present reality, it terrified him.

"I think Betty has a real estate license," Lacey replied.

"I'll call her."

"What are you up to today?" Lacey asked.

"Nothing," Paul replied.

"When you find the time to break away from nothing, you might want to start packing," Lacey said, and then ended the call.

Paul's answer was true. While he previously had plans to investigate the highly suspicious yet deceased Harry Lakes, Brandy convinced him otherwise. She explained that while Lakes was probably up to no good, he was certainly not the link that explained the series of killings in Mercer. Paul was glad for a reason not to take a drive. In fact, he was glad for a reason not to do anything at all. He parked himself in front of the TV and watched a marathon of *Mythmatch*. After he asked Brandy to fetch him his third beer, she tried to get him out of the house. She even suggested a hike, an unusual proposal from someone with a compromised gait, but Paul couldn't be budged from the comfort of the sofa.

Brandy prayed that her betrothed's lethargy was simply a response to all the recent stress, but in the back of her mind it occurred to her that she might have hitched her wagon to a dull, aimless man with a little bit of cash tucked away.

Lacey packed well into the evening until complete exhaustion set in. Surrounded by a sea of boxes, she climbed into her bed and thought she'd take a quick nap before she continued.

Something stirred her awake a few hours later. She first checked the clock and noticed it was just past midnight.

She had a feeling she was not alone.

A familiar shape was perched on top of a big box by the window. While some people experience the phenomenon of being unable to distinguish between waking and dream life, Lacey was not one of them. She was wide awake.

"You're alive," she said.

"Surprised?" he replied.

"Yes."

"What happened?" she heard herself asking.

Hart sat down on the edge of Lacey's bed. She could see his face through the light in the window. He had a few days' stubble and his hair was growing out from an amateurish bleach job. Despite herself, she was almost happy to see him.

"I'm not dead," he said.

"I figured out that part," Lacey replied. "But I *saw* you."

"Did you?"

"You had your mother's ring. The tattoo on your wrist . . ." she trailed off, trying to think of something else that proved what she'd once believed. But there was nothing.

"It wasn't me," Hart said.

"Obviously. Who was it?" Lacey asked.

"Some kid," Hart replied.

"Did he have a name?"

"Everybody has a name."

"What was it, Hart?"

"Brice."

"He's been missing."

"Not exactly," Hart casually replied.

"How did he die?"

"Peacefully."

"The tattoo? Was that a coincidence?"

"His choice."

"How many shots of whiskey did it take to be his choice?"

"About a dozen. The drinks cost more than the tattoo, I'll tell you that."

"I don't understand," Lacey said. She tried to keep her voice even. If Hart sensed fear, she would be next. "Why did the body keep coming back?"

"Because without a head, I needed someone to identify me. I needed *you* to identify me. I thought you'd find the tattoo the first time around and recognize the shirt."

"The shirt?" Lacey repeated.

"You gave it to me, remember? Two years ago for my birthday."

"Oh yeah," Lacey replied. "But couldn't they identify the body through the fingerprints?"

"The fingerprint database is only for convicted criminals. Believe it or not, I've never been charged with a crime."

"I still don't understand why you did it, Hart."

"I did it for you. And me. We have money now. We can go anywhere we want."

Hart removed a quartered envelope from his back pocket and passed it to Lacey.

"This arrived for you today."

Lacey peeked inside and saw that it was the check from Hart's life insurance policy. Lacey tried to hand it back to him, but he told her to keep it.

"Did you kill Terry?" she asked.

"Technically a pulmonary embolism did."

"Why?"

"Because I knew he'd give the land back to you."

"What about Harry?"

"He was going to ruin everything," Hart replied. "He knew Shady Acres was worth nothing. He found details in Terry's files. He would have made you pay him off. I know his kind."

"Right. What about Doc Egan?"

"Sorry that was so brutal," Hart said. "I had to make it fast."

"But why'd you kill him?"

"I thought I'd get rid of him before you got too attached."

"I wasn't getting attached."

"Then let's just say it was his time."

"Anyone else?" Lacey asked.

Hart casually searched his memory bank, as if it were possible he killed someone and did not recall.

"I think that's it."

"So you didn't have anything to do with Doc Holland's plane crashing?"

"Sometimes planes just crash, Lacey."

"Right."

"Can't say I'm broken up about it," Hart said, letting a smile creep over his face.

"Did Holland kill my parents?" Lacey asked.

"Yes. Why do you think he was paying me off all those years?"

"Because he wasn't a real doctor."

"Nope. That's what Sook thought. But if that was all Holland had done, he would have moved to another town that needed a quack. I had him by the balls for years. But then I had to lay low when I was working out this plan. As soon as he thought I was out of the picture, he made a run for it. Then the new doc moved to town."

"That was his son. Did you know that?"

"I did not," Hart said, clearly taken aback. "You know, that makes me feel better about killing him and all. Karma."

As Hart stared at his ex-fiancée, Lacey did her best to avoid any display of the tangled emotions that were fighting to surface.

"What do you say we get out of here?" Hart casually suggested.

"Sure," Lacey replied. "Just let me finish packing."

"One suitcase," Hart said. "Anything else we need, we can buy. Between the two of us, we got all the money we need."

Hart picked up a grungy backpack that was on the floor next to the window. He unzipped it, revealing several bundles of hundred-dollar bills.

"How much is in there?" Lacey asked.

"One hundred and eighty-five thousand."

"All that money you got from Doc Holland?"

"And a few other business ventures. But don't worry, darling. Wherever we end up, I plan on going legit. We'll be just like your all-American family. I'm thinking picket fence, 1.5 children, barbecues, soccer games, maybe I'll even buy a lawn mower. The kind you can sit on and drive around. And I'll have a real job."

"Doing what?" Lacey asked.

"I'm thinking about starting a hedge fund."

Lacey and Hart could hear a truck stirring up gravel on the driveway. Then the engine died.

"You expecting someone?" Hart asked.

Lacey raced to the window and peered out.

"It's Paul," she said. "You should hide."

"Hide? I haven't seen Paul in ages. We have a lot of catching up to do."

"Please don't kill him."

"Got any beer?" Hart said, disappearing into the kitchen.

———————

Lacey opened the front door as she heard Paul fumbling with his keys.

"Stay calm," she said.

"I am calm," Paul replied.

Paul pushed his way past his sister, just as Hart exited the kitchen uncapping a Budweiser.

"Fuck," Paul said, quickly losing his calm.

"Long time no see," said Hart with a smile.

"I thought you were dead."

"Nope. That was somebody else."

"Lacey, have you called the cops?" Paul asked.

"Nobody's calling anybody," Hart replied.

"I think you're mistaken," said Paul. He started patting his pockets, looking for his cell phone. "Damn, must have left it in the car. Where's the phone, Lace?"

Paul headed for the kitchen. Lacey blocked his path.

"Let's stay calm, Paul."

After the events of the past few weeks, Lacey's nerves had flatlined. She hardly had to fake it anymore. She was almost calm.

"I got that the first time, Lace. What's going on here?"

"I wouldn't know where to begin or end," Lacey said.

"How about you start with the headless guy. Who was that?"

"Brice," Lacey said.

"Nice guy," Hart said. "It's a shame he had to die. Under a different set of circumstances, we might have become good friends."

Until this point, Paul thought he was looking at a ghost. When he realized he was looking at a killer, rage took over.

Paul launched himself at Hart and tackled him onto the coffee table. He landed a few rough blows before Hart could retaliate. But Hart had been getting in scrapes since he was five. Hart kicked Paul in the groin and threw him off. While Paul was curled in a fetal position, moaning,

Hart kicked him in the kidneys. When Paul rolled over on his back, Hart stomped on his ribs.

Paul opened his mouth to scream for help, but got clipped in the jaw by Hart's steel-toed boot. Hart then rested his knee on Paul's broken ribs and pummeled his face until it was covered in blood.

"Stop," Lacey said, standing over the two men. Her expression was even—the only evidence of fear was the slight rattle of the gun in her hand. Lacey pulled back the hammer on Sook's gun and aimed it at the center of Hart's chest.

Hart looked at Lacey, amused.

"Sweetheart, what are you doing?"

"What does it look like I'm doing?"

"Don't aim a gun at a man unless you plan on using it," Hart said, getting to his feet.

"You think I won't shoot you?"

"You don't have it in you, Lacey."

"Now I do," Lacey replied.

She pulled the trigger. Hart looked down at the hole in his belly and smiled, as if he suddenly realized that he and Lacey had more in common than he thought. Lacey pulled the trigger again because the smile unsettled her. Then she pulled it one more time because Hart was still standing.

And then he wasn't standing anymore.

While Paul held an ice pack to the side of his face and winced from the collection of injuries he had amassed, Lacey told him everything she knew. Every unsolved murder was now solved. There was no audible clicking, but it's fair to say everything did indeed click into place. Now there was only a mess to clean up.

"What now?" Paul asked.

"We could call the cops," Lacey said.

"We could do that," Paul dully replied. "Any other options?"

"We could bury the body, clean up this mess, and get out of town."

Paul was stumped. "How do we decide?"

Lacey pulled a quarter from her pocket.

"We could leave it up to chance," she said. She interpreted Paul's silence as agreement. "Heads we bury him. Tails we call the cops. Okay?"

Lacey flipped the coin and smacked it on the back of her hand.

"Heads," she said, stuffing the quarter back in her pocket. "Well, at least this time we know what we're doing."

Paul would never learn that the quarter came up tails.

Lacey and Paul got a second wind when they realized that there was an end in sight. Lacey stuffed her hair into a baseball cap, donned gardening gloves, and covered them with plastic dishwashing gloves. Paul pulled an old tent from the garage and used it as a tarp to wrap up the body. He pulled the truck deep into their driveway in a direct line from their back door. They dragged the dead weight through the kitchen and along the back porch to the truck. Lacey counted to three and they hauled the body onto the truck bed.

At no moment did Lacey even think to cry. As far as she was concerned, Hart had been dead for months. She couldn't begin to imagine what she ever saw in that guy.

Even though he'd thought Hart dead for weeks, Paul found himself wondering if anyone would really miss Hart. His mother was the only person who came to mind. He pitied her, but after all the damage Hart had done, he couldn't summon any emotion other than that.

The living room had that distinct metallic odor of blood. A thick pool of deep crimson began to seep into the hardwood floor.

"How will you clean this up?" Paul asked.

"I like how you assume that I'm going to clean it up," Lacey replied.

"I am severely injured," Paul said.

Neither of them made a move. They had watched far too many episodes of Nightcrimes to know that this amount of DNA would be impossible to wash away.

"I have an idea," Paul said.

———

Lacey packed her car with only the bare essentials—one suitcase and their family photo album. Everything else, she figured, would just be a bad memory. Paul took his stereo, CDs, his entire DVD collection, and a shovel, all of which he loaded in the back of the truck on top of Hart's body. They scrubbed their hands and changed into clean clothes.

Paul traveled throughout their rambler, pouring gasoline in every bedroom and exiting through the back door. He lit a match and tossed it inside. He watched the flames snake through the house and suddenly become a massive blaze. This part almost made Lacey cry. Almost. She tossed Hart's insurance check into the bonfire. As they watched the flames, a thought occurred to Lacey.

"Paul, why'd you come back to the house tonight?"

"Brandy kicked me out. Said I had no ambition or intellectual curiosity. That I drank too much beer. The usual."

"Will she take you back?"

"Sure. I just got to get ambition and intellectual curiosity."

"Huh. How will you do that?"

"She wants me to read War and Peace."

"Big book."

"She likes the Russians."

"There's always CliffsNotes," Lacey replied.

Paul coughed from the smoke fumes.

"Time to go," Lacey said.

"I'll see you there." Paul got into his truck and drove away.

Lacey watched the flames for a little while longer. She felt a surprising satisfaction in watching her whole life burn to the ground.

The siblings convened at the first site where they had tried to dispose of the body previously known as Hart. They figured it was as good a place as any.

And it's not like anyone was going to go hunting for a dead guy. They dragged the corpse about a half-mile down the trail and then dropped him over the edge. They hiked down the woodsy ravine and started digging a grave. About two hours of hard labor had passed, mostly Lacey's, when they felt satisfied that Hart could remain interred there. When the earth had swallowed the body, Lacey and Paul hiked back up the trail and, once again, dusted away their footprints with a tree branch. They could hear the sirens of fire engines in the distance.

When Paul and Lacey reached the parking lot of the rest stop, they loitered by Paul's truck. They hadn't thought about it before, but they were going to say good-bye. At least for a long while.

"Where are you going?" Paul said.

"I have no idea," Lacey replied.

"Sounds nice. I hope you're happy there."

"And I hope you're happy wherever you end up. Even if it is with Brandy."

"Thank you," Paul replied.

"I'm sorry about how things turned out," Lacey said.

"Me too."

"But it wasn't all bad, was it?" Lacey asked.

"No. Not all of it."

"We didn't die, did we?"

"No. We didn't die."

"See you later, Paul."

"Not if I see you first."

They hugged awkwardly. Then Paul got into his truck, pulled it onto the road, and headed north to Tulac. Lacey turned south, back into town. She had one more errand to run before she could leave for good.

She parked on the side of the road, outside Mapleshade. Her flashlight guided her through the woods and she followed the ribbon markers left by Sook. She found the patch of unsettled dirt where Sook hid his stash and dug it up with her hands. She buried Hart's money with Sook's gun.

Even though she wanted no part of it, there was no good reason all that cash should go to waste.

No one saw her come or go. As she was driving away, she left a message on Sook's cell phone.

"Sook, it's me. You might want to disinter your petty cash in the near future. Be good," she said.

And then she took the first road heading east, because she could drive the farthest in that direction.

She turned to her passenger and said, "I hope you're up for an adventure, Irving."

Irving was just a cat, so he didn't respond.

NOTES:

Dave,

    Sorry about Irving. I decided to keep him. I wish you the best in all your future endeavors. Really, I do.

      Lisa

ACKNOWLEDGMENTS

David Hayward wishes to thank Tom and Quinn for the save, Matt for the science, Frank and Ben for the encouragement, Marysue and Stephanie for the guidance, Matthew and Joey for the support, Robin for the bus ride, Gerard for the Gerard,[49] and Lisa for everything.

Lisa Lutz would like to thank Marysue and Stephanie for their patience and friendship; the entire LGLA team for all their hard work; Morgan, Steve, and Julie for too many things to list; Jay and Anastasia for Sanjit (R.I.P.); Warren for *The Fop*; Kate for her brain; Pedram for the medicine; Las Hermanas for the peace and quiet; and Dave for being "game."

---

[49]Really? You're thanking a cat!